OBUMBRATE

BOOK TWO IN THE ILLUMINE SERIES

OBUMBRATE

BOOK TWO IN THE ILLUMINE SERIES

OBUMBRATE

BOOK TWO IN THE ILLUMINE SERIES

ALIVIA ANDERS

RED ALICE PRESS

OBUMBRATE
ISBN 978-0-9911-9475-9

The publisher acknowledges the copyright holder of the individual works as follows:

RIVEN
Copyright © 2012 by Alivia Anders

Cover design: Regina Wamba
Interior design: White Rabbit Designs
Interior formatting: White Rabbit Designs

Red Alice Press
www.redalicepress.com
Logo design: Kathryn Quinn

Manufactured in the United States of America

OBUMBRATE

| BOOK TWO IN THE ILLUMINE SERIES |

PROLOGUE
THUNDER

In one second, everything can change.

Life can bloom like a flower, exposing petals of a raw and unyielding beauty. Death can touch and silence a voice, leaving an abyss in place of a familiar soul.

Gripping the steering wheel of her car, Bethanie knew all too well how precious time was. It was a fickle thing, working against her in ways she had only ever seen as a curse, aimed to destroy her lone chances at redeeming herself in her short life. Her foot pressed harder against the gas pedal, wheels tearing through the thick and muddy back roads as it poured relentlessly.

Against the back of her mind, she knew it didn't make much sense to be driving in the madness of the weather. Rain pounded at the windshield, making it virtually impossible to see anything before her. Yet the continuing *tick-tock* of the silver pocket watch resting on her lap reminded her that she had a place to be, a place she would never reach in time.

Once again, time was working against her.

She closed her eyes for one gratifying moment, perfectly recalling the hands that had given her the silver pocket watch. Hands that belonged to someone she had spent all her life trying to get close to, desperate to admit the way his skin electrified hers. Desperate to say how much she ached to know the taste of his lips. Desperate to hear her name leave his tongue until time robbed him of the ability to speak. Desperate to hear that iconic message, three little words that could make or break a heart.

Lightning blazed through the sky, illuminating the world in a hazy blue-tinted glow. It was then that she saw the familiar back of an old, yellow car, that her heart stopped.

She pulled over to the side, her door thrown open before the car had come to a complete stop. Her chest tightened at the sight spread before her; car lights still on, driver door hanging wide open, all the signs of something terrible, but no body to prove it.

Bethanie scrambled around the car, ignoring her slip of feet and short-lived crash in the growing mud puddles. He was here, she could feel it. Her eyes started to search around the road and field of crops, when she spotted a parting in the field.

She ran, sprinting and screaming into the waist high spread, spotting his body only a dozen feet in. He lay eagle-spread, eyes vacant and unmoving as they stared into the swirling black mass hanging in the sky.

"*No!*" She screamed louder, dropping to her knees beside the freshly dead corpse. She grabbed at his arms, shoulders, chest, and face, anything to bring a response out of the boy she had carelessly wander from her sight.

Smacking at his face once more with rattled hands, her screams continued. "You don't get to die like this, not here, not now. You have a bigger cause. Do you hear me? You do not *get to die.*"

In that moment, everything stopped.

Like a tear in time, the world seemed to pause on itself, waiting for the push to move forward. She looked around, tears still running over her cheeks, waiting for a sign, a charge she could react to. Overhead the sky rumbled, the crackling of thunder the only thing creating sound other than her.

Bethanie fished for something against her chest, finding a small brass key woven entirely from wire. With a kiss, she placed it on his chest, then wrapped herself around the boy's limb body.

A cold draft rushed over the small clip of field, a twisting sensation starting in Bethanie's chest. Icicles collected on the tips of the grass, a veil of snow gathering on her shoulders and hair, as her once damp tears turned sharp and solid on her face. With a final breath, she exhaled those three powerful words to the chilled body beneath her.

And lightning struck them both.

ONE
BREAK ME DOWN

Once upon a time, on a cold winters night
A young and fair maiden was given a fright
She had awoken to chaos beyond her control
A horrorful sight, a new world to behold
The ocean sealed under a mass of chains
While perched atop, one coffin remains
A circlet of fire wrapped about like a cage
As muffled screams sounded desperate with rage
Yet the only comfort the maiden received
Was watching the white roses burn as she grieved

"Miss Hanley."

I jolted against my plastic-backed chair, muscles clenched. The pencil in my hand froze mid-stroke as my mind went blank. I dared the chance to look up. Mr. Whitley, my Biology teacher, gave me a disapproving stare, lips pulled tightly across his aged face. Behind him, my classmates all stared at me, stone-cold silence filling the room.

Instantly I relaxed. A man like Whitley was about as threatening as a newborn hamster. I kept a cool face as I asked, "Was there something you needed?"

Behind him, I heard some of the kids snicker. Whitley did his best to appear intimidating, puffing out his chest and letting his glasses dangle precariously on the edge of his nose, but only succeeded in looking like a moth-eaten teddy bear. "I was going to commend you on your excellent note-taking for the final next week. Thankfully, I held my tongue." His hand rested lightly on the edge of my desk, tapping it twice at the paper on my desk. "It *is* good to know though, that you won't be failing your art final."

I glanced down at the paper in front of me. A large human eye encompassed the whole sheet from corner to corner, dark lashes framing a detailed interior sketch of chains settling over ocean waves, a sole hand reaching out from under the surface. Above the chains rested a coffin white roses lain on top, fire licking around the base. It was a scene straight from a macabre book.

"Uh, thanks? The idea sort of stemmed from a poem, I think." I half-shrugged, not really sure where I got the idea from. Whitley didn't seem to notice, or care for that matter.

"I'd put the drawings away and lay off the Edgar Allen Poe, Miss Hanley. You missed a lot while daydreaming away. Unless your wish is to have my class again next year, your peers all off at college, leaving you behind in this tiny town," he straightened and moved his hand off my desk, returning up to the white board at the front, continuing to map out the portions of our upcoming final.

Tugging the sleeves of my cream sweater over my hands, I tried to focus on the board in front of me. My eyes however, had another plan. They continued to drift down to the drawing laid out before me. It was one of dozens I had completed in the last two weeks, each one more detailed than the last. It always started with the same almond eye shape; same curve of the pencil under my hand, same smudging and detailing, everything perfectly identical, save for one thing. Some of the eyes told stories of black birds and blood, others told stories of sunlight and fire. The aching part was that each had been created while I revisited Leo's death in my mind.

I snapped my notebook shut to hide the drawings out of sight. Lips clenched tight, I made sure to pay extreme attention to the white board and write down as much as I could before the bell rang ten minutes later. Whitley seemed pleased when I passed by him to leave, apparently taking my sudden interest in last-minute note-taking was on his accord. Maybe he thought I'd taken his words seriously, like the notion of having to repeat a year in a public education system was the most terrifying thing that could happen to me.

Hah. If only he knew. One look in my head and he'd see school was one of the last good blessings I had left.

In the hallway I stood in front of my open locker, staring at its contents without really seeing. I half-pretended to debate on what books would be most important to take home with me for studying, but what exactly mattered when you knew death was knocking on your door? Even if I did give a damn, I could still fail all of my finals and graduate with a low C-average in every class. I had to give it to my grandparents. If it hadn't been for them pushing me into one of NYC's select private schools, I wouldn't have the luxury of slacking off like I had been. Again, that was still assuming it meant something. The idea of even seeing graduation rested on the assumption that I'd live long enough to actually make it down the aisle and take that diploma, that maybe they'd teach me something useful for my limited existence. Seeing as they didn't teach me the ins and outs of being half of a mythical creature, and how to save myself from a fiery death, I was betting that would never happen.

Nothing had gone right since I'd set foot in Belfast. And that was putting it lightly. Just as I has started to settle into my old home I had learned a bitter truth; that every part of my life had been a sick, crafted lie. From the second I came into existence, I had been shuffled and shoved, picked on by a lunatic mother, abandoned by an unimaginable, alleged heavenly being of a father. I had learned that running from your past only brings it front and center, hungry with a vengeance. Life, to me, felt like a tragic painting. I felt like a sparrow with clipped wings, still believing it could fly.

I sighed and pressed my forehead to my locker. Since coming home from the hospital in Charon, day to day life had been practically impossible. It was hard enough learning I wasn't the human I thought I was, but add in a demon that was constantly looking for a weak-point in my instinctive defenses to kill me, and I was already in over my head. Kayden, Ursula, and Abigail had all agreed to let the past fall behind us and to never speak of it again. Leo wasn't dead to anyone but us, and as far as everyone else knew he was off in New Zealand for a student exchange program.

Leo... he was gone. Everything had happened so fast, my mind was still trying to wrap itself around the reality of it. A cold shiver raised goosebumps on my skin, scattered fragments of that night playing out in my head. One minute, it had been about dressing up and having fun, embracing a side of me I didn't know was possible to love.

Then it had all turned to blood, so much blood.

Blood on my hands, dark red liquid staining my palms, embedding itself deep in the cracks and cuticles of my fingers. Blood on my white dress and on Leo's button-up, sticky and slick as it clung to his paling skin, clouded eyes staring blankly at the ceiling as his final breath exhaled from his lips.

I wanted to mourn him, honor his death, but everywhere I turned someone was watching me. Kayden rarely left my side at school, and when I would think I'm alone at home the floorboards would creak and give away Jayson silently listening in to my stifled sobs. Jayson quickly caught on that something was different when I came home from what he thought had been an innocent sleepover at Ursula's. Maybe it had been the way I started sobbing the first time I picked up my sketchbook, days after his death. Maybe it had been the night he found me sobbing on the bathroom floor, my hands scrubbed raw to the point of bleeding all over the linoleum floor. He had silently been watching me fall to pieces, completely unaware of the weight on my shoulders, completely unaware of how I wanted to tell him everything. Instead I had lied, citing that finals was taking a toll on me, that Abigail would know exactly how to help. After all, she was my shoulder to lean on.

Too bad Abigail wasn't an option.

It may have been only two weeks since Chase nearly succeeded in killing me again, but his violent attack left only a fraction of the sting Abigail's words had. By the time I noticed she had been in the hospital by my side the entire time, I had thought I was delusional. How could a mortal be in a mythical realm? She was human, or so I had assumed.

Fool me once, shame on me. Fool me twice, shame on me twice as hard.

A light cough came off from my left, my eyes spotting an unmistakable pair of Doc Martens standing next to me. "Are you coming down to lunch today?"

I shut my locker, wiggling the handle to make sure it was locked. I made sure not to look at her as I passed her to make my way down the hall. "I'd rather not, Abigail." I winced as her name passed my lips.

Abigail followed behind me, her long peasant skirt making swishing sounds against the sides of her legs. "Essallie, it's been two weeks. Enough is enough." She tried to match my stride as I walked faster until she couldn't take it. Hands grabbed at my sweater and turned me around. "So I'm a little weird, like you didn't already know. If it makes you feel better, I'll say I'm sorry."

"That's just it, Abby. I didn't." My eyes began to prickle, tears threatening to make a show. But I couldn't cry, not with several students still in the hallway with us. I shook my head. I felt like an overused bleeding heart, shocked to life too many times to count. "I can't accept your half-assed apology. You're not sorry you kept everything from me because it was 'good for me'. You're sorry you were ousted. You could have told me."

Abigail pursed her lips. I watched her lip curl upward as her trademark sneer and eye-roll made its appearance. "What did you think, Essie? That we became such fast friends because we connected so well?" She paused and tucked a stray piece of dark red hair behind her ear, deafening silence pounding between us. When she spoke, it was quiet and low. "I didn't mean it like that."

"Then tell me how you did mean it." I fought to control the volume of my voice. My fingers began to twitch as I fought the need to let my knees buckle from the quivering that ran rampant in my joints. "You know, I'm not some fragile little thing that's too delicate to hear the truth. I should have known anyone who was close to me was bound to be tired to my freakish side."

"I wanted to tell you, I really did." Abigail still spoke in a low-tone. "But it wasn't my call."

Red began to bleed into my sight, clouding my view. Every beat of my heart matched the pounding in my head. I spoke in a hiss. "Of course not. It's never your call. It's always someone else's. I'm sorry I ever trusted you, ever knew you." I rocked back on my heels and reached up to press my fingers against my temples. "God, why is every freaking person around me some kind of supernatural *freak?*" My voice cracked at the end, and I lost my hold on the scream built in the back of my throat.

It was only the two of us now, all the other students having shuffled off and away from the scene we- I was making.

"Listen-"

"No, *you* listen. I don't want to hear your sob story of how you kept me in the dark for my own protection. This isn't some stupid vampire novel where everyone keeps the squishy little human from knowing anything." Fire sparked on my fingertips, a familiar dull ache spreading through my veins. I wanted to release it, let the full force consume the hallway and both of us in it. "I can set anyone on fire in a given moment, burn forests to the ground, reduce buildings to ash! Is that why you couldn't tell me anything? Because I'm like a Molotov cocktail?"

Abigail moved to answer, but I shoved a flaming finger centimeters away from her face, silencing her with a gasp for air. "No more lies, Abigail. You're going to tell me everything, or nothing will stop me from setting you ablaze."

"It wasn't her choice, Essallie. It was mine," Kayden's voice called from the end of the hallway. I looked up to see him approach us, each step bringing his shifting silhouette into sharper focus. His dark black hair spiked on his head stood in sharp contrast to his rich tanned skin, eyes a spinning mist of hazel and black. Even dressed in an everyday get up of a windbreaker, t-shirt and jeans he looked like a dark immortal, the kind of person you'd swoon over under the bleachers and dreamt about at night. If I hadn't known better I'd have called him seductive, cunning, a mystery I'd long to find more about.

Eyes locked on Kayden, he stopped as a brilliant arc of flames erupted on my second hand, engulfing it whole. It spun into a ball and cradled in my palm as I held it in his direction. "You stay out of this. I'll pick my battle with you next, *demon.*" I gave him a piercing stare. He had been someone to trust, to tell me everything and help me navigate this new power I could barely contain. Instead, it felt like he'd thrown me to the wolves. My attention moved back to Abigail. "Who else is weird like me, like us? My brother? Thomas? Jessica?"

Abigail took a step backward, hesitation written across her face. She stole a quick glance at Kayden, who shook his head silently.

"Oh my God. Jessica?" I hissed. "Is that why she's still in Portland? Did she even *go* to Portland?"

"I can't say."

"Dammit Abigail!"

Like flipping on a switch, fire shot from my hands. A wall of bright blue flame instantly separated them from me, my fire acting like a barricade. Abigail reacted in barely enough time; stumbling into the lockers behind, her she quickly put out the fire that started on the hem of her skirt. Kayden silently joined her, swirls of black smoke curling at his feet.

"How am I to know anything you tell me is what's really going on? Or am I just supposed to trust you both, the demon and the sneak, both holding your own goals at heart," I hissed, backing down the hall to make for the exit to the parking lot.

"Essie, this is enough. You can't keep doing this," Kayden snapped as he stood alongside Abigail. "This is what it's like being different, you have to accept that. People live and people die. Leo was only the beginning. The sooner you accept that, the sooner we can plan."

I felt a stab at my heart as he said Leo's name aloud. He shouldn't have been allowed to speak that name, the name of that brilliant life I let die. Grief washed over me in waves that was almost too painful to hold back. The urge to let fire engulf the whole hall crossed my mind again. "Plan for what? How much more have you kept from me? I can't trust either of you, not after what happened." I turned to face Abigail, fighting the urge to cry again. "Was any of our friendship real? Or was Kayden using you to get to me from the beginning?"

Abigail turned her gaze to Kayden and started to speak. He instantly drowned her out, eyes never left my face. "By all means, get even more pissed. Blow yourself up and kill everyone here. It'll be their blood on your hands. You think Leo's death was hard, try living with the knowledge you killed hundreds."

I looked down to my blazing hands, watching the fire roll over my skin harmlessly. "You know what? I like the sound of that." I flexed my fingers, letting coils of the flame lash out at them from the blaze between us. With the pressure of my body I launched the wall straight at them. Kayden wrapped himself around Abigail as she screamed just as the fire raced around Kayden, burning him in seconds. It dawned on me that Kayden could be gone from that burst, or that Abigail could be burned to the point of deformity, maybe even death. Yet somehow, I didn't care. Every feeling I had was locked in a box within my soul, leaving me with a hollow sensation I couldn't place.

Spinning sharply on my heels, I crossed the parking lot and slid inside my car. The growing roar of the engine felt oddly satisfying, the rumble just enough to match the quakes and quivers of my body. For a second I looked back to the building, my neck tilted to see inside the doors where I had abandoned the two traitors. My car had just inched past the double glass doors when I spotted a burst of black smoke fill the hallway.

The skin on my knuckles flared white against the steering wheel as I navigated through the streets of Belfast. I was searching for something, anything to distract me from setting fire to the whole town. School was too risky, too many potential events that could trigger my anger and hurt someone innocent. Home was just as dangerous, as Jayson was bound to ask me why I was so uptight, and I didn't want to hurt him. I was barely keeping my temper in check as I drove, and I knew that at any point I could lose it and blow up the car. I needed some place quiet, somewhere the fresh air could hit my lungs and tame my thoughts with a gentle breeze.

I crossed past the same church three times over before I settled on parking. It was mid-afternoon, so no services were being held. I made sure to pull my sketchbook from my messenger bag before I left the car. Connected to the small church was an equally small graveyard, the perfect place to go for a quiet moment. After all, who's quieter than the dead?

Only the sound of my footsteps sounded around me as I rounded the headstones one by one. Most of them were faded, crumbling from age and weather, and the new ones stood out in sharp contrast. My fingertips brushed over the black marble of a new headstone naming an older woman who had died four years ago. Instantly I was enraged. Leo deserved one of these, he deserved to be buried and rest. But the stupid facade Kayden and his parents agreed to all put on made that impossible. All because no one wanted to cause a panic in the town.

Between the hospital and home I had learned there was much more to the eyes of Leo than anyone had let on. His family held a key role in gate-keeping the entrances to Charon. They decided when new entrances could be placed and who held control over them for safe passage. Leo had been the last of his blood line. Now, with him gone, the question was who would take over when his parents pass.

Finding space between two aged headstones, I found a

comfortable place on the grass to sit, my sketchbook propped up on my legs for support. Slowly I turned the pages, taking cursory glances over the abstract designs. It used to be something I loved, an outlet for my frustration. Now all I saw was Leo. Images of his hands reaching for my pencil, his happy smile as he showed me Charon, it all blurred behind a wall of haze in my mind. I had it shut it out- all of it -if I was to ever function again. So much easier said than done when you've seen two violent deaths before your eyes.

My fingers found the pencil I kept in the ringed binding and before I knew it, I was drawing. Sheer impulse drove the pencil against paper, framing a beautiful almond-shaped eye with a dark iris, small arcs of light breaking through the black smudges of lead. It wasn't an eye I openly recognized. Most of my drawings were normally manga related; cartoon eyes with dramatic eyelashes and open messages displayed in their large stare. This one was human, a real life eye.

"I didn't know you enjoyed my gaze that much, Nephilim." A female voice softly purred behind me. Instantly I snapped out of my haze, like breaking through a watery surface with force. I looked around to see the graveyard had turned darker, shadows pulling towards the headstones and swirling around me. Slowly they spun upward, framing in a delicate woman I had only met once.

I waited for the initial shock of wear off before I used my voice. The Queen looked as ornate and elegant as she had the night of the circus disaster. A flowing gown of the blackest of fabrics cut with a sweetheart top swallowed her petite frame. Gloves of the same fabric were decorated with sparkling pearls and Swarovski crystals. Beautifully dressed or not, it was her pale face framed by curtains of black hair that stood out. "Your gaze?"

She glided over with inhuman grace and gently crouched down to point at the picture I had been working on. "Correct me if I'm wrong, but I believe that would be my eye." She stared at me with curiosity. "Do you carry the Sight, as well?"

I stared up at her face and back to the photo. Sure enough, the photo I had been instinctively scribbling had been of her eyes. Maybe I was psychic? More likely than not I had remembered her face in my subconscious when I was revisiting that night in my memories. Then again, it wouldn't be the first time I was surprise by my own hidden abilities.

I shrugged and brushed off her question. I was in no mood to deal with any kind of mind games she might try to enact on me. "Did you need something? Or do you just enjoy taking afternoon strolls in the mortal realm?"

The Queen appeared unfazed by my cold shoulder. "Kayden said you were brash. I can see he was right." She smiled. "Do you speak to him like this as well?"

"You answer my question, and I'll answer yours."

Her smile faltered by a fraction before she recovered with poised grace. "Very well, then. I came to see you. You had left in such haste after the... incident. I was worried for your well being."

Her lies lingered in the air like bitter puffs of sulfur, strong enough to taste, strong enough to gag on. "Two weeks is an awfully long time to wait. You could have just been honest and said you wanted to see if I was dead yet."

She opened her mouth slightly to speak, only to close it. Rich honey brown eyes narrowed at me. "You haven't answered my question, Nephilim."

"Essallie. It's Essallie," I corrected with a snap.

"Essallie it is, then. You haven't answered my question."

I turned my eyes back to the drawing on my lap. With a jerk of the paper, I ripped it from the sketchbook, crumbled it into a wad and chucked over my shoulder.

"Only those who smell to high heavens of bullshit and ulterior motives." I rose to my feet and faced her, heat lancing through my veins like spears ready for the fight. "Spit it out. You didn't come here to check on me. So why are you here?"

Her eyes widened in surprise as I stood there, waiting. After today's nonsense with Abigail and Kayden, I had heard enough bullshit to span my lifetime six times over. Queen or no Queen, I didn't owe her anything. If anything, she owed me her life. It had been my hands covered in Chase's blood, not hers. For sacrificing my own lifespan to a torture of burning veins so her and all her little supernatural freaks could continue on in their meaningless existence.

Finally, she spoke. "You're smart. Smart enough to know not to trust me." Brushing past me, I watched as the shadows moved with her, forming a small pool around the hem of her dress. "I am, however, surprised to see you trust a demon of all things. Especially someone like Kayden."

It was bait, I knew it. She was testing to see if I'd wait to see the shoe drop off the other foot. Fire spread from my fingers and washed over my hands. I pointed an emblazoned finger at her. "Your simple mind tricks won't work on me. I'm not interested in playing your petty game."

A horrid smile spread so far across her face, I thought it might split in half. She laughed as she stepped closer, until all I could see was the kohl lining the rims of her narrowed eyes. "Oh, you'll play my game whether you like it or not."

God, she sounded like a freaking cartoon villain. I started to turn and leave, my hands still engulfed in the angelic flame. "Sure thing, Queenie."

Shadows erupted from the ground, bursting skyward in sharp, jagged spikes. They spiraled together until a thick black cocoon sealed around the graveyard. I pushed a burst of flame through my veins to light up the inside when I saw a glimmering black spear launch into my hand. I screamed and the shadows launched into a fury, dozens of them stabbing at my hands, my arms, anywhere the fire pulsed from my body.

As I screamed and thrashed, the Queen spoke. "You see, Essallie, there isn't an option to ignore my voice. When you control the dark and all its splendor, you'll find many are willing to listen if it means their lives will be spared, if but for a moment."

Pressure crushed my chest as I fought to breathe. Breathy whispers spoke to me, like wind whistling through barren tree tops. My fire was gone, swallowed by the stabbing shadows that sunk into every inch of me. Emptiness seeped into my pores and filled me with a hollow sensation. Everything was so dark, so empty, so lost.

The shadows retreated, and I collapsed onto the ground. I watched through watery eyes as they took their place just under the Queen, shifting and swirling. She reached down and ran her hand across the shadows in a loving gesture. Some of them had spun up and into the fabric of her gown, forming swirls of deep violet against the black. "Now, let's chat."

I unsteadily rose to my feet, every inch of my body shaking. I felt like a leaf in the wind- powerless, frail, empty. The burn inside of my veins was gone, cooled to an bitter icy sensation that spread throughout my body. I reached deep inside to trigger the fire only to find a cold hollow instead. My fire was gone.

"What," my voice cracked. "What did you do to me?"

The corners of her lips hitched into the vague image of a smile. She breezed past me to sit on a thick headstone several rows over. Her hand beckoned me to follow. "Teenagers these days, " I heard her say. "Always so eager to start a fight. No doubt the hormones compel you to do it." Sitting on the etched granite, she looked up at me with a sympathetic gaze. "It must be hard, being so young and having this power you can barely control. I almost wish I could relate."

I stared down to my shaking, open hands. Hormones were the least of my worries. When you played with fire, you were bound to be burned. She could never understand, no matter how tied to her magic she was. "You don't know anything about this. Just go, leave me alone."

She let out a barely audible laugh. "You underestimate my ability to feel. Most demons lose their ability to harness emotion after centuries of seclusion from humanity, but there are a small few who never forget. I know more than you'll ever understand, Essallie." I looked up in time to watch her face harden, her mouth set into a thin line. Something stirred behind her eyes. "Some of us experience things that can never be erased. You think it was painful watching a friend die-"

"He wasn't a friend. He was so much more than I'll ever be able to explain," I spoke faster than I could think, the words rolling off my tongue with violent force. My hands shook as I missed the comfort of my inner fire. "Everyone keeps telling he was someone I barely knew, had little time with, and because of that I'm supposed to get over his death just like everyone else. They don't understand. When he died, it felt like part of me went with him. This goes deeper than some friend dying, this was someone tied to my soul."

For a moment, the Queen stayed silent. Only the subdued sound of her shadows filled the empty space between us. "I lost a daughter. So yes, I do know what it is like to lose a part of your soul, your spirit, or whatever it is we supernaturals have inside us. I know what it's like to feel yourself rip in half." A haunted look stirred in her eyes as she spoke through a thin lipped smile. "She looked just like you. That's why the night at the circus I was so guarded. I had thought for sure that my mind was trying to do me in."

My stomach dropped into my feet the same moment my chest let off a jolt of pain. Embarrassment and humiliation washed over me in waves. Here I stood, complaining over someone who may or may not have been tied to my soul, and yet she harbored a deeper secret than I had. A daughter, someone of true flesh and blood, lost to the ashes and dust.

The image of a jackass came to mind. I didn't linger on the thought for long, but I did add the loss of her daughter to the list of things Kayden had failed to fill me in with. And that list was growing awfully damn fast.

"Kayden never mentioned anything like that." I gently replied. I wasn't sure what to say past that. I'm sorry your daughter died and I'm pissing and moaning over a boy? My apologies I'm a selfish hot-headed teenager?

The lack of apology didn't seem to faze the Queen. A faint smile tugged at her lips as she let out a huff of laughter. "I can see Kayden hasn't told you nearly as much as you think he has. Tell me, what did he say about me?"

That she was cruel. Anyone who got on her bad side was as good as dead. All the things you'd tell someone to keep them from speaking to another. "Nothing redeeming."

She nodded, running a hand through her hair and twirling the ends around her index finger. "What reason does he have for staying by your side?"

"What do you mean?"

"I simply find it a little odd," she began, speaking slow to my narrowed gaze. "I've known Kayden for over seven hundred years, and not once has he been the type to simply stay with a fledgling, a newcomer, unless there was something to be gained."

But I knew what was keeping him. I was the only one with the key to his freedom. My still-beating heart ensured his connection to me, our uncanny bond. As long as I lived and breathed, he would continue to remain in the shadows, waiting for his chance to finish the charge assigned to him.

"I think he was wrong." I heard her say, surfacing me from my thoughts. When I looked up at her, she was shaking her head. "You don't seem to be easily manipulated. Then again, I didn't kiss you like he had."

For the second time today, I felt the air leave my lungs. My mind instantly brought me back images of his molten gaze, the smooth sound of his voice. I banished the pictures from my mind and ignored the heat on my face. That was supposed to have been our private moment. I hadn't told anyone of the kiss. "How- how do you know about that?"

"Essallie, do not tell me that you thought that kiss was real." The Queen came down to my level, swaths of black fabric and energy-hungry shadows licking at the edge of my feet. She stared at me intently. "I can see it in your eyes and the red on your cheeks. You're fond of him."

Fever in the form of blush colored my cheeks, my heart beating to the tune of a painful pitter-patter. "Answer me! Who told you about the kiss?"

"Who else would have told me, but the demon who did it himself."

I was starting to think my gut-punch reaction to everything I had learned recently was becoming a habit. Forcing myself to keep breathing, I ran my hands through my hair. Anything to keep myself from trying to punch a decade-old headstone.

The Queen continued, her face carefully kept neutral. "He had laughed and told me I hadn't to worry about you. That any chance of you ascending was gone because of a *little magic* he'd done before you had all arrived." She frowned as she spoke, no doubt from seeing the physical pain I was struggling to keep inside the more she revealed. "No war could come from a dying angel, he'd said."

"He, he said he would help me." A curious numbing sensation began to spread from my chest to my fingertips. He had offered to help, that he would make it fair before trying to kill me. That's what was supposed to make this interesting. But if he'd purposely made me focus on him instead of Leo... if I had never kissed Kayden, would Leo and I have connected? Would he still be here, guiding me, saving me from myself?

"I'm sorry, but I need to go," I said, standing on my shaking limbs. The numbing sensation was starting to turn into sharp jabs of cold, sinking deep into my gut and heart. "I'm sorry about your daughter."

She held out a hand to stop me, but didn't grab or push at me. "Don't you want your gift back? Your fire?"

I shivered and stared at the ground. A bitter taste coated my tongue when I spoke. "Probably not. Unless you're giving me the okay to kill Kayden."

The Queen came to stand before me, mere inches left between us. Hands cupped just under her chest, she gently extended them outward toward me, a small blue flame flickering in her palm. It shot straight for my chest, lancing into me with instant effect. Warmth spread through every inch of my body, replacing the numbing, hollow sensation that had been there moments ago.

"You may leave," the Queen said. "but before you do, a warning. Kayden is not a person to be trusted. He'll only use you for his own gain in the end."

"Like I didn't already know."

"And one more thing. Do be careful." Her voice sounded almost resembled something of sympathy and genuine concern. "When it comes to the race of Nephilim, the world reacts in two ways. None will take kindly to your angelic blood; there will be those who will seek to harvest your blood for their own gain. Others will want you dead, no matter the cost."

Wariness crept over my skin. "Why would you tell me this?"

"Because one of the last Nephilim was killed at the hands of a madwoman. A woman who tried to harvest the blood of Nephilim to create the perfect race."

TWO
ALL I HAVE LEFT

I drove home in a daze, the warmth of my inner fire the only thing grounding me. I was conflicted; the more I went over my conversation with the Queen, the less it made sense. Right out of the gate she told me she wasn't to be trusted, yet she offered me a piece of detail surrounding Kayden that suddenly made everything fall into place. Her words made me call into question all of Kayden's recent actions- the distance, the bitterness, the lack of affection after kidding me like it was just us and the world-

I slammed on the breaks, and just in time. Any further and I'd have missed the turn off for home. I pulled into the driveway and made sure everything was locked before heading inside. As I cracked open the door, the sound of the local TV news station played out of the kitchen. As I got closer, a not-so-pleasant fishy smell hit me in the face.

"Jayson? You in the kitchen?" I dumped my messenger bag at the foot of the stairs and started my way down the hall.

"Who else cooks lobster ravioli and lives in this house?" I heard him shout back over the news broadcast talking about the recent power surges in Portland. "You want some?"

"Very funny, but pass," I said. Opening the door to the kitchen, I made a face of disgust. Jayson was standing in front of the stove, gently prodding at the stuffed ravioli cooking on the stove. He wore a laced apron that said 'Ready To Catch Some Tail' on it in pink cursive font.

I nearly lost it as soon as I laid eyes on him. "Did you lose a bet?"

Jayson place a hand to his chest and took a step back, a look of mock wounding on his face. "I'm offended! This was given to me by Sylvia."

Ah, his new pretty little girlfriend was already breaking him in. I had only met her a handful of times since they started dating two weeks ago, and she seemed nice enough. Part of me wondered if Jayson was trying to get the two of us girls to bond, in some hidden hope that I'd tell her what was eating me alive.

I wiggled my eyebrows mischievously. "And suddenly, I approve of it so much more."

"Essallie Miranda Lillian Hanley," Jayson said with actual shock this time. "Are you making a dirty joke about my apron?" He tugged at the girly print, pointing to a lobster tail I had conveniently missed before. "You do know where it says 'tail' it means lobster tail, right? Not having-"

"Ah, no! Don't you finish that sentence!" I plugged my ears in protest, ready to sing as loud as needed to block out my bother talking about sex.

He placed a hand on his forehead and stuck his head up to the sky dramatically. "My own sister, a vulgar-minded teenager. I'll never look at you the same way again!" He paused and gave his ravioli a quick stir around the pan. "When you told me that joke about the bakery and buttered muffin the other day-"

"I'm not answering that."

He stared at me in horror, one hand slowly rising to cover his mouth. "I thought you meant an actual bakery and muffin!" He groaned. "No wonder the woman at the bakery thought I was gross when I told her the joke!"

I pressed the heels of my palms into my eyes and laughed hysterically. Sometimes I wondered if my brother was like any normal boy on the planet. He could cook, clean, had a girlfriend, didn't live for sports or politics; he was sort of like those dream come true boys you read about in chic-lit paperbacks at the checkout line in the grocery store. I was lucky to have him.

"Jayson, don't ever change." I said amidst the laughter. When I eventually caught my breath, I noticed he was staring at me with a weird look on his face.

"What, was it something I said?" I asked.

He shook his head, the weird face still going on. "Now that's the Essallie I've missed lately." I realized his weird face was his attempt at a kindred gaze. His smile touched his eyes, lighting up his whole face as he continued to beam. "I wish you'd tell me who put a damper on that fire of yours. I'd love nothing more than to see them burn."

Yeah, me too. Shame the list was far too long and impossible to achieve. I couldn't see Jayson holding his own against two demons, a super-ninja, a succubus, and my own blood.

Thumbing the edge of the table, I mumbled. "I didn't go anywhere. I just took a backseat to moody and ungrateful Essallie."

"Well, what ever Essallie you are, you're still my sister, understand? You can tell me anything, even if you think you can't."

"Thanks Jayson. I'm going to head upstairs and study. You, uh, might want to check on that before it burns some more."

As Jayson turned back to the stove, I made my exit. I dragged my messenger bag up the stairs and into my room, tossing it onto my bed with a thud.

Standing in the middle of my room, I thought back to Abigail's words earlier today. I wanted to call her so bad, say I'm sorry, but part of my was holding back. I was so fed up with all the secrets, the hiding, and the lies. It just wasn't right to go along with it.

"Less moody than before?" The shadows in a corner of my room shifted. Kayden materialized into my room, looking a little worse for wear. His normally tanned skin had paled, and a dark scruff covered most of his jaw line. Small purplish bruises bagged under his eyes, while his cheekbones stuck out further than I could ever recall seeing them. In a few hours he looked like he had aged at least thirty years.

"I'll be less moody if you stop lying to me," I replied coolly. I gave him a quick once-over with minimal interest. "You look like hell."

"When you're made of fire and brimstone-"

"Yeah, whatever. Unless you're here to say you're sorry, you can go. I've had enough crap to deal with today. First school, Ursula giving me death stares at all times, you being you, Abigail being some crazy ass ninja, it goes on. It's just too much."

"She's not some crazy ass ninja, she's a Satrix. She was only doing what she's been trained to do from birth."

"I don't care if she's a stripper working the corner of Suhtreex or-"

"Satrix, Essallie, and it's not a corner, it's a nickname. Be thankful you weren't around when it was customary to call them by their full name. Saying *Fidei Defensatrix* every time you had to reference to them got real old, fast."

"Ugh, whatever. Can we not talk about Abby?" I sat down on the middle of my bed with my arms on my knees, hands splayed palms up toward the ceiling. My eyes lingered on Kayden's hands, and I instinctively wished he'd take my hands into his and tell me everything would be okay. That the rampant chaos running my reality was all a terrible, horrible nightmare.

His voice brought me back from my wishful thinking. I watched as he ran a hand through his hair repeatedly. "She was just trying to help. It's in her blood." He came over to sit next to me, careful that we didn't touch in case we set the bed on fire. "Would you preferred being undefended?"

"I wasn't *undefended*. You were there," I pointed out.

"Yes, I was. But I was nowhere near you, Essie. If Abigail hadn't been there, you'd be dead. Would you rather she let you die?"

Yes, yes I would. My death could have been the end of all of this. A war everyone believes is coming now, all because of me. The countless deaths that could and would occur. Kayden had said Leo was just the beginning. Who else would I lose that meant everything to me?

I changed subject. "The Queen came to see me today."

Shoulders bunched, his body tensed at the mention of her. When he looked at me, I noticed his eyes had returned to the color of coal. I could barely make the words through his tightened jaw. "What did she want?"

"To warn me of people who may hurt me," I said carefully. His body tensed tighter, wound like a metal coil prepared to spring at the slightest snap. Cords of black smoke rose from his skin, as if he were barbecuing alive on my bed. I did my best to keep my lips pressed tight as I watched him. The Queen's words repeated in my head with a growing force.

You don't seem to be easily manipulated. Then again, I didn't kiss you like he had.

"You don't like her." The words slipped from off my tongue faster than I could catch them.

Kayden's eyes locked onto mine. His shoulders slowly deflated, tendrils of smoke dissipating into thin air. When he spoke, his voice sounded calm, but I could still hear the pressure it took him to keep his tone in check.

"Lucretia," he began with a barely contained sneer, "is like the Queen piece on a chess board. She has every move available in her arsenal, and any piece could be hers."

In that moment I wished I could see into his mind and understand the tumbling of emotions lying under his mask. Someone with such a level of dislike for a person had to have a reason for it.

Even though it was like re-opening a fresh wound, I couldn't help it; I had to know more about why he disliked her so deeply. "She mentioned you. I was told that you were distrustful." The words carefully left my tongue. "Dangerous, even."

"Sounds like the pot calling the kettle black to me."

I leaned in closer to get a better look at him, but he only shifted further from me. This was the game of cat and mouse we'd been tentatively playing since that night outside the bookshop portal to Charon. Ever since the kiss he'd been aloof, distant. It was almost as if he'd reverted back to the Kayden I'd met in New York, not the Kayden who'd helped me understand what I was. Not the Kayden who'd encouraged me, pushed me to better myself, to prepare for the inevitable I still wasn't ready to accept.

An impulsive thought rooted in my brain. "Kiss me, Kayden."

He looked like I had asked him to lick the bottom of a salt barrel. "Are you that desperate?"

I was taken aback as his look brought on a sharp sensation of pain in my chest. "Of course not," I whispered quietly. I kept my eyes on my fists, watching them clench over, the skin over the knuckles parchment white. "Do you have a problem kissing me?"

"There's no need." He brushed me off so easily, and practically with a dash of humor. "Unless you've been poisoned by your new friend in the Queen. I see she's done a number on your mind, has she done it to your body too?"

I let my shoulders drop. Of course he wouldn't kiss me, there wasn't someone like Leo between us. Not with him six feet under in a cemetery in Charon. I swallowed down the bitter taste in my throat, rolling my shoulders to shake off my embarrassment. Of course Kayden had only kissed me to his own benefit; how could I have thought for a moment that maybe, just maybe, something made him care inside his black-smoke of a soul?

The wounded beat of my heart told me I had been played a Fiddler's Fool.

"I should have known better." I stood up and crossed the room, counting the small steps until I came to a stop in front of the open window. Outside, silhouettes of trees shrouded my view of the moon. Small beams of milky light broke through the barrier the trees had created. "She told me, you know. And here I thought she was bluffing just to get a rise."

"What did she tell you?" The creak of floorboards under his weight told me he was standing, probably waiting for me to turn around and face him.

"That I was a fool for thinking you had a heart." I used my hands to lean against the window frame. Cool air tickled my face. I thought out my next words carefully, selecting them in hopes he'd make the crushing pressure in my chest vanish like the smoke that made up his body. "Tell me she's wrong, Kayden. Tell me that you would never stoop so low as to *manipulate* me so I wouldn't see the connection forming with Leo right in front of me."

Silence. It seemed to stretch on forever, and with it, my heart sank lower into the pit of my twisted stomach.

"I had to do what was right for me," he said, starting low. "I never meant for you to take our physical contact as... something more."

I spun around to face him, livid. Hot tears stung as they ran down the sides of my face. In one breath, everything had been ruined. The memory of that night would forever haunt me, remind me I fell for the trap of a demon. "How was I supposed to take it? Like it's normal to kiss you on a random basis? Like its normal to feel what happened between us?"

"Please," he sneered, laughing at me. "Did you really think those feelings were real? I merely did the same thing Ursula does with any human. I *made* you feel, and I don't regret it. I don't regret one second of manipulating you."

I pressed against the wall, leaning my head up in a last ditch effort to stop crying. Inside, it felt like I was dying all over again. "Did you know Leo was going to die, or was that a lucky gift that conveniently appeared in your deck of cards?"

"A lucky hand, if you will." He started to come closer to me, then thought better of it. Not an ounce of shame crossed his face, any form of guilt or humility nonexistent. "Trust me when I say this; you're better off not coming into your powers. You're better off not knowing that kind of battle for the rest of your life."

"Who are you to dictate my life?" I fought to control myself from screaming. Digging my nails into the skin of my palms, I rode the waves of pain so I didn't act on anger and set Kayden on fire. Above us, the bedroom light started to flicker. "I'm supposed to trust you now. What was your plan if he hadn't died? That you'd pretend to fall in love with me? Use me just like Ursula uses a human? Enrapture me until you could find another way to keep Leo out of my picture?"

"Is it so wrong to want to be free?'

"You're damn right it is," I growled. "It is when you put your own selfish immortal ass before the dying half-angel and the life of an innocent."

Once again, the room fell silent, only the sound of my beating heart filling the empty gaps. But I couldn't let the thought of Kayden planning my death die. It had to be a lie, just had to. I couldn't take another person I held feelings for set me up to die at their benefit.

My voice sounded barely above a whisper. "You kissed me to distract me from Leo. You killed him just so I could burn and you be free? Do you have any idea how convoluted that sounds? Whether I live for another five hundred years or die tomorrow you will still be an immortal. One way or another you would have been freed."

"One day you'll understand, Essallie," Kayden replied, not an ounce of an apology with it. The last fragment of my heart shattered into dust, bleeding for him as he went on. "We all do what we must to survive in our realm. If that means sacrificing a few to gain an upper hand, we do it."

I stared at him, jaw set. "Never. I never will do that to someone."

"Someday, you will."

Heat lanced at my fingertips, ready for a blood bath. It was all I could do to not see red. I imagined Kayden leaving my house later, joining his demon friends and laughing as he shared his tale that he fooled the gullible half-angel.

I let the words fire with force. "Get out. Just, get out, and never come back." When he didn't leave, I screamed at him louder, fire igniting my hands. "I never want to see you again."

He stared at me for one last second before he vanished, leaving me alone. I waited for the spoils of his black smoke trail out of window before I sunk to the floor and sobbed, my walls and flickering light the only comfort to my name. I kept my hand sealed over my mouth as I let the sobs shake my body. Because of me, everything has gone wrong. Because of me, someone died. My creation was unraveling everyone's lives, destroying everyone I came in contact with. Only a soulless, heartless monster could do such a thing and still want to live.

Monster. It seemed pretty accurate. Seeing as after this, I was fairly sure I didn't have a heart left to break.

THREE

PAINTED ON MY MEMORY

Tuesday had turned into one of the best weather days in months. The sun stayed strong, bright and luminescent. What little traces of snow that had remained vanished as the temperature climbed, revealing fresh patches of rich grass and budding flowers. Belfast had turned into a colorful paradise practically overnight, and everyone was celebrating it. Everyone but me.

The last week had dissolved into a blur, a chunk of time lost to the masses. My fight with Kayden still stung like a freshly grazed wound, torn at the edges and too weak to heal. He kept to my words since I screamed at him to never come back. He didn't show up for finals, for any of the local parties held by seniors. Just gone, like ashes scattered to the wind.

My graduation ceremony went without a hitch. One second I had been stage-side, waiting for my name. The next, a thin little book rested in my hands as I joined the others before me back in the crowd. Jayson made sure to stand up and whistle when I stepped onto the stage and accepted my diploma. We'd gone to a little dinner out in Portland, his treat, and back home to a small party he'd thrown together to surprise me. But without Abigail there to snicker by my side, it felt pointless.

I'd slowly made my way up the steps and to my room for a moment of peace. Door shut behind me, I sat on the edge of my bed and stared out through the window, my funny little piece of paper twirling in my hands. It all felt fake. My dress, the party, Jayson's beaming smile at how proud he was of me, it all felt off.

There was a gentle knock at my door before it opened. I turned around to see Jayson poking his head in. His hair was a mess, tousled locks starting to fall into his eyes.

"Can I come in?"

I looked back down to the paper in my hands and nodded. He stepped inside, making sure to shut the door behind him, and came over to the edge of the bed to sit alongside me. For a few minutes, neither of us spoke, the silence oddly comforting yet equally smothering.

"It's funny," Jayson said, shattering the silence. "The memories of this place as a child were so terrifying."

It had been like he read my mind. My eyes landed on a small photo on the window ledge, two kids smiling at each other, covered in cake icing. "Do you remember my fourth birthday? How mad Mom was when we smashed my cake before she could take a photo?"

He chucked, a haunted smile lifting his lips. "How could I not? After that beating I swore I would never be able to sit again."

"I can't remember why we decided to tear into it, though."

"You said you hated the picture on top," Jayson's face took on a far-away look. "Mom had drawn on horns on your name when you had insisted on wings."

My face fell as the dim memory of plunging my hands

into a cake made by spiteful mother played in my mind. With it came flashbacks of dark nights, hiding in hallway closets and flowerbeds to avoid a woman gone off the deep end. Everything turned back to her, and how she'd known from the start that she'd carried a half-breed for a daughter. A black mark on her pristine relationship with an angel named Michael.

"House of Horror was so befitting for this place," I barely whispered. No amount of bright paint or re-done kitchens could ever replace the nightmares I had experienced in this place. It had set me up for a life of time-ticking death. Some days, I wished she had aborted me when she had the chance.

"Jayson," I began. "If I don't come back after the summer-"

"*When* you come back," he corrected me, holding up a hand to silence me. "It doesn't have to be this summer, or fall, or winter. It could be next week, or five years from now. But when you decide to come back, remember you'll always have a home here."

"I'm just so surprised how a piece of paper with words on it can mean so much to the world."

His hand rested over both of mine, and I could hear him struggle with the right words to say. "We really do have a twisted way of needing proof people can do things. But you should be proud." His tone turned stronger, more confident and elated. "Several months ago no one thought you'd be here."

I pursed my lips and did my best not to sound sullen. "I guess Gram and Pop still didn't think so."

Jayson spoke soft. "I'm sure they're still on vacation."

"And I'm sure they're not."

"What makes you say that?"

"Because I know their schedule."

He sounded like a cross between half-amused, half-incredulous. "You have their lives pinpointed down to a schedule?"

I stared at him. "They come home the third week of May, every year like clockwork." My eyes turned to stare at the small suitcase propped against the wall as I shrugged.

When Jayson didn't answer right away, I looked back. He too had noticed the luggage that hadn't been there a few days ago. He strained to keep his tone pleasant. "Of course. Your home with them, back in New York."

Guilt washed over me instantly. I felt like I had just gut punched him, only to spit in his face and laugh as he curled into a defeated ball on the ground. "I didn't mean it like-"

"No, it's okay. Really, it's fine." He smiled, but it clearly didn't touch his eyes. "But you'll come and visit some time, right?"

"Count on it," I told him, wrapping my arms around his shoulders and giving a short squeeze.

I wasn't sure what to expect when I came home to New York. That maybe there would be a chance of finding two loving grandparents waiting for me to see that I was no longer this catatonic and introverted granddaughter that they had seen shuffled off to Maine only a matter of months ago. As I narrowed on the highway, and took the route down, I let my mind drift. I thought back to one of my first days at the small school in New York. It was a tiny little private place. One that held maybe a group of fifty kids per class. An elitist school, my grandfather would smugly say over his morning breakfast and paper. The kind of school you'd only dream to get in. And it felt like just like, a dream. I went through private school smoother than a sheet of water, cleaner than a sheet of glass. It wasn't until the event with Chase that I had been perfect, that I had been normal. I couldn't remember having any kind of oddities or events. I couldn't remember anything standing out about me until that night. That was when I felt like everything had turned. Like every pair of eyes turned to stop and stare at me. That no body left me room to breathe.

My previous home in New York had been a lavishly decorated one. My grandmother wasn't exactly the kind of person to skimp and cut corners. Everything held that neoclassical style with just a touch of Victorian accents you knew she picked up from private auctions for an easy six figure price. I remember spending most of my childhood unable to touch anything in that home, for fear of receiving a wrath like no other for ruining her 'precious' things.

As I entered the building, I gave a small nod to the bell boy, strolled to the elevator, and hit the number. Those two minutes riding in the elevator felt like forever. I suddenly realized I had no idea what I was going to say to them when I came face to face. Did I want to start off accusing and hot-headed, telling them of my fears that they hadn't believed I would ever return home, sound of mind? Or did I simply take them into my open arms and let it all fall to the wayside?

I looked up to see the elevator doors were wide open. I hadn't even heard the bell ring. Stepping off into the hallway, I watched the elevator shut the door behind me, leaving me alone with nothing but four walls to greet me. As I went down the hallway, it became clear I didn't want to start off things on the wrong foot with them, I didn't want things to be harsh and uncomfortable like they were with my Mother. I was tired of turning people away, my grandparents as far as I knew were perhaps the only remaining family who, aside from Jayson, actually cared about me, and not about some unexplained gift that was bestowed upon me.

I reached over to the door and looked down and stopped. It was slightly open, as if someone had forgotten to shut it. I could hear the soft sounds of orchestra music, no doubt coming from my Grandfather's study. Giving the door a small nudge, I stepped inside, leaving my bag sit at the door.

"Grand? Gram?" I called out. Nobody greeted me back.

It was unusual. They definitely had to be home. There was no way they left the door open, and a regular burglar was out of the question; the complex we lived in had enough security that made airports blush.

I looked over into the living room and saw the first sign of distress. A red flag shot up in my mind as one of my grandmother's prized vases had been smashed, shattered chunks of porcelain lying scattered on the floor. The couch had been slightly turned to an angle. I followed the path of destruction to the hallway off to my left, finding more destruction to greet me. A turned over end table blocked down the hall. I turned it over to set it back only to see one of its four legs was missing.

An odd ringing sensation started in my ears as I walked down the hallway. The pounding of blood in my head growing louder and louder, stronger with each overpowered thump. My bedroom door had been closed, the bathroom door closed as well. My grandparent's bedroom at the end of the hall also appeared shut. Only one room was ajar.

The swells of orchestra music grew louder as I inched closer to the door, my body quivering with an instinctive fear. For a second the ringing and music meshed into a noise so powerful I thought I'd never hear anything else. As I got closer, I saw no light coming from the room.

Stepping closer to the frame, I pushed open the door to fully expose his study. Hallway light blasted in, revealing a grizzly scene painted before me. A silhouette of a human slumped in the brown leather chair sat in the far corner. On top the desk, haloed in the light, lay my grandmother's corpse, her torso ripped open exactly like Chase's had been the night he had died. Red smeared over the scattered papers on the desk. I stumbled back into the door, screaming, and fell.

Scrambling to get back up, I felt a dampness cover most of my legs and arms. I let out another scream before bounding out the door faster than I could think, stumbling into the walls, smearing bloody handprints all over the creamscicle walls in my wake. I made it just to the kitchen sink before I threw my head into it and heaved everything in my stomach. I began to scrub furiously, pouring dish soap all over my hands as I did anything I could to get the blood off my hands. Red, so much red.

I don't know how long I stood there scrubbing, turning the water hotter and hotter until my skin seared and screamed in agony. I turned off the faucets and sank down to the ground, looking down at my sodden appearance. Blood smudged and smeared over my jeans, my jacket soaked by blood. I couldn't believe it. Just how many people was I going to lose? How many more people were going to hurt me and those surrounding me?

There was a small crunch of something across the room. I immediately snapped up to attention, the ringing in my ears replaced by the fluttering effect of my heart, beating faster than a hummingbird's wings. Inching myself off the floor, I peered over the counter. A small figure dressed head to toe in black stood in the mess of my living room, eyes curiously examining a shard of the broken vase I had first seen. A small red heart was emblazoned on the jacket of her shoulder, the only source of color on her.

I gasped, and she instantly laid eyes on me. I went cold. Her eyes were a solid obsidian, no form of iris or pupil to speak. It was as if she were an incarnate of the devil herself.

Every instinct in my body told me to run, my veins burning with the need to put as much distance between myself and this person as I could physically manage. I never felt such an overwhelming urge to move in all my life.

48

The person took one step forward, I took one step back.

Suddenly the game shifted, and she leapt toward me, clearing the distance from the living room to where I stood in an instant. My body reacted before my mind could, racing for the front door. I burst through it and down the hallway, slamming into the wall and smacking the elevator button in the same breath. There was no way it would open in time before that... thing joined me in the hall. My eyes landed on the door to the staircase, and I flung myself through it.

I don't know how many floors I cleared before I looked up. She was practically right behind me, clearing steps in multiples with ease. I had no idea how she was doing it; my lungs burned, a rigid ache settling in my chest and throat, and at some point I knew I would have to stop to breathe. But the rising fear that she'd catch me kept me moving, willing me to avoid capture or even death.

I managed to get down the steps and out the front door, ignoring the gasps and shocked stares that followed me. My mind was racing almost as fast as my heart continued to pound, the streets signs passing by me in mixed blurs. Before I knew it, I had cleared several blocks and found myself in a street corner alleyway, alone.

I pressed myself against a cold and damp brick wall, wedging myself between two large dumpster cans. This was insane, my mind told me, absolutely insane. I had just cleared through a corner of Times Square, most likely running from a demon, like a zebra fleeing from a hungry lion. Every inch of my body burned and ached, yet I had nothing to show for it but some bloody clothes and beads of sweat.

Half-angel or not, you weren't supposed to run from the enemy. You were supposed to fight them, kill them.

All of Kayden's words buzzed at the front of my brain. He had asked me point-blank if I would be ready for this, ready to fight against masses of demons intent on killing me for their own benefit. At first, I had thought he was exaggerating; we weren't in the 1600's any more, battling with swords and crude weapons. Now, I wasn't so sure.

I wanted to tell someone, instinctively involve the police. But what exactly could a mortal officer do for a supernatural battle over me?

My eyes spotted a piece of broken mirror, and I picked it up. One quick look told me I wasn't going to get far with all this blood on me. I started to remove my jacket when I felt a familiar lump in the one side pocket. Pulling it out, I stared at the glint of shiny plastic and metal, my cell phone left in my palm.

My heart leapt into my throat, and I was dialing a number before I even realized who it was. Kayden's number rang a couple of times before sending me to voicemail. I hung up and tried again, only this time I dialed the one person I knew would pick up.

Jayson's voice sounded through my phone on the third ring. "Essallie! You made it there safely?"

"Jayson," I started, only to stop. My voice quivered and cracked, I sounded horrible. "Jayson, I-"

He caught the sound of my choked sobs. "Essallie, what's going on? Are you hurt?"

"No, I- I'm fine," I stammered out, clenching a fist and smacking the cold wall behind me. The words came in a rush, spilling from my lips in a snowballing effect. "Gram and Gran are dead, Jayson. They're dead, murdered, blood everywhere, and I saw it, and it's everywhere, and I don't know what to do and- and- and-"

I heard something crash behind me. Instantly I spun around, scream clutched in my throat. An emaciated street cat scurried across the alleyway into an open container.

I zeroed back in on the phone in my hand. Jayson was screaming at me, trying to get my attention.

"Essallie, Essallie are you still there?"

"I'm still here."

"Listen to me, right now. You need to go to the police. Let them know what you saw. I'm getting in the car right now."

"Jayson, if I go to the police, they'll arrest me on the spot. It's too much like Chase's death. How coincidental can you get? The second I'm home, and they're dead?"

"Running from the police is the last thing you want to do-"

"And turning myself in is on the same list," I sighed. "It's me they're after, not Gram, not Gran, not Chase."

"Who's after you, Essie?"

I started to answer when another set of footsteps sounded behind me. I turned around to come face-to-face with the woman I'd spotted in the apartment. Slowly, I lowered the phone from my face, pressing it against my leg so Jayson couldn't hear.

"Who are you?"

"Now, must we start with all the tense formalities? Or can we skip them and get straight to the part where you come along with me?"

I held out my free hand and ignited a ball of brilliant blue flame. "Why does nobody answer my questions?"

She gave me a sharp, cryptic smile. "Who I am is none of your concern." She extended a hand out to me, flicking tresses from her long ponytail over her shoulder. "This can be done easily or painfully. I'd rather take you in whole, and not in a jar. But I can promise you that, voluntary or not, we will get what we want from you."

"What is it you want?"

"The same thing everyone wants. Your blood." Her fingers wiggled at me impatiently. "It'll be over before you know it, just come with me."

My eyes locked on her outstretched hand. I studied the curvature of her fingers, the slender black nails sharpened to small points at the top. Just at the peak, a fleck of dried blood clung to a single one. I thought of my grandfather and grandmother, fighting off the woman before me, her nails slashing through skin and muscle and veins, their blood forever on her hands.

I exploded.

Fire expelled from my body, a sheet of flame arcing down the alleyway. I could hear the woman curse before exploding into smoke the exact same time I raced to make my exit. Kicking several piles of trash behind me, I ran down the opposite end, phone locked tight in my hand.

As soon as I had darted down another alley, I brought the phone back up to my ear. "Jayson, are you still there?"

"What the hell is going on?" He screamed on the other end. "Who the heck was that and why the hell was she talking about your blood?"

"I think she's an unhinged mental patient," I lied between breaths, running through the darker end of an alley. "Listen, you can't come here, it's too dangerous." I had no idea how this woman was tracking me, but I had a good feeling that it had something to do with my blood.

Jayson started to angrily reply when a high-pitched whistle blew out all other sound around me. Something hot and sharp sliced across my cheek, taking the cell phone with it. I let out a scream of terror as the phone ricocheted at the far end of the wall. It burst into crunched glass and plastic fragments. Behind me, the woman laughed with sinister glee.

Rage built in my chest, hot spikes ready to release. My veins throbbed just beneath the skin. The time to run was over, I had to defend myself.

Scrapping my heels into the gravel, I turned around to face my captor. She grinned wickedly in relish of the challenge, releasing her nails to long black spikes as she leapt up to attack. My body reacted instinctively, the click of fire igniting over my palms in defense. I threw myself into a slide against the ground, bringing my hands in front of my face. The image of a flame-blower came to mind and I breathed, blowing off a burst of blue fire at the woman.

She shrieked and curled inward, collapsing onto the ground in a smoldering heap. I barely had time to scramble to my feet before she was on hers, charging at me once more. I twisted my body to the side, barely missing the talons of her hands. I pushed a jolt of fire at her, catching the end of her ponytail as she spun back, pressing herself to the wall opposite me and using it as a springboard to crouch against.

"You have a death-wish I see, Nephilim," she hissed, crawling up the wall like an insect. What ever spell that had been keeping her looking human had now faded, revealing her form. Her face was no longer the creamy pale perfection she'd sported before. Now it was scaly and deep murky green with sharp, jutting angles making up her cheeks and nose while providing deep hollows for her black eyes. Her lips had been pulled back across the lower half of her face, revealing multiple rows of jagged teeth, stained and discolored with a mix of blood and pus-like goo.

"Not nearly as badly as you do." I stepped back, keeping to the balls of my feet. I felt like a spring, ready to launch at any given moment. "Should have turned around before I decided to fight back."

She laughed, twisting her arms to impossible extensions, the scratching of her nails against the wall shudder worthy. "You won't say that when we finish slaughtering everyone you love. I pick my teeth with loved ones of Nephilim, ever since your filthy kind was created."

I could feel the pressure in my veins, each heartbeat making the sensation overwhelming. Pictures of Jayson, dangling in this creature's grasp like a petrified rag doll, brought my rage to a boil. If I didn't release it soon, someone was going to pay. I was going to lose control.

"Tell you what," I started, craning my neck while keeping my guard up. "I'll make you a deal. My blood for my life. You can leave with your life and do whatever you want with the blood. I leave and you never see me again."

She seemed to mull over the offering, twisting her head at me with curiosity. She scuttled down the wall a few feet, drooling as she got closer to me. "Can't do. Master promised me your flesh when they would be done with you." One of her eyes changed color to a bright chartreuse. "Delicacy, flesh is. Those two mortals were delicious, smelled just like you. Appetizer to the main meal."

"Shame I have to disappoint," I replied sarcastically. "But your days of murder are over."

She screeched and launched off the wall straight for me. I had a second to spin around and curl inward, squeezing my eyes tight. I forced all the energy through my back just as the alleyway exploded into a luminescent bath of sparkling light.

The effect was instant; It felt like an extension of my soul had been pulled from my body, wrapping me into a cocoon of pure energy. The woman had screamed in horror, leaping back from the light as fire laced up her limbs with merciless speed. I turned to face her and she lashed out, nails scrapping across my face and knocking me to the ground.

Against the vines of burning light, she stood on her two feet and took a third lunge for me. This time I couldn't fend her off. Teeth sunk into my abdomen, tearing into the side with my scar. The pain was beyond anything I'd ever felt, the sensation like hot screws driving into my flesh. One of my wings flung at her, knocking her off me while adding to the fire pressing upon her body.

I scrambled back to my feet and added distance between

us. Crafting a fireball I launched it, watching the brilliant blue mesh with the white flames, burning her skin as far as bone. The creature screamed and writhed, flailing her melting limbs in a desperate attempt to reach me.

I stood there, watching the fire char her body as if I was from afar. Skin peeled back like curling paper, revealing layers of the same pus-like ooze that drooled from her mouth, while the layers of muscle and fat melted away. I stood there until nothing but bones remained. Until I was sure she was dead, never coming back. One reincarnated demon was enough for my lifetime.

I walked out of the alleyway and down the main streets, oblivious to anyone who chose to stare. Chances were my outside appearance reflected how I felt on the inside; bruised, weak, drained. The crystal wings and blue fire both had vanished, leaving a hollow feeling extending deep inside of me. My head swam with everything, repeating my alien actions. Kayden had never taught me any of those things, yet my body knew exactly what to do as if I had it built into my DNA.

Turning onto a new street, I spotted a diner I'd never seen before. Wedged perfectly between two fast food shops it looked quaint, lost in the frame of an older time. I walked inside and slid into a nearby booth, keeping my head down to avoid any more stares.

My ribs ached, and as I yanked away the fabric of my torn shirt I quickly understood why. A half-crescent shape of teeth marks framed my colored scar. The skin around it was inflamed and tender, probably infected. Oddly enough, not a single drop of blood escaped from the wound. It wasn't nearly as painful as Chase's assault had been on me, either. I wondered if there was more than one type of demon blood.

A waitress came over to the booth, a bored expression glued to her face until she took in my disheveled appearance.

Her amber eyes enlarged in a mixture of horror and curiosity. "Dear God, are you dying?"

I let out a weak, low laugh. "Most likely. But until I do, can I get a cup of coffee?" I thought about it for a moment. "And use your phone?"

She gave a jerky nod of her head, dark brown curls bouncing. "You'll have to come to the counter to use the phone, it's corded. Just don't tell my boss. We're not supposed to let customers use it unless it's an emergency."

Biting back the urge to tell her that this definitely was an emergency, I forced a smile in place of my sarcastic remark. She turned to leave as I stood to follow her, but I stopped. Between the back half of her uniform swished a long, thin red tail coated in small sharp barbs. The second I blinked, it vanished. Maybe the poison was already taking effect.

My fingers ran over the countertop as the waitress came over with the phone and a cup of coffee. Setting both down, she gave me a small smile before heading over to the other end of the diner, taking an order of an elderly couple. I punched in Jayson's cell number, and he picked up on the first ring.

"Essallie?" He sounded shaken, and I could practically picture the look of worry on his face.

I took a deep, steadying breath. "Yes, it's me."

And just like that, he started spouting words. "What the hell is going on, Essie? Abigail told me you're fine, that your phone died and Kayden was on his way to get you and bring you home. You're not telling me something, I know it. I called the police up there and they're on the way to you house and-"

"Jayson."

"Essallie-"

"Jayson, listen to me." I closed my eyes, envisioning him as if he were right beside me. "I need you to go home. Please, don't drive here. I've lost too much, I can't bear to lose you too."

Silence stretched on the receiving end for over a minute before he started to plead. "Come home, Essallie. Please. I don't want to lose you, either. We can do this together, whatever it is. I meant it when I said you could tell me anything."

I covered the receiver and took in a shaky breath. He couldn't get involved in this, that much I knew. He'd only be fodder against the creatures searching for me.

Removing my hand from the speaker, I kept my voice low and calm. "Everything will be okay. Just please, go home. Be safe, keep close to Abigail. I promise to tell you as much as I can, soon."

"Essie, please," he begged, and I nearly shattered. But I held my ground. Seconds that felt like centuries ticked by as he realized I wasn't going to budge. "Remember what we used to tell each other before nightfall? Our little safe-keeping phrase?"

I let out a weak laugh, hot tears escaping from my eyes. "Batten the hatches, love you bunches."

"You remember. Don't ever forget, I love you bunches. Be safe."

"I'm so sorry, Jayson. Goodbye."

I placed the phone back on its base, staring at the receiver with a bitter and empty feeling filling my chest. My heart felt as if someone had struck it with a mallet, steamrolled it, and tossed it into a hole to be filled over in wet cement.

Tearing my eyes from the phone, I stole a quick glance around the diner. Most of the booths had been quickly filled during my phone call; groups of families and friends huddling over cups of coffee or hot chocolate topped with whipped cream, laughing and smiling. Sharp gusts of wind rushed into the room every time someone came in, filling the room with a mix of hot and cold air. My heart let out a painful beat. Until now those smiling faces could have been Jayson and I, two people blissfully unaware of the horrors lingering in the shadows of another world pressing against each other.

"Miss, mind if I put the phone back?"

I jerked my head back to the phone, a hand resting lightly above it. A busboy stood behind the counter, his face caught between a mixture of shock at my appearance and fear that I might snatch the phone. But it neither the boy nor the phone that left me staring. It was the purple horns, a pair of them protruding out of his forehead, that caught my eye. And this time when I blinked, they were still there.

"What *are* you?" I asked.

The boy looked taken aback. He laughed nervously, a hand reaching up to touch his horns reflexively before he controlled himself.

"I'm afraid I don't understand, Miss," he said.

My gaze turned harder, lips pressing into a thin smile as a light bulb turned on in my head. "I think you do." I brought my hands in front of my chest, keeping them just in his eyesight. Slowly I opened them, revealing a flicker of blue flames cupped inside. "You understand very well."

The container of dishes nearly slipped out of his hands and crashed to the floor. "Please don't do that- you'll scare them. They don't take too kindly to Nephilim-"

"Like your horns wouldn't scare them all?" I extinguished the fire between my hands and traded for a small flame cradling my index fingernail. The flame lazily spread halfway down my finger until I stopped it. "I bet you'd hate to have everyone here know you're a demon of some sort. Or worse, that you talked to the dreaded half-angel everyone seems to hate."

The effect of my words was instantaneous. Color drained from his face, his eyes bugging out of their sockets with paranoia. "My horns? But they won't... Please, what do you want?"

There was only one thing in life I wanted, and that was to be free of being half of some creature. But for the moment I'd settle for some information I was sure the little scaredy cat would cough up. "You answer some questions, I'll leave. Easy as that."

He nodded enthusiastically. "No problem, sure."

"Why are there so many supernatural creatures here?"

His eyes ran across the room quickly, no doubt making sure we were the only two in the conversation. "No offense, but you do know where we are, right?" When I shook my head, he started to chuckle. "This is a corner of the demon end of New York City. You won't find any mortals around here, least not a mortal who isn't tied to one of us."

"But, the groups-" I started to say, turning around for a moment to look at the people in the diner. Sure enough, the busboy was right; no one in the diner was human, all wore different levels of glamours. A collection of various colored scales, feathers, tentacles, and more stood out like large billboards against the bleak, common backdrop of the diner. People who I had originally thought to be normal were demons, faeries, and succubi.

"Okay, that takes care of that embarrassing question," I mumbled under my breath, turning back to face a grinning busboy. His horns had grown considerably since I had pointed them out. Now they stood about six inches off his forehead, purple leeching into his skin and filling in the corner creases of his eyes. "Next. Is there a... demon who dresses in all black? With a red heart on the shoulder?" I traced a heart on my right shoulder to show him.

He nodded, completely nonchalant about it. "It's a private demon, someone who's hired personally, like a mortal PI. They're called Venator Privatus, but we just call them the

Vens." Scratching his head, he nibbled on a side of his lower lip for a moment. "There's usually two symbols on their sleeves. One is the heart, that shows they're Vens, and the symbol underneath tells you who's hired them."

So someone had hired a Vens to capture me? What, were we in some communistic society where you could pluck someone off the street and no one question you? I marveled in horror at the thought. Running a hand through my short hair, I tried to think what Kayden would say if we were both stuck in this predicament.

Wait a minute. Why did I need to know what Kayden would do? I was my own person, after all, wasn't I? Did I not have the ability to make my own choices in life? I didn't need someone to lead me by the hand and decide what I needed to do. I would be strong, and stand up for myself. This was my destiny, and I would take it head on.

I seized the first idea that came to mind and spoke. "You have a name?"

"Darren."

"Alright Darren, how about do me one more favor and then I'll vanish from your hair, er, horns," I amended, staring at the rapidly evolving cones on his face. More purple spikes had started to protrude from his face, forming half circles around his ears like decorative piercings. "With this being such a high-supernatural region, I'm sure there's a portal nearby."

He nodded again. "There's two. One at the local club, Sphynx, but that doesn't open until nightfall. The second," he trailed off, then looked down away from my gaze. "I can't take you to."

"Why?"

"It's in my boss' office." His face looked strained. "He'd freak if I let someone use it- it's supposed to be private."

"Private shmivate. I know the family that owns control

over all of them, and their son." I refused to say Leo's name aloud, worried it might start a wave of emotion I couldn't control. Instead, I transferred my possible sadness into anger. My gaze narrowed to thin slits. "Denying me access could revoke his right to even have the portal. You wouldn't want me to report your boss, would you?"

Darren's eyes widened, and I swear I saw him flinch in fear. His voice was barely audible. "He'd fire me, banish me from the quarter." It didn't take long for the resolve to form in his face, his shoulders slumping in defeat. "I'll do it. Quickly, though, before he comes back from his luncheon."

I nodded and followed him through the double doors leading to the back half of the diner. The kitchen appeared as if it was in anarchy, food flying left and right as two men with seven hands each tried furiously to keep up with different orders. Timers blared left and right, pots bubbling over the lids as several other bodies scrambled to put plates in order and serve them out.

"Guess it was a good thing I didn't order food?" I joked over the noise, following Darren through the kitchen to a mahogany door at the end.

Over the sound of someone swearing in a guttural language, he laughed. "Not to shoot my boss in the foot, but I wouldn't eat here if I could help it." He fashioned out a little brass key to unlock the door, swinging it open and gesturing to me. "Ladies first."

Following him inside, he shut the door, sealing all the noise out with it. I turned on a table lamp for a little more light. The office had no windows, no real natural light to open up the room. The carpet beneath us reeked of mold, the walls cold and damp to the touch. Sparse furniture of a desk, chair, and bookcase were the only three things in the room.

Darren motioned to the bookcase. "This is it. But I don't know what one opens the switch."

I came to stand in front of the shelf, running my eyes over the covers and spines. Most of the books looked ordinary; self-help, succeeding in business, some on supernatural beings and identifying factors. But one small, cobalt blue book stood out against the rest. Just like the one at the bookshop Leo used to own.

I looked over my shoulder and gave Darren a wink. "I've got it from here, no worries."

He nodded, offering me a small smile. "Before you go, some advice?"

"Yeah?"

"Be wary," he said, something in his tone instantly worrying me. "You're stepping into the lion's den unprotected."

I had to laugh; was everyone going to tell me what I already knew? It had been clear early on that I would spend the rest of my life alone, fighting to stay in one breathing, living piece.

"Please, give me some credit," I replied with a smirk. "You ever seen what these hands can do?"

He fumbled for words, but I didn't give him a chance to answer. Stepping into the light, gravity tossed me through the portal, landing me in the middle the last place I'd ever expect to be.

FOUR

A LIFETIME OF YESTERDAYS

I was pretty sure I landed on a body.

Everything around me was dark, a bottomless pit with no light. For a moment I had thought for sure I had gotten lost to the time space continuum or some awkward conundrum, when something beneath me moved. And groaned.

"Jipskie, what the gravy-and-potatoes are you doing?" The body, a male judging by the voice, hissed. "Are you supposed to be on?"

"What the hell is a Jipskie?"

The person stopped moving. "...*who the hell are you?*"

"I could ask you the same thing!" I started to squirm, catching my shoulders on the sides of the small and cramped space we were stuck in. "Stupid portal and it's stupid faulty crap-"

"Stop it! Hey, knock it off! You're going to break it!" He sounded fearful. Hands clumsily came into contact with my face as he tried to stop me from wiggling around.

"Break what?" I managed to get out before the door burst open. A blast of lights clouded my view as we tumbled onto the floor in a mess of limbs and fabric.

"What the hell is going on here?"

Blinking, my vision started to clear, putting me face-to-face with at least a dozen people all in various stages of attire. Crowds of people carrying props, dabbing on makeup, and marking the floor in chalk hurried by our group huddled in the middle, unmoving. A rich, burgundy velvet curtain hung behind all of them, but did little to dull the noise of a growing crowd anticipating a good show.

Oh crap. I was on a stage.

"Well?" The same guy who had asked what was going on snapped. He had tan, olive colored skin covered in bursts of black polka dots, and eyes a shimmering ocean green that matched perfectly to the ruffled blouse he wore. Placing hands on his hips, he glared. "Tusk, who's your lovely little companion and why is she intruding on my show?"

I had almost completely forgotten I wasn't alone. Half-buried in the waves of multi-colored fabric surrounding us sat a boy. He looked no younger than a teenager with his wide, open violet eyes and smooth pink lips, his hair a shocking mess of black and silver spikes sprouting from his head.

The boy, Tusk, spoke in a panicked rush. "I don't know, sir. I was just getting into the cabinet for my scene when she appeared from thin air!"

"I thought all portals had designated locations?" Speaking up, I started to peel off the various heaps of fabric weighing me to the floor. "You know, solid bases so people could come and go as needed?"

Overly-flamboyant man snapped his fingers, which I noticed were more like claws than actual human digits. "You used Frederick's portal, I see." He let out an irritated huff, rolling his eyes in maximum drama queen style. "I thought I had gotten through to his thick skull that he can't use it for the next eight weeks!"

Eight weeks? I thought about asking him why it had to be eight weeks, when it sort of occurred to me that I didn't exactly need to know. Or hear his sob story about how some riffraff was disgracing his preparing performance. Getting to my feet, I ignored the widening eyes and small gasps few had tried to contain over seeing my appearance.

"My stars, you're that, that," one of the female stage performers started to sputter. Her lips curled into a sneer just as she found breath. "That *Nephilim* from the circus!"

My face blanched. Eyes either narrowed in disgust or widened in shock as recognition crossed their faces. Looks like Kayden lied yet again on the whole 'no one saw you' ordeal.

"Well, trust me when I say I have no intentions of bothering you past this. Err, break a leg?" I offered the colorfully dressed man an awkward handshake and tried not to flinch while touching his clammy claws. Shuffling past him and the rest of the frozen pack, I quietly slipped out the nearest exit and onto the streets of Charon.

Two weeks hadn't been enough time to wash away the mesmerizing effect the place still had on me. Like marbleized version of Tokyo, Charon held the appearance of an ethereal palace, a serene setting stretching into a never-ending horizon. Tall, intimidating towers of sparkling pearl and creamy white ascended into the skies above, clouds their only neighbors. Even below on the ground it sparkled, homes of all shapes and sizes the same smooth and cool marble as above. If fairytales had a home, this is the place I would have imagined they'd all join together.

My heart still called out to the decadent beauty, like a lonely soul would to its other half. I knew deep down I belonged here, belonged with the faeries and demons and whatever else existed in the magical end of things. It's just that I never felt welcome.

I stared down both ends of the street in search of a street

sign, anything to tell me what and where I was. Instead, I was greeted with cold grey buildings. I found it odd; all of the buildings I had seen before in Charon were sparkling white, a glimmering marble like none other. Yet every building on this street was a light, bitter grey. It was almost as if the buildings were dirty and needed a good scrub.

I made my way down the street, doing my best to appear as non-creepy as possible while checking inside windows for signs of life. Most of the homes had their curtains drawn, and the few that didn't were vacant. I sighed. Looked like I would be on my own.

Gazing up to the overcast sky, I tried to spot something to help direct me to the main strip I knew. Sure enough, there in the sky at due east stood a tall pillar, a scaffold of white nearly blinding. I turned down various streets, making sure to keep the pillar in sight, watching it grow closer. As I got closer to the tall tower, I noticed the buildings began to lighten too, what little pigment of grey turning into a brilliant, dazzling white. People started appearing from thin air, chatting animatedly on freshly tailored lawns or walking down the street towards the same direction I was headed.

Flashbacks from the first time I had set foot in Charon washed over me, and it wasn't long before the my heart thumped painfully in my chest. The first time I had seen the buildings I had pinched myself, waiting for the dream to end. Now, I'd do anything to make all of this all just some bad nightmare.

A sharp jab in my gut reminded me this wasn't a dream, that I was very much awake and alive. My fingers gently pulled back a corner of my shirt, revealing a bigger wound that hadn't been there before. Inside my stomach twisted, nausea rolling over me as I spotted the splotches of yellow and green marring my skin. The wound was spreading, tenderness now extending all the way up to under my chest. At this rate,

I'd have a couple hours before it would kill me, tops.

Tugging my shirt back down and biting back a whimper, I continued forward. Familiar tawny cobblestones appeared under my feet, and before I knew it I had found the main street of Charon. I spotted an all-too familiar sign for a pub and ducked inside. If any place was going to help me in my search, a pub certainly would. Inside, purple and yellow banners for a performance decorated the walls, and I instantly recognized the model as the flamboyantly dressed man from the stage.

"They say his rendition is going to be the best in the last three-hundred years." I turned to see a girl standing next to me, pointing at the poster. At first glance, she looked completely average and human, until you looked in her eyes. Cats eye and icy blue, it was the only thing that gave away her inhuman genetics. The rest of her was normal, from the long elegant blonde hair and fair, pale skin. "Did you get a ticket?"

"I'm not much of a theater gal," I replied, looking back at the poster. Aside from the man standing up front, two people stood in the back, hands clasped together. Both had a display of elegant, white feathered wings. "What's it about?"

"*Chant du Cygne*? It's tragic, really, but we always consider it a comedy," said the girl. "It's about a pair of Nephilim that fall in love, but the one is slain by a demon before they can perform the bonding ritual and live happily ever after for all eternity."

"Doesn't sound very funny to me."

She shrugged. "Different strokes for different folks."

My gut twisted, but I wasn't sure if it was from the demon poison spreading inside of me or the image of a demon slaying me that did it. "Why does the demon slay them? Why not let them exist elsewhere in their happiness?"

She laughed, but it was sad. "In this world, no one can be happy. It's always kill or be killed."

"Sounds about right." We stood in silence for about a minute, both gazing at the banner with minimal interest. If it hadn't been for the tick-tock of the clock reminding me that I was one step closer to dying, I wouldn't have bothered to move. "Say, you don't happen to know-"

"Where to find a cure for demon poison?" She finished my sentence without pause. I froze; how did she know what was wrong with me? Tapping her nose, he answered my unspoken question. "I can smell it. My guess is you got on the wrong side of something nasty, judging by the poison used."

"I'm going to ignore the level of creepiness that just happened and be straightforward. Where can I find a remedy for this?"

She shook her head, small tresses of her blonde hair swaying over her shoulders. "You won't be able to put the salve on yourself. Do you have anywhere to stay for the night?"

My mouth opened to say yes, until I remembered the bodies I had left behind in New York, let alone the Vens I had burned to a crisp. "I'll figure something out."

"So that's a no."

"Fine. No, I don't have somewhere to stay."

The girl nodded thoughtfully. "I have a small place close to the border, you're more than welcome to stay while the salve draws out the poison."

"That's okay, I'll be fine," I shook my head and turned for the door. My fingers had just wrapped around the knob when it opened from the outside, a familiar face with fair green skin and wild, unruly hair staring at me in shock.

"Essallie?" Serena asked, her eyes still as wide as saucers. Her fingers reached up to touch the blue blemish over part of her face, crimson nails resting lightly against her cheek. "I thought you had returned to the mortal realm."

I glanced over my shoulder to the girl with blonde hair,

but she had already crossed the room to sit in a corner booth shrouded in the shadows. "I did," I answered distractedly at first, then fully turned back to look at Serena. "But some complications came up. Demons, dead bodies, you know."

"No, truthfully I don't."

Awkward pause. "Oh." Why did I think every supernatural being had to deal with wild bouts of murder and strife?

Serena let out a small laugh, shrugging her shoulders and stepping back in the same fluid move. "It was good to see you again, but I really must be going..."

So soon? But she just got here. A light bulb went off in my head. "Wait, do you have a minute? Maybe you could help me out."

She stunned me by shaking her head, caramel curls bouncing as she moved. "I'm sorry, I really do have to leave." Faster than I could react, she turned around and vanished, leaving me standing between the open door and pub entrance.

"Serena, wait!" I called after her, stumbling outside as a sudden spike of pain gripped at my insides. I doubled over in pain, biting my lower lip in a weak attempt not to scream. Through watery eyes I tried to spot her head among the crowds of people. Just at the end of a building, a mess of curls and green skin caught my eye.

I pulled myself up and raced through the throng of people, ignoring the blatant glares and snarky remarks as people bumped into me. People packed tighter, shutting me off from catching up to Serena. At this rate, I wasn't going to get to her.

An idea rooted in my brain. I acted on it before I could think it over, fire blazing over my knuckles in a blatant display of power. Those who had been standing before me stepped back, fear and horror mixed on their faces. I leapt through the parting crowd, hands in front. I wanted my message to be clear; get in my way and you were going to get burned.

With the fire on my hands, I cleared the path to where I had first spotted Serena easily, but she was already gone. My eyes scanned the thinning crowd, landing on the faint image of her ducking into the apothecary we had first met.

I was there in a second, flinging open the door to a startled couple hovering over a small purple bottle. Serena stood in the doorway, halfway through the curtains behind the main desk.

"Serena, wait," I started. The startled couple, the shop owner and her husband, came to stand in front of the desk, blocking Serena from view.

"You again," the woman I remembered as Lorena, spoke with a quiver. Opal eyes held a mix of resentment and fear. "Haven't you done enough?"

I pointed a emblazoned finger at her. "You're one to talk. Step aside and let me speak to Serena alone."

"Not a chance." She glanced over her shoulder at the willowy girl and gave a curt nod before turning back to me. A look of pain crossed Serena's face just as she vanished through the waves of fabric. "You're not going to bring another innocent into your crosshairs."

I felt my eyes practically bulge out of my head. Her, innocent? Was everyone drinking the poisoned party drink these days? "*She's* the one who told me about myself! There's nothing innocent about her. She knows more than you think, now get out of my way."

"Or what?" Lorena took a faint step toward me, lips pursed. "You'll silence me? Be the monster every person knows you are and destroy our way of life?" I watched as a blade materialized in her hand, a silver dagger no more than six inches, the hilt covered in different engraved patterns. "You, filthy Nephilim, are a stain on this world. Your very inception is a blemish of corruption and disgust. Your kind only exists to cause us misery and pain with your *rules* and *limitations*."

"Lorena," her husband pitifully tried to calm her.

She cut him off. "No Bernard, I'm done playing these games! All Cassandra had to do was end her life before she gave birth to her little spawn of vermin! None of our lives would have fallen apart if she hadn't existed. Our family is gone because of her, frayed into nothing, and none of it can be woven back together as long as she exists!"

"So it's my fault I was born? Do you have any idea how messed up that sounds?" I asked her, incredulous.

"No. It's that wretch of a woman you call *Mother's* fault that you were born. She knew what she was getting into, what kind of curse she was bringing into this world by having you. The fault falls on *you* for not having died in New York when your time came!"

Shock rippled through me, like an aftereffect of taking a bullet to the chest. For a moment it felt like I would never breathe again, just like Lorena wanted. I could stop, let my lips turn blue and bitter as every cell within me died. I could grant her the relief she so desperately wanted.

Too bad I wasn't suicidal. Or mental.

Bernard turned to fully face his wife, violet eyes brimming with tears. "Lorena, please, think about this." He held out a small photograph with a shaking hand. "The means will not get your desired end. We knew that from the start."

She gave him an icy, empty stare. "It's the only way. We have to turn her over. Otherwise..."

"You don't know that."

"I do, Bernard, you know I do." Lorena's shoulders dropped in misery. The posture of her body made it look like she carried the weight of the world on her shoulders. "I may be old, but I still carry the Sight just as I had when we first met. There is no other way out of this that doesn't involve turning her in."

Fear grabbed at my heart, forcing it into a pounding frenzy. The lights, both candle and electric, began to wildly flicker. "Lorena, listen to your husband," I said, hoping she was still able to reason. "Condemning a person to death won't save your family."

"Spoken like a true person who has no real family to speak of." Her hand with the dagger raised, pointing straight at my heart. "You have nothing to lose."

"I have *everything* to lose!" My voice cracked as I bit back the urge to screech. "Dysfunctional or not, I have a family, I have friends! I stand to lose them all if you sign me off because of some prejudice."

Deep down, I knew it was no use. Lorena would continue to barter for time by arguing with me, baiting me with the same jabs at my vanishing life. I thought of Abigail, and how heartbroken she'd be if I died before resolving our fight. I pictured Jayson, face obscured by shadows as he stood before three caskets, knowing he'd forever torture himself because he didn't come for me. Even Kayden meant something, no matter how little he meant to me in this moment. I wouldn't let her win, I couldn't let her win.

Fire shot from my fingertips, and Lorena screamed, stumbling into the desk behind her. She dropped the dagger and clutched her wrist against her chest. With my other free hand I flung my fire at the blade, turning it to ash within seconds.

"Bernard, do something-" she croaked out.

I shot Bernard a glare. "You do nothing, understand? All you're going to do is tell me where Serena left for, and I will leave. But lie to me, and what happened to the dagger will happen to your shop."

Bernard flinched, and for a moment I felt bad. I didn't

enjoy looking heartless and cold; it only reinforced the black history Nephilim apparently had.

"Where is she, Bernard?"

He sighed, closing his eyes in sadness. "She has left for the back tunnels surrounding the market. You will find her in a small flower shop, purple roses outside."

I gave a short nod, passing by the two of them just as Lorena had snatched the photograph from her husband's hands, sobbing. Part of me wondered just what had happened to their beautiful family, and if the photo showed just how fallen apart things had become. The poison in my side reminded me I didn't have any more time to spare.

I passed through the curtain, revealing a thin and narrow hallway leading to a back exit door. Outside, sun glimmered on the horizon, warning me of the quickly approaching night. If nightfall came and I still had not found Serena... well, I didn't want to finish that thought.

Following Bernard's directions, I walked down several damp and dimly lit tunnels framed in discolored and aged cobblestone. Out of the corner of my eyes, silhouettes of cloaked figures loomed in the shadows, emanating a wave of fear strong enough to make my stomach roll. As soon as I spotted the hint of purple I picked up speed, nearly flinging myself inside the broom closet sized florist shop.

The contrast between outside and inside was like burning sun and pitch-black night; stunning, powerful bursts of colors covered every inch of the store, flowers of all shapes and sizes in full bloom. Tulips, daisies, roses, and more, each one intermingled with the next as they wrapped up posts and spread across the ceiling.

"Looks like someone found where the Hatter gets his colorful ideas," I whispered under my breath. Carefully I reached out and touched a silky petal of a elegantly blossomed orange rose, slowly running my fingertips over it. The smell of tangerines filled the air, small orange bubbles drifting from the ceiling like a misting confetti. It was unlike anything I had ever seen in my whole life.

"Curious, isn't it?" A small voice said from across the room, and I looked up to see Serena staring back at me, her eyes full of discontent. In her hands she held a blue and white spotted lily, its petals spreading as wide as her palm. "To find so much beauty in such a negative space."

Setting the flower down, she ran her fingers over the edges of the petals before walking toward me. The flower shuddered for a moment, then sealed itself tightly. Serena came to stand in front of me, and for the first time today I could see that something had taken its toll on her; Dark, bruised circles ran under her red and puffy eyes; her springy curls were limp and lifeless; and her skin looked blotched and irritated. Like a pristine piece of china lost to the sea, Serena was weathered.

"Sometimes the most beautiful star in the sky hides behind the blackest night." I sighed and touched the orange rose again. A new cascade of bubbles danced around the air, flying around the two of us with glee. It was a sharp contrast to the way we both felt on the inside. "Serena, why did you run?"

"Because I cannot help you," she suddenly snapped. She glared at me bitterly, hands clenched to fists at her sides. "You shouldn't have come here. By staying here you are putting everyone in danger."

"How?" I threw my hands in the air, rolling my eyes at her cryptic statement. "Everyone keeps telling me I'm dooming people by being here, but no one exactly tells me why. Kind of hard to understand the warning signs if you don't speak the language."

"Who else has said this to you?"

I pinched the bridge of my nose, forcing myself to breathe evenly. Fire stirred inside my chest, and my palm gave off a dull ache. "The Queen, Bernard and Lorena-"

"No one should know about the situation aside from a select few."

"I'm sure Kayden warned me at some point, then there's the Vens that tried to capture me-"

"What?" Serena nearly shouted. She grabbed my upper arms and stared at me in sheer terror. "A Vens tried to capture you? Here, in Charon?"

I winced; her long nails were starting to dig into my skin. "No, back home in the mortal realm. That's why I came here-someone told me that I could find who hired the Vens. I have to stop them before they..." My throat turned to sandpaper, and I could feel the start of tears. "Before they kill everyone in my family."

She stared at me for a moment until my words sunk in. Her eyes casted downward, voice thick with sorrow and sympathy. Slowly she released her hands from my arms. "They traced your scent to your loved ones."

I nodded even though she couldn't see it. "The two who had raised me almost my whole life." I swallowed painfully against my dry throat. "Please, Serena, help me. I can't let them find my brother, he's the last real piece of family I have left."

"You don't understand," she said, shaking her head solemnly. "It isn't that I do not want to help you, it's that I physically cannot."

"But you knew so much about before we had even met," I started.

She held up a hand, silencing me. "That was not my doing. Seventeen years ago, I met a prophet who told me that one day I would cross paths with a Nephilim who would be lost. Everything I have told you was what the prophet had told me."

I thought about it. A prophet using Serena as a messenger

just to string me along with little information except on how I'd die. It sounded a lot like something Kayden would do, but I doubt he really knew about me because of how shocked he'd been when I exploded and revealed my wings. But if the prophet knew about me...

"But you said Leo was my Watcher," I said. "Did the prophet tell you that, too?"

She shook her head. "It was only a guess. The level of energy that came off both of you when paired together was incredible. A K-Vamp would have lasted off it for months."

"What the heck's a K-Vamp? You know what, nevermind." I shook my head. "We're getting off topic. Serena, I-" Pain shot up the side of my body, the force of it so intense that I collapsed to the ground. Hot bursts of pain like scalding knives attacked every inch of my skin, my insides felt like they would expel from my gut.

Almost immediately Serena dropped down to catch me, holding my head with one hand while the other restrained my flailing body. "Essallie, speak to me!"

The pain was too much for me. I tried to tell her it was too much, but all I could manage was a high-pitched scream. My body shivered and shook, bones cracking and popping with sharp force. It went on for what felt like hours, Serena stroking my cheek and bidding me to hush while I fitfully tried to claw at the source of my agonizing pain.

As soon as I could speak, I gasped out the words. "I'm dying, Serena. Demon poison."

Her stare darkened with confusion. "What poison?" She followed my twitching hand to my side, where my fingers dared not to touch the swollen and festering wound.

Slowly and as gently as she could, she lifted back the edge of my shirt. I saw a nauseating blend of colors covering the skin she had exposed, and nearly gagged.

"How long have you had this? Why didn't you tell me

you were infected?" She looked panicked. Immediately she helped me to my feet. "A Vens' poison can-"

"Kill you, I know," I finished with a gasp, breathing against the sensation of heavy pressure weighing on my chest. My vision started to dim. "There's a salve, though, right?"

She gave a jerky nod of the head. "Yes, I have some at home in an emergency kit. We have to get you there immediately."

Everything was starting to blur together. Rainbow swirls danced in front of my eyes, and I willed myself not to barf. "But you said, you said you couldn't help." My voice felt thick, submerged underwater. "I have to get back to my brother..."

"You can return to your brother in the morning, Essallie." Serena shuffled forward as I leaned on her. "You're in no condition to help him, anyway."

I started to mumble something to her, but someone had shut off the lights. Darkness surrounded me, plunging me into a solitude of emptiness.

And for once, I was grateful.

FIVE

WE WILL NEVER FALL

Leo was watching me.

He looked just as I had last remembered him; black tuxedo nicely pressed, blonde hair ruffled and carelessly tossed about. When he reached out a hand to help me up, I noticed I was wearing my mother's white gown again, not a trace of blood on either of us.

"Well don't you look enchanting?" Leo spun me into his arms, beaming. Dipping me low, he placed a gentle kiss against my collarbone and softly murmured. "Why I didn't do this sooner I'll never know."

"Leo," I gasped, heat scorching my cheeks to a rosy tint. "Ursula, she's going to see this-"

"To hell with Ursula. To hell with everyone but us, Essie."

I pulled back from Leo as he went to place another kiss on my collarbone. His eyes sparkled as he looked at me, a blazing fire of exultation. Happiness radiated off of him, and he shined as bright as the sun.

"You know I'd never leave you, Essie." He stood up, bringing me up too, until both feet were firmly planted on the ground. His hands found my cheeks, thumbs rubbing small circles over my skin. "You're too important to me to lose."

Staring into his eyes, I almost believed him. Until I looked around at our surroundings. Nothing but white, stretched as far the eye could see. Like an empty canvas, we were the only thing in the middle of a vast expanse of my imagination.

I did my best to not to cry, but tears had already run over my cheeks and onto Leo's fingers. "Leo, none of this is real."

He grinned and gave me the same crooked smile I recalled. "Of course it's real. We're both alive, how can this not be real?"

"Because," I whispered. "You died."

Leo stepped back, shaking his head and giving a weak laugh. He opened his mouth to speak, when blood started to spread across his chest, covering his white shirt in a bright red. With a shudder, he collapsed onto the floor, wheezing until nothing but silence echoed around me.

That's when I started to scream.

I gasped.

My eyes flung open as I shot myself forward, sitting sharply upright in bed. Sheets laid in a tangled heap around my feet, twisting around like a snake slithering up its prey. My chest rose and fell, each breath a struggle to finish.

I gave up; clamping my hands over my eyes, I let out a choked sob. Leo. Leo, Leo, freaking dead-and-never-coming-back Leo. Why couldn't I stop dreaming about him? Thinking about him brought the fire to life inside me, a riot building on the edge of a cliff.

My dreams seemed to be caught between premonitions and memories anymore. If it wasn't Leo I was dreaming about, it was Kayden luring me to my own violent death. Last time I had dreamt of Leo had been two days before I left for

New York. I ended up discarding the sheets in secret and buying new ones, the shock from having set them on fire too much to handle in the moment. I had lied to Jayson, told him I had used the sheets for art class or something. The dreams were seeming to only be getting worse as time went on, as if the product of my imagination wanted to see me go insane like my Mother had.

Judging by where I was, I almost thought I had gone mad. The twin-size bed I was on had basic, cream colored sheets and comforter set. The bed frame looked dated but still in good condition, the dark wood posts carved to resemble vines twisting up the sides and into the canopy above. A small bedside table made of the same wood had a glass jug, some rags, and a bowl of purple goop inside of it. Purple goop withstanding, everything looked incredibly normal. Had I gone home without realizing it? I tried to think back; the last thing I could remember was Serena inching us to the door out of the flower shop, just before everything went black.

I gave the wad of sheets at my feet a little kick and got out of bed. A small vanity I had missed earlier stood in the corner, several different hairbrushes and mirrors on top. Picking up the largest mirror, I got a full look at myself since the alleyway. I had a good feeling I resembled a traumatized homeless vagrant; One look in the mirror told me I hadn't been far off. A thin, superficial cut ran across my cheek where my phone had been as I had called Jayson. Mixtures of dirt and dried blood stained my clothes and matted part of my hair to my scalp. Hollow, desolate eyes stared back at me, reminding me of a corpse. At the bottom hem of my t-shirt, a purple stain gave a dash of color against the filth and grime. Something pushed at my mind, and I lifted my shirt up.

The bite marks from the Vens was still visible, but barely. All of the blotched and swollen skin had vanished. Only the permanent black-and-blue bruise from Chase stayed the same.

That meant that Serena had gotten me here, used the purple salve, and saved my life.

Downstairs, I could hear her voice, softly singing in a language I didn't know. Crossing the room, I opened the door to a small landing, a set of tightly wound spiral steps laced with the same carved vine pattern leading downstairs. I took the steps easily and followed the sound of Serena's voice.

As I got closer, I could hear that she wasn't actually singing; she was talking to someone. Keeping back, I did my best to say silent and overhear the exchange.

Serena sighed furiously, the sound of china being set on a table. "She thinks I can save her."

"Of course she thinks you can. You came to her in the wake of a defining moment," a male voice replied. "You gave her answers no other soul would and caught her in a critical time." He paused and took a small inhale, a rustle of fabric as he moved in his seat. "I am curious though..."

"Be curious all you want, but I have no way to explain what happened," Serena spoke firmly, tone clipped and thickly accented. "I cannot explain the phenomenon that occurred."

"Maybe there's a chance she's already ascended?"

"Impossible," I heard her say. I imagined her shaking her head in disagreement. "Her gift is wild, uncontrollable. She's as unreasonable with her power as a mortal female would be with body chemistry." There was a sound of chairs moving across the floor. "She claims to have killed a Vens."

"Essallie?" Disbelief colored the male's voice. I strained to hear as it dropped lower, softer. I knew him from somewhere, that much I was sure. "There's no way. You said so yourself, she's wild. The level of control required to do that..."

"I know, but how else can the poison be explained?"

"I'm not saying she didn't come into contact with a Vens, but defeat one? Improbable."

The sound of feet on the floor as a chair pushed back. "I had better check on her."

"Serena, sit." The male voice chastised lazily. "She has legs, doesn't she? Let her come down when she's ready." Another chair moved just as the sound of china clinked gently together. "I'll fetch more tea, heaven knows you could use some."

"I wouldn't be this tense if," Serena stopped abruptly. "If things were-"

"If you didn't have a loose cannon for a Nephilim in your home?"

Silence.

"That's not what I meant," she said softly.

The male spoke again, gentler than before. "Just relax. I came here to help, and that's what I intend on doing."

I waited until the sound of feet trailed off before allowing myself to breathe. Serena was going to owe me some serious explanations, especially after last night.

Stepping into the room, I had to blink a few times to adjust. Serena was perched in a sunken living room eerily resembling a tea room from the 1900's; ornately patterned furniture and drapes of coordinating colors of gold, green, and brown blended the room into a picture straight from a movie. Little trinkets sat on small shelves around the room, appearing delicate and crafted from thin and colored glass.

A small spindle of sunlight trickled in through the heavy drapes. "Serena?"

She jolted in her seat, shoulders bunching into her neck as she stiffened. Looking up at me, she smiled and slowly unwound. "How are you feeling?"

"You want the real answer?" I laughed bitterly. "Picture a steamroller flattening me. That's probably the most accurate way to answer your question."

"So, then it's like any other day?" She winked, and this

time I genuinely laughed.

"Same story, different day of the week." I sat down on the edge of an ornately patterned chair, leaning forward. A small dark wood coffee table with mint green engraved carvings rested between us, sporting a small white tea cup and matching plate. It was all a little overwhelming to take in. "I didn't take you for the old fashioned type."

She took a glance around the room, a fond smile on her lips. "Yes, I guess you could say I miss older times."

"Is everyone's home in Charon like this?"

"Not even close." She gestured to one of the shelves decorated in the delicate glass trinkets. "This was once my father's home, as was his before that. I wanted to preserve the memory of family, not favor the idea of an empty existence. That's why I still run his flower shop."

My eyebrows rose. "That place was your father's?"

She nodded. "Not much has changed for my branch of the family, not here or in Charon, for the last several centuries." Her tone dropped as her gaze darkened. "But many have changed their perceptions and views on how things should be in the world. They've bought into the lies the higher ups continue to feed them."

I glanced around the room nervously. Even in the real world, I wasn't one for politics, and the last thing I wanted was a lecture on offices in Charon. "Serena, earlier I heard-"

"For example? That *Queen*," Serena continued to rattle on, sneering in disgust at the mention of the Queen. "Is a bottom-feeding, mind-bending, manipulative excuse for a ruler. You'd do well to never trust a word that comes from her mouth."

I started to object about the Queen, and how she had given me the secrets of Kayden's ulterior motives, when she sighed. Her hand came to rest on my knee as she looked at me wistfully. "She'll do anything to have a power as strong as yours, even in a raw state."

Yeah, my power was raw alright. Raw enough to soon burn me to death from the inside out. "I'll die before that ever happens."

And how true that was.

A deep clearing of throat stopped the chit-chat between us. I turned my head to the open archway leading from the kitchen to see a boy standing still, a tea tray held in his hands. He looked eerily familiar; something about his peachy skin, muscular frame, and brilliant platinum blonde hair set off every alarm bell within my head. I could practically hear Paul Revere galloping on a horse in my head, crying out, "The memories are coming! The memories are coming!"

He set the tray down on the coffee table, handing Serena a new cup of smoldering tea, then extended one to me.

I felt the air whoosh out of my lungs the second our eyes met. Like a final piece of the puzzle being put into place, my mind instantly transported me back to the first day I had woken up in Charon's hospital. Faces had come and gone, secrets had been dumped on my shoulders with little warning, but one person had sat in the confines of my mind, nearly lost in the haze of those few painful days.

Ari blinked his stormy teal eyes, a question stirring within. "Are you alright?"

Staring up and down his frame, I tried to unlock my tongue from the roof of my mouth. "You're not wearing the white gloves you last had on."

His eyebrows rose just as the corners of his mouth hitched. "So you do remember me."

"Not exactly hard to forget someone when they claim to be something as damning as Nephilim."

"There should be some level of irony in using 'damning' in the same sentence as 'Nephilim'."

"I'm sure there is, but the joke is on us, unfortunately."

He was fighting it now; his lips had grown to a full smile bordering on outbursts of laughter. "What part? The part where everyone expects us to be vile and slithering demons, or angelic dancing cherubs clothed in loincloths?"

My grin started to match his. "Oh, the cherub part, undoubtedly. I'll take being called a demon any day over wearing a strip of cloth and floating in the clouds, waiting for the cold to freeze my ass off and perk my-"

"Essallie," Serena interrupted with a high-pitched squeak. Bright pink blush bruised her cheeks. "I think Ari gets it."

Ari dragged one of the expensive chairs alongside me. He dropped into it smoother than a hot knife skimming through butter. He spared Serena a small apologetic glance before turning back to lock eyes with me. "It's good to know your memory is intact."

I nodded while trying to raise the cup of tea to my lips. "You didn't exactly earn points for being courteous, but you earned a few for startling the hell out of me."

"I'd say I did a good job, then. Nephilim shouldn't really carry the enemy within," he said with a smirk.

My gaze turned down to stare at the teacup resting in my hands. I wasn't sure about carrying the enemy, but I sure felt like there were plenty of demons to battle in all aspects of my life. It had only taken a matter of weeks to watch everyone around me get tossed into the sea of nightmares, and now I was scrambling to save them all.

Looking back up to Ari, I pulled out the memories of what happened the moment we met.

"Excuse me?"

I sat up in bed, staring at the guy across from me in the door frame. War? Nephilim?

In a single take of breath it all came flooding back. Chase and Cassie. Demons and angels. Fire and wings. Jayson and

Mother. My whole world unraveled in a period of weeks, burned to the ground before my very eyes.

Oh, right.

The guy with the impeccable blonde hair, Ari was his name, leaned off of the frame in a smooth move I would have expected a real angel to do. His eyes carefully searched mine before looking over my exposed skin, settling on the dark streaks just under the surface. His hands were covered with white leather gloves and tucked just inside the pockets of his jeans. "You still have some of the poison inside of you."

"Gee, captain obvious, did you figure that one out all on your own?" *I snapped, making sure to shove any showing skin under the folds of cream blankets. His gaze made me instantly feel uncomfortable, as if he was undressing every thought in my head. Like he knew me before we had even met. It was a tender gaze, breaking inside of my crumbling heart.*

He stepped a little closer. "Demon poison is guaranteed to kill. The only way to save yourself from it is to cut off the limb where the poison was inserted." *His teal eyes were piercing, questions jumping all around inside of them.* "How on Earth did you survive?"

"That's enough," *Kayden stepped in, jaw set. In a single stride he stood chest-to-chest with Ari, eyes blazing.* "She's alive, that's all that needs to be said. You said so yourself. If you accelerate her heart there's a chance it'll trigger the venom to spread back into her body."

Ari's eyes narrowed to thin slits. His hands began to move from his pockets, only to stop as a small smile appeared on his lips. "I can see the scars, you know. She might not have the guts to kill you, but I'll set you on fire and watch you melt into nothing without a second thought." *He craned his neck to look over Kayden's shoulder, eyes resting on me.* "When you're ready to find me and know more than this shrub can teach you, you'll know where to look, Essallie."

Kayden stood rigid until Ari turned around and walked out, clicking the door shut softly behind him. I counted off twenty heartbeats before he spoke. "Did he just call me a shrub?"

I couldn't help it, the sarcastic remark slipping off my lips. "Well, you are the perfect kindling for a half-angel's fire." My head rested back onto the pillow behind me, closing my eyes. I didn't have time to be thinking of some renegade who came storming into my room, claiming to be the very thing I wished I wasn't. I yanked the bed sheets closer to my body, shivering involuntarily.

"Essallie?"

I jumped in my seat, Ari's voice pulling me from the depths of my memory.

I gave my heart a moment to settle before speaking softly. "You were right."

Ari tilted his head to the side curiously. "About what?"

"I knew just where to go looking for you."

There was a short pause before he started to laugh. "Hate to burst your bubble, darling, but Serena here found me looking for you." He ran a hand through his hair before settling back on me with his startling eyes. "You're not that easy to track. Lilix almost had a heart attack when she said she'd lost you at the pub."

The pretty blonde with icy blue eyes instantly came to mind. "She works with you?"

Ari nodded and gestured to Serena, who had been watching our conversation silently. "Serena sent her my way shortly after I came to Charon. I bet you know exactly why, too."

Sneaking a sip of tea before answering, the response nearly tumbled from my lips. "Because no one trusts Nephilim."

"Or anyone associated with them, as I'm sure you've experienced too."

The memory of the apothecary couple surfaced, and I nodded. "More than I'd care to know."

"Good, that means we're on the same page." Clasping his hand together on his lap, he leaned closer to me. "Now that I've finally found you, we can finally work on finding your Watcher."

Finishing the last bit of tea, I carefully set the cup onto the tray before rising up from my chair. "And that's where you're wrong. There is no Watcher for me in this world. Now, I have a brother to go home and protect while I still can, excuse me."

I walked past an open-mouthed Serena, who looked from me to Ari in shock. Descending up the steps, I ignored the terse whispers coming from the living room, urging Ari to follow me.

My hand had just begun to swing the bedroom door shut when something blocked it. I stared down to see a broken-in cowboy boot wedged between the door and its frame.

"Essallie, hear me out," Ari pleaded softly.

"There's nothing to hear out," I said, releasing the door and crossing the room to stop alongside the bed. "I'm thankful Serena brought you to me, really I am, but you're wasting your time."

"Are you so sure of that?"

"Yes, I am."

"Then why did you come here?" Ari came closer. "Why return to a place that labels you an outcast?"

"I... I don't know." My fingertips brushed over the crumpled sheets. I couldn't look him in the eyes, for the truth was even I didn't know exactly why I'd come here. "Serena just seemed like the only person who could help me at the time."

"From what?"

"From everything! Anywhere I turn I'm joined at the hip

with demons trying to kill me. Demons killing my family and leaving me to pick up the bloody mess. So pardon me, but I need to get home to the last family member that means something to me, before another creature tries to leave me a corpse in place of someone I love."

"Is he really your brother?"

I paused. "Oh yes, thank you for reminding me of my Mother's discrepancy. Brother or half-brother, it doesn't matter. He's all I have left."

Something in my desperate stare must have triggered a thought in Ari's mind. "So your Watcher means nothing to you?"

"I already told you, I don't have one," I snapped.

His eyebrows bunched in confusion. "Then you've already ascended?"

I shook my head, and Ari looked even more confused than before. My chest rose and fell in a long, desperately needed sigh, my body collapsing in a crumbled heap onto the bed. "He died before we could bond. A demon killed him."

A flicker of emotions crossed his face, finally settling for a mix between pain and sympathy. Crossing the room, he settled alongside me. "I'm sorry."

"So am I." I chewed on my upper lip, anything to stop the burning sensation of tears collecting in my eyes. "He was the one who showed me this place, this world, not once with an ulterior motive at hand. He was a gentleman, and will forever be missed."

"If he's as good as you say he is, then I'm betting he died doing the noble thing." Ari reached forward to take my hand, using his free one to swipe just under my eyes. "He wouldn't want you to cry."

I hiccuped and stared at Ari, numbly nodding my head. He had a point; if Leo saw me like this, blubbering every time he was mentioned, I had no doubt he would have teased me.

But it was so much more than Leo now- my grandparents, Kayden, Abigail, Jayson- so many people had been dragged under my wings, and I was supposed to protect and appease them when I could barely protect myself.

"There was an instant connection between us, like two magnets clicking together. I had never felt such a thing. I'm certain he was my Watcher."

"Wait," Ari started, his face turning into a puzzling mask of confusion yet again. "You aren't certain he was yours?"

"Not officially, no-" I said warily.

He pulled back from me, eyebrows as high as his hair line. "Essallie, are you telling me you've been throwing your life away on an *assumption* that this one person, out of *eight billion*, was the magical one for you? Did you not consult the scriptures?"

His question was sharp, like a smack to the bare skin during a blizzard in the North Pole. "I'm almost positive he was mine! No one else connected with me on such an immediate level."

"So what? If I connect with a puppy in the pound, does that mean I have to take it home, even if I'm certain to be allergic?" Ari rolled his eyes to the heavens, muttering in a language I didn't understand. His glowering eyes came back to rest on me. "There are ways to make sure you have the right person, Essallie. A list is complied and updated any time a new child of Nephilim comes into birth."

"It doesn't matter!" I stood up, throwing my hand skyward. "You're missing the point. I have the last important part of my family back home, no doubt going mad from the cryptic way I ended things yesterday because I thought I was going to die. The game has changed, and Jayson needs me. I can't imagine him defending himself against a bloodthirsty demon following my scent, much like I couldn't imagine my grandparents doing so before they died."

"You should listen to yourself," Ari scolded me, and I couldn't contain my shock. "You're surrendering your life on the basis of a circumstantial feeling! Even if this person was your Watcher and he is dead-"

"He's most definitely dead."

"-you can't just give up and quit life. That's not how living works, sorry to piss on your pity party. When a cancer patient gets a diagnosis, they don't simply just stop living life. They fight, Essallie, fight like hell against every mutant cell in their body. From the moment I met you I knew you were a fighter, now I'm not so sure someone so weak and pitiful could have ever been a fighter."

"You," I jabbed a finger at his face, vivid. "You know *nothing* about me. You don't know the level of pain and misery I have had to endure my entire life! You weren't there the nights my Mother would chase me throughout the house, trying to kill me because she knew I was a poison that had infiltrated her home." Fire sparked, engulfing my knuckles in a bright display of blue hues. "You weren't there the day I watched my first love try to sell me to a demon for eternal youth. You weren't there, slipping and sliding in the puddles of blood, finding my my two lifelong guardians gutted like wild game for dinner. So take your assumptions of me not being able to fight and shove it right up your ass!"

I waited for him to jump back at me, to rebut my snarky defense and belittle me further. Instead, he gave a small and soft clap, his eyes a smoldering aquamarine. "Now that," he said. "Is the Essallie I met. About time, too. I was beginning to lose hope."

My jaw dropped. I had walked right into his trap and bit the bait; he had been antagonizing me, waiting for the fury to ignite from within. As much as I wanted to be infuriated with him, I had to give him a hand in his undermining behavior.

Extinguishing the flames from my hands, I crossed them

91

over my chest, feet still firmly planted on the floor. "This changes nothing. I'm still going home to my brother."

"Do you think he's in immediate danger?"

"Yes."

"And do you think he'd be okay with you coming home to protect him, if he knew you would be sacrificing your life in the process?"

I hesitated. "Yes."

"Essallie."

"Okay, okay," I bitterly replied, narrowing my eyes. "No, he wouldn't."

"Good," he nodded. "We're clear of one lie, now let's clear the other. Is he in immediate danger?"

I started to say yes again, only to stop. In our last phone conversation, I had instructed him to go straight to Abigail and to stay near her. No explanation why, just to do it. And deep down I knew, even though he was a stubborn boy, he would have listened and gone to her. Abigail would have instantly understood why, and probably would have told Kayden too. Despite Abigail's lack of sensibility, I knew she'd have Jayson's best interest at heart and protect him until I would return.

Sighing, I said, "No."

A triumphant smile spread over Ari's lips. "Excellent. Then I'm sure he won't mind you gone for a few days while we find out about your Watcher." He rose off the bed, coming to stand directly in front of me, both hands gently placed on my shoulders. "And if this person really was yours, then we'll figure things out from there."

Against the burning urge to sneer at him, I gave a small smile and relaxed the tension in my shoulders. A glimmer of hope, like a diamond among the rough, seemed to peek out from under the surface of my daunting nightmare for a life. Maybe there was a chance that, against all odds, something good could come from my odd and undesired existence. And if not, I could always watch them all burn.

SIX
BEATING HEART

"This looks absolutely ridiculous."

I was standing in the middle of the sunken living room, arms crossed in resistance over my chest. Long, spinning twists of navy fabric covered every inch of my body in an elegant high-collared robe. It instantly reminded me of something a witch or sorceress would wear while hovering over a book of incantations, weaving a spell of eternal love between herself and a ravishing stable boy.

Serena glared at me under her beautiful black lashes. She had been crouched low, doing her best to hem the robe without butchering it.

I turned my head to look at the clock on the mantle. Ari had taken off for a little, promising to be back within the hour, and it had already been over an hour and a half. Where in the hell could he be?

I started to shift my weight when I felt a sharp tap sting my leg. "Do you ever stand still?" Serena grumbled under her breath.

"Hey, I'm not the one that decided new clothes were in

order," I coolly remarked, making faces at her. "My shirt and pants were perfectly fine."

"Of course they were," Serena packed as much sarcasm as she could into the four little words. "If you want everyone in Charon to know who you are. At least while you wear this you'll have a little coverage. Smell less like death, too."

"I did not smell like death."

"Oh, you certainly did." She pulled out a pair of scissors from the small sewing box alongside her. "And at least that scar of yours is covered up, too."

Blowing out the air from my cheeks, I muttered an offensive word under my breath. Serena began to cut into the fabric using a part of household scissors, carefully snipping so the remaining half of the dress brushed the tips of my toes.

"Serena?"

"Hrmm?"

"Why do the buildings get darker the further you leave the main road in Charon?"

The sound of cutting fabric came to a stop, and I looked down to see her free hand comb through the mess of caramel curls on her head. She seemed to consider my question for a minute, mulling over the answer edging on her tongue.

"Centuries upon millennia ago, when Charon was first formed, it was like a crystal paradise," Serena began, her eyes glazing over to a faraway stare. Her fingers inched down to her cheek, absentmindedly tracing the edges of her blue mark. "The first Queen, the True Queen as we call her, made it into a place of love, of endless possibilities. She was one of the first Nephilim to have been created.

"For countless lifetimes, she reigned with a pure heart and angelic soul. She married another Nephilim, and together they created two daughters, Harmony and Ebony. Harmony had tragically passed in an accident, leaving Ebony the sole heir to the throne. When her mother eventually passed, legend has it she made Ebony promise to keep their bloodline true, and marry another Nephilim. It would never happen."

It was as if Serena had painted a picture for us both to step into; I imagined an even more beautiful, crystal version of Charon, suspended in a state of perfection for centuries. Lead by a gentle, but powerful woman who did everything in her power to embrace the sacred blood in her veins.

Serena went on, her words continuing the visual in my head. "What Ebony had never shared with her mother is that she rejected her bloodline, and all the purity that came with it. As her name is dark, she aimed to be slathered in ink, and in her ultimate defiance on her mother's dying wish, married a demon and gave birth to his child. A corruption, a half-breed torn between two worlds at ultimate extremes."

"But would that child not be of three? Human, angel, and demon?"

She nodded. "Indeed, the child was, and for centuries after, the line continued, fathered by demons, all children born male. Until Lucretia. She is the last of the legacy, and unable to have children."

I felt like my head was crunching in on itself. Chewing on the inside of my cheek, I tried to wrap my mind around the problem Serena was trying to spell out in front of me. "So Nephilim can have children, and demon can have children too, but mix them together and they can't?"

"In a sense, yes. A hybrid of Nephilim and demon who is male can have children, but a female cannot."

The light bulb went off in my head. "And Lucretia is a female, and a mix of both."

Serena's faint smile told me I was on the same page. "Exactly. At first, no one knew, and who could have expected it when all the males could produce children?"

Of course no one would know. Never once had there been a question that a Nephilim-demon mix could father a child, and the last female had been Ebony, who had only been Nephilim. I wondered if there was a type of genetic incompatibility between the two when bound together in a female.

My mind circled back to the original question at hand. "But how does the history of the throne have to do with the buildings being grey?"

"I wasn't finished," she flicked my kneecap, resisting the urge to roll her eyes. "When Queen Lucretia took her place on the throne, we knew things would be different in Charon. Over time, our kingdom had tarnished and dulled, ruined by the negative energy. Lucretia had decided to instate a new plot for the land, and had all the buildings redone in white marble. However, the residue from the demonic presence and negative energy within Charon has stained the town. Only the center strip had been unaffected, no doubt by some work of magic the True Queen had implemented all those years ago."

Was that why Nephilim were so heavily disliked in Charon? Because we were the beginning of a long, dark existence in the murky undertow? I couldn't help but feel sad for the people who chose to think such things; being of one species, mixed or not, didn't make you a monster. It's the actions and decisions people make that turn them into monsters, not their blood.

Serena had just finished snipping off the last end of fabric when the sound of the door opening and closing reached our ears. Ari bounded into the room, a small black box tucked under an arm. I noticed he had changed out of the clothes he'd been wearing earlier, having traded in the all-black get up for a casual white t-shirt, worn in jeans, and the dark brown leather jacket I had first seen him in. A small golden chain peeked from the collar of his t-shirt.

He reached up to scratch his head before giving me a small smile and concealed wink. "Sorry, took a little longer than I thought." Leaning at an angle to see around the billowing waves of fabric, he spotted Serena. "Are you done playing with your pretty life-size doll?"

She stood up and pouted, staring at me through half-lidded eyes. "I just wish she had hair to work with. You can't really do anything with what she's got going on."

I reached up to touch the ends of my short cut, frowning. "Hey, I like my hair, thank you very much."

"Obviously, you didn't like it enough," she half-mocked, sticking her tongue out at me.

"Oh hush before I give you a matching crop," I pretended to threaten her. With wide eyes, she instantly rose her hands to grab at the mass of hair framing her petite face. I turned my attention to the black box Ari still held under his arm. "What's in the box?"

Wiggling his eyebrows, he challenged me. "Do you *really* want to know what's in a small, compact, black box?"

I ran through a quick list in my head, then nodded. "Worst case scenario, it's a sex toy or dead shrunken heads." My face scrunched up in disgust. "Or fish. On second thought, let it be dead shrunken heads."

He blinked at me in complete disbelief. "Wow. How often does your mind circle the gutter?"

"Circle the gutter?" I let out a loud laugh. "Hate to shatter your perfect image, but I don't circle the gutter. I do, however, live in the sewer of dirty minds, and the smell never leaves you no matter how far you climb out of it."

Mouth opening to speak, he took a step forward, then backtracked and shook his head. "I can already see you pulling jokes in a desperate situation just to liven the mood. Great."

Serena stepped forward, snatching the box from the crook of Ari's arm. "You two bicker and banter like a married pair, good heavens. And all over a..." She lifted the lid of the box and looked down, trailing off. Her eyes flickered up to Ari's. "How did you manage to get these?"

Taking the box back from her hands, he offered a graceful shrug of the shoulders. "Just a little twisting of the arm, nothing more. I had Lilix call in a few favors." Reaching into the box, he pulled out a matching pair of dark green teardrop earrings, each one individually wire wrapped like my glass heart pendant.

"Assuming I have to wear them," I said, reaching out for the pair. "What do they do?"

"They're a cloaking device, well, sort of." Ari frowned, pulling his eyebrows together as his face looked pinched. "Think part cloaking device, part decoy item. They don't really cover you like an invisibility cloak, but they distract everyone who looks at you into thinking you're either someone else or not really there at all."

Carefully taking one of the earrings, I examined it curiously in my outstretched palm. The same swirl sat at the clasp of the earring, matching perfectly to my pendant. As if in reply, the small heart on my chest began to glow, small waves of heat radiating off of it.

I heard Ari gasp, and looked up. He had a wicked, triumphant smile on his face as he watched me, as if he had just found his own diamond in the rough. Against the glow he looked like a true angel, from the rich and even tone of his unblemished skin to the brilliance glimmering in his eyes.

"Even better," he said when the glowing had finally stopped. "Both objects have been gifted by the same angel. Now I know you'll be alright." Handing me the second earring, I put on both. "Only the best Vens in all of Charon could spot you, and I highly doubt the Queen is out to kill you, otherwise you'd have been dead by now for sure."

My fingers brushed over the pendant around my neck. Gifted by the same angel, the very one that created me. A man I've never met, or at the very least can't even recall. Small waves of sadness brought my shoulders to a slump, and I couldn't help but wish I could meet the person responsible for making me.

"So this is what we're going to do," Ari's voice broke through my melancholy rift, and I instantly straightened up. "We've only got to go to the shop directly alongside the apothecary's- it's easy enough, but we're better off being safe than sorry. That's why you're dressed up."

I did a double take over his current outfit. "You don't look like you're wearing any special trinkets."

"Didn't anyone ever tell you?" Ari had come closer, leaning in until I could feel his breath on the side of my neck. "There's always more than meets the eye."

I pulled back and shook my head, clearing the sneaky thoughts of seeing more than meets my eyes on him out of my head. This wasn't a time to let my hormones play battlefield with my heart. Not when both my life was at stake.

Giving Serena a grateful smile, I started for the door. "Thank you, again. You didn't have to help me."

"Of course not," she said matter-of-factly, striding past me and opening the door. "But I did. Guess you could say I carry a wounded soul for what's good in this world."

Ari went out first, giving Serena a curt nod with both hands tucked in his pockets. Before I stepped out with him, I stopped in the doorway, my toes brushing the bottom of the frame in hesitation.

My eyes locked with hers as I grasped one of her hands. "Be careful, please."

She made no motion to pull her hand away from mine, but the strained look in her face said she wanted to. Still, she did her best to smile and nod. "I should be saying that to you, if there really is someone aiming to pierce your heart."

I laughed darkly. "The more I learn about myself, the

more I see someone has always been out for my heart, immortal or not."

She peeked around the frame, her face beginning to pull into an emotionless stare. "You should go," she said. "Before he leaves you behind." Her hand pulled free from mine to push at my back, forcing me out into the sun-blessed field around her home.

Ari had already started through the waist-high grass, moving through without a look over his shoulder. I hurried to catch up but continued to lag behind, unable to stop looking back at the little grey home covered in bright flowers. My stomach twisted at the thought of something happening to the beautiful woman inside that house, captured or tortured or killed, all because she had kept me hidden.

"Get up alongside me," Ari's voice floated back to me. I snapped up to see he had already put twice the distance between us. "Unless you're aiming to become demon fodder once we hit the main road."

Sneering at his back, I grabbed two handfuls of my skirts to hike up and jogged up to his side. Heat pricked at the back of my neck, the sun glaring vengefully from above. With no wind to keep me cool, the combination of heavy fabric and cloudless sky made it feel like we were standing on Mercury.

I dropped my skirt to wipe the sweat off my forehead with my arm. It came back drenched. "You do know I've already walked the streets around here, and I'm not exactly dead, am I?"

He shook his head while pushing up the sleeves of his jacket to his elbows. "Luck, my dear, no more or less. I have a feeling this time we won't be so lucky, not with two Nephilim paired together."

I pinched the bridge of my nose, breathing deep from my mouth. All of this demon-warding crap was going to drive me insane. What happened to school and college and my psychotic mother being the most stressful things in my life? This calling, if I could even call it that, had taken all of my life and tossed it into a landfill, then told me to start from scratch. Not exactly something to be happy about, unless you're an axe murder and trying to avoid capture, I guess.

But this wasn't just about me anymore. There wasn't a doubt in my mind that Ari had a family, too. He probably made just as many sacrifices as I had, if not more. Sneaking a quick look at him, I guessed he had to be around my age, one or two years older, tops.

"I bet your family misses you," I thought aloud, staring forward as the street got closer. "Any brothers or sisters?"

"My family's dead."

The harshness of his words left me off guard. I knew it wasn't right to poke at someone's past, especially when the dead were involved, but the curiosity overwhelmed me. "How did they die?"

A solid minute passed before he answered. Still, the tension in his voice was thick enough to cut steel. "Mom died in a car crash. Dad was murdered. No siblings."

Nothing past that was said until our feet hit pavement. "I'm sorry," I whispered.

He shrugged, the move as fluid as water. "Life happens. People aren't kidding when they say to live it to the fullest."

We walked down the left hand side of the street, inching closer to the heaven-high white tower looming on the horizon. My mind started to run circles around itself, wondering just how much Ari had seen and gone through before he stuck himself with me, something I still couldn't comprehend.

"Ari?" I looked at him from the corner of my eyes. "Why did you come looking for me?"

He met my gaze, his expression softening slightly. "I wish I knew." His shoulders rose and fell again. "My Watcher had told me to find you, and help in any way I can, but she never explained why."

I frowned in thought. "Lilix is your Watcher?"

Shock crossed his face, and he smacked a hand to his forehead in a bought of nervous laughter. "Heavens no! Demons can't be Watchers, only mortals."

"I don't see any mortals with us." To prove my point, I looked around.

"She wouldn't be here," he said, something changing in his eyes. A glimpse of sadness, deep and haunting, filled his eyes. "It's a long story."

"Well, no offense, but we're not exactly short on time here." I pointed to the building in the distance. "That monster of a tower isn't exactly getting any closer right now."

"Not now." His words were firm, but not sharp. "Another time, maybe. We're starting to get into more populated areas." We passed a corner home and turned onto a new street. Ari reached out to pull me closer, sparing me a quick glance. "You have the earrings on?"

I nodded, twisting my head from side to side so he could see the large stones on each ear. I had expected them to feel heavy and weighted, but instead they were light and airy, almost as if I didn't have them on at all.

Moving down the street, I kept close to his side, trying my best to sneakily use him for support. The sweltering heat had drained me, the dress not helping the situation one bit. I barely noticed the placement of his fingers on my waist.

People started springing up left and right, just like they had when I made my way down these streets before. One moment it was only three bodies, then twelve, then thirty and more. The closer we inched to the center of town, the more demons and supernaturals we came across.

I kept my eyes squinted, ready to fight on cue. The burning sensation in my veins lay tightly coiled in my chest, like a protective barrier around my heart. An all-too familiar itching started to grow in my palms, accompanied by the dull ache in my fingertips.

But the fight never came. Every time someone walked close along my path, something distracted them or they got confused and walked away. A woman covered in quills seemed to be walking right up to me, until she got within five feet of me. Like magic, she blinked in confusion, turned right and walked out of my path. I was stunned.

Ari must have seen the surprised look on my face, for he started to laugh. "Did you not think they'd work?"

I dimly shook my head. "Who the hell's ever heard of magical repelling earrings?"

"No one, that's the point." He acknowledged the heart pendant around my neck. "Our gifts are unique. Others might create their own versions, imitations, but the power bound in ours far exceeds any other. Yours work twice as well because they came from the same angel."

The same angel? My mystery father, Michael? I absentmindedly reached up to touch one of the earrings. "How do you know that?"

"The Nephilim that got these was a son of Michael."

"I have a sibling?" The thought of having another brother never crossed my mind. When I thought of a brother, Jayson was always the first and only to come to mind.

"*Had*," Ari corrected me. "Remember, the last Nephilim lived over three hundred years ago." A humorous grin graced his lips. "We're like the canned meat Spam. Supposedly real, no real evidence to support the claims."

I bit back a laugh, passing a half-mermaid half-faerie person. Against the clear blue day, I could make out the tower looming off into the endless sky above. It was much closer now, maybe only another two or three blocks. My thoughts shifted from imagining a dinosaur in a pond to the task at hand.

"So how is this all going to work?" I started adding up some pieces in my head, from getting there to reading whatever we were going to read, then leaving. All of it had to be done with minimal exposure to people, just in case someone unwanted was lurking nearby, like another Vens.

"I can't remember the name of the place," he admitted sheepishly. "But I do know what it looks like. There's a brass plate above the door with some inscription in Latin. That's where we want to go."

I started to picture a place like Leo's bookshop; small on the outside, huge and swallowing on the inside. If it was as large as I thought, things could get messy if we were ambushed.

A sudden, unexplainable fear seized at my gut. My breath quickened in my throat, the sound of my heart mimicking helicopter blades. "What if he wasn't my Watcher?" I stared up at Ari, all of my strength replaced with ice cold fear. "What if he died in vain?"

Ari gradually came to a stop, bringing me with him. Turning to face me, he placed his hands on my upper arms. They were warm, almost comforting in a way.

"Listen to me," he said gently, the emotion in his eyes matching the soft tone of his voice. "If he was, he was. If he wasn't, then you still have time to find yours before it's too late. Either way, I promise you, he didn't die in vain. You said he protected you, right?" He asked, watching me nod. "Then there isn't a single chance he died in vain. But I'm telling you, the more you dwell on this, the more you're tarnishing his memory."

Slowly he moved his hands away, instead reaching down and taking my hand into both of his. "You need to live. You're strong enough to do this, all of this."

My voice quivered. "I don't think I'm strong enough for

any of this."

"Yes you are," he countered. He let my hand drop back to my side. "It's there, buried under everything. All you have to do is unearth it."

I watched him for several minutes, waiting to see his eyes change. He said the same things everyone else had, but unlike everyone else, there wasn't a trace of doubt in his words or gaze. Every inch of him believed I could, and would, be strong enough for whatever we would unearth.

Giving him a slight nod, we continued forward. Ari reached out for me again, but I shook him off. I needed a couple minutes of no-contact to get my act together.

Walking directly behind him, we turned onto the main street of Charon. It still looked as perfect and pristine as always, photograph worthy. Weaving through the crowds and pockets of people, it didn't take us long to get to the end of the street.

Immediately I locked onto the building of the apothecary. For the first time I noticed the outside had a large wooden sign, carved into the shape of a vial and painted purple. Funny how excitement can make you so narrow-minded in a moment of curiosity.

Eyes off the purple sign, I looked at the building next to it. This one was very narrow, but spiraled tall and high like a vanilla soft-serve ice cream cone. At the top of the door frame sat a small, worn in brass plate, just like Ari had said, but that was the only noticeable mark on the building. Opening the door, he motioned for me to follow.

Inside, the room looked as big as I had imagined. The first room was basic; only one piece of furniture, a desk, stood in the middle of the room. Glossy black ceiling and walls gave the room an eerie feeling, like we were suspended in the middle of a waterfall at night. I inched closer to Ari, ignoring the fear slithering in my gut.

As we approached the desk closer, the top of a balding man's head came into view. Upon closer investigation we saw his whole body, all two and a half feet of it. The man was dressed in a small, old-fashioned tux, and had a monocle wedged into his face just over his left eye.

The original fear quickly turned to a fit of giggles after seeing this. Only two minutes inside and already I didn't know what to make of it.

Ari nudged my side. I couldn't tell if his eyes were glaring at me or if it was the glossy walls reflecting in his eyes.

"You have to state your name," he said, whispering with a snap.

"Why me?"

"Because I'm not Essallie Hanley, you are, dunce."

"No need for insults, *Ari*head," I fired back at him. I turned my attention to the man in front of me, took a breath, and started to say my name. "Essal-"

"Left hall, second floor," the man cut me off, replying with a lazy drone. I took a quick glance around the room before pursing my lips. His directions wouldn't have been so complicated, if there had actually been a hall to go down.

I gazed over my shoulder at Ari, but he only shrugged. Facing the desk once more, I tried to speak. "What hall-"

"If you are a true Nephilim, your little bauble will guide you," the man cut me off again, tone just as lazy and uninterested as before.

"And if not?" I demanded, hands on hips.

"Impossible," he replied, bored. "Otherwise you couldn't have entered."

I looked over my shoulder to Ari for the second time. My fingers wrapped around the pendant on my chest. "He said my necklace will guide me. But it doesn't even feel hot."

"Give it a second?" He suggested, putting his hands out in a 'I don't know' sort of gesture.

I sighed bitterly; this was ridiculous. Who in their right mind thought it would be cool to make all these rules and stipulations up in a magical world? I had a good mind to give them a foot right where the sun don't shine.

Neck tilted, I stared at the glossy wall to my left. The longer I looked at it, the more the eerie feeling began to crawl over my skin. I had just started to turn away when an idea popped in my head.

I walked over, stood in front of the wall, and reached out to touch it. My hand went through and I gasped as a bitter, shocking cold raced up my arm, spreading across my body. Pushing past the cold, I raised my other hand to the wall and plunged it forward, the effect instantly making me feel like I'd been standing outside on a glacier, naked.

I could hear my teeth chattering over everything, muffling out the rapid pounding of my heart, the words I hissed under my breath, and anything else around me. My lungs began to feel tired, overworked. My eyes began to shut. Thoughts of sleep prodded my mind, telling me it would be better to give in and give up, to let the cold swallow me whole.

A final shuddering breath was inhaled, and I closed my mouth. I focused on the beacon of warmth circling in my chest, fighting to stay alive under the confines of my self-imposed barrier. With one thought, I let the fire loose.

Flames rippled off my skin, engulfing me in a giant blue blaze. Like giving a great sigh, it all released off my body, spirals of the potent flame racing down my limbs and attacking any location it could. Whispers trailed around me like smoke lingering in a parlor room, telling me to let the whole place burn.

I took a sharp exhale, flinging my eyes open. A brilliant firework display of fire seared at the cold covering me, sounds of buckling metal and pressured space resonating through the room. The wall shattered, fragments of the glossy wall flinging in every direction.

Arms back at my sides, I tempered the flames down to just my hands. I made sure to give Ari my slyest glance possible.

"Well? We don't have all day," I teased him before turning back and walking down the hall. His awkward combination of awe and shock expressed on his face would be one I'd cherish for a long time.

About a quarter of a mile into the hall, I came to a stop. Behind me came the sound of Ari's cowboy boots clip-clopping on the ground as he caught up, his grumbles coming to a hush when he stopped alongside me. A bright gold door stood in front of us, symbols and swirls of inky black decorating the door with a classy look. The only difference was the knob, which was colored a bright fire-engine red.

"Any idea what to do?" I asked, not taking my eyes off the knob.

Beside me, I heard Ari snicker. He tried his best impersonation of me. "Well whatever you do, *don't take all day.*"

I elbowed him, forcing myself not to pout. Something about the door told me that you didn't want to touch that knob, and it wasn't the red paint. The same uneasiness that had come from the glossy walls returned.

Tentatively I walked forward, keeping on the balls of my feet. A dull rumble began to grow, steadily building from background noise to full-on earthquake shaking. It seemed that with each step, the room became more intense, more determined to shake me loose.

When I finally reached close enough to touch the door, I froze. Blistering heat blew off the door in waves, and I knew just from it that trying to touch the door would end in one hell of a painful burn.

I planted my feet apart on the quaking ground in an

attempt to steady myself, but it failed. The shaking was too strong, and I collapsed onto my knees, every inch of my body vibrating with the rumbling inside the room.

I barely heard Ari shouting my name over the shaking. Turning to my side, I watched him grab the golden chain around his neck and pull out a brass key. He then shouted something else, but I couldn't make it out.

Dropping to his knees, he tried to scramble over to me before he flung his hand at my chest. I screamed and tried to pull away, until I saw he wasn't being weird. In his hand was my pendant, burning as hot as my own personal sun.

He pressed his lips up to my ear and screamed. "Press it into the center notch!"

I pulled back from him, confused, and turned to look at the door. I could barely make it out, but in the center of the door was a small, heart-shaped nook, perfectly sized for my pendant.

Unclasping the necklace from my neck, I held the pendant tightly in my palm. I knew the second I got to my feet and moved for the door that the whole place would up-heave, so I would have to be quick. One shot, one chance, like a basketball game with two seconds on the clock and one score short of victory.

I crouched down, arched onto the tips of my feet, and threw myself at the door, hand with the pendant outstretched. Like flint striking tinder, the door instantly engulfed into flames, the burst of energy powerful enough to knock me onto the ground, sailing past Ari.

The effects of the impact were immediate. Black spots clustered my view while pain spiked through every nerve in my body. I lost all sense of hearing in replace of a high-pitched whistling that seemed to scratch at the inside of my skull.

Ari scrambled over to me, looking down at my sprawled

position. He placed a hand on my cheek, his mouth moving in the same pattern, like a broken record playing the same beat. Worry was etched into his eyes, the crease around his mouth, the way his eyebrows pulled together in a panicked flurry.

I noted several things as I laid on the ground, staring above. One, the ground had stopped shaking. Two, I was definitely going to bruise from the fall. And three, something about the look in Ari's eyes brought a nervous case of butterflies swarming in my insides.

My eyes fluttered shut, and for a moment I simply reveled in the feel of his heated skin against mine. It was the first time I realized that he could touch me, unlike Kayden, and not spark my fire. Ari could be someone I could kiss, could hug, could spend the night curled against for comfort. But Kayden, I could not.

Kayden. Why was I thinking about him in a time like this? He was part of the reason I was in this mess. One of the very real reasons why I was fighting against everyone, trying to understand my place in the shattered picture of my life. The very photo he shattered for me. It made no sense to wonder about him while I was laying flat on my back, waiting to catch up with the world.

Waves of sound started to filter back into my ears, and bit by bit the rest of the world came to join my injured senses. I let my eyes flicker back open in time to see Ari still repeating the same phrase, only this time it had sound accompanied to it.

"Essallie, tell me you're okay." He sounded anxious, bordering on hysterical.

I cracked a smile, ignoring the pain that came with showing my happiness. "Still think you're pissing on my pity party?"

Ari stared at me for a moment, caught between emotions.

A nervous laugh slipped by as he started to speak. "Not even close."

I started to sit up but quickly found the pain from the fall was still very much present. So I kept my head on the ground for a little longer.

"Tell me what you see," I said to Ari. "Where the door was."

Taking his eyes off of me, he looked at where the door stood. From the floor I watched his eyes widen, his expression mystified. "Did you-?" I waited for him to finish. "Did you do that on purpose?"

Using him for support, I carefully moved up into a sitting position. Just as I had been placing the pendant into the door, my hand had come in contact with the gold and ignited into a smoldering frenzy. That's what had caused the explosion. My fire had burned everything as if it were the body of a Vens attacking me, and it showed.

What was left standing of the door consisted of spirals left untouched by my fire. The gold had been reduced to burnt honey colored flakes, swirling around the room like leaves on a blustery fall afternoon. And in the center of the half-fire carved door rested my pendant, completely untouched.

Ari helped me up to my feet, one hand locked tightly around my waist while the other held one of my hands. We shuffled forward, coming within inches of the frame. Using my free hand, I reached out and plucked the pendant free from its notch.

There was a sudden jolt within the room, like a fresh heartbeat on a monitor. The door refilled itself, turning into the golden solid it had first looked like, but with a black knob in place of the red.

I didn't miss a beat. Grasping the knob and giving it a twist, I pushed the door open to reveal an elevator interior. Ari moved us inside, pressing the only button on the control panel and watching the door close us in. The elevator gave a little groan before finally moving along, gradually moving upward.

"I swear, they pull a Sailor Moon and I will so be done with this crap," I grumbled, wincing as I slid down the wall and onto the floor. "No elevator shenanigans."

Ari stood alongside me, staring ahead at the door with an expressionless face. I clasped my necklace back on just as the elevator came to a stop, the door sliding open. My heart began to pound inside my ribcage, floundering against the tiny space like a bird trying to fly free from its cage. This was it.

Looking out past the door, my heartbeat stopped.

SEVEN
THROUGH THE FEAR

You would think, after turning into a bomb and imitation earthquakes, I would have came to the easy part in this moment.

Not a chance.

Staring forward, a new hallway stretched out before us, its walls and floors the same glossy black with minimal lighting. A bright burst of light lay ahead, just cresting over the floor where the hallway vanished.

I got up onto my legs, shaking and swearing at the same time. Every part of me ached, sleep sounded like a sweet treat to the levels of pain I had already endured.

"Ari, please tell me it was difficult like this for you," I bit my lip, swallowing down a small gasp of pain. Patches of purplish marks littered my body, the after-effects of using huge bursts of power at a time. I looked and felt like a walking, bleeding bruise.

He extended a hand to steady me before shaking his head. "Not like this. But the bookkeeper said everyone's task in getting here would be different."

We stepped out of the elevator, slowly walking down the hallway. I did my best to use Ari for support without completely collapsing on him.

"So what," I huffed out, forcing my jelly legs to stay straight. "What did you face?"

"A field of dead flowers and tombstones." He stared ahead, refusing to meet my gaze. I noticed the twitch in his mouth, the lock of his set jaw, and the stone-cold bitterness in his eyes. There was definitely more than he was letting on.

"Did you burn the flowers?" I asked innocently.

He didn't reply.

Continuing forward in silence, I tried not to mull over all his open-ended answers he'd given me. Flowers, family, his Watcher, it all sounded like he was hiding a deeper end, a darker meaning tucked behind his words. Had his Watcher been killed by his family? Family killed by his Watcher? Maybe they had all died in a tragic event, and Ari had never ascended either. If that were true, it would almost be like kismet; two half-angels with timers glued to their chests and no bomb squad to help diffuse them.

Ari gave me a little shake, nodding forward to the hall. The light was getting bigger, growing outward and spread towards us. Small waves of heats rolled past us. It was a warning, like the tide pulling out before a tsunami rolls in.

I pushed off his side and came to a stand on my own, both hands out in front of me. Fire instantly sparked on my palms, racing in rivulets around my arms and blazing off my shoulders. In another five seconds the light would engulf us, and whatever else came along with it.

"You ready?" I asked, looking over at him. He nodded; he was already standing the same way as me, white fire covering him from the neck down like a suit of protection.

Five...

I grounded my feet a little better as a roar began to drown

out all noise.

Four...

My heart began to pick up its pace once more, the beat mimicking an erratic twitch.

Three...

A glow shined from my chest and ears; both the pendant and earrings were blazing.

Two...

Ari said something, and I turned my head to see him mouthing something to me that I couldn't hear over the roar.

One...

Eyes closed, I screamed.

"Petrified?"

I opened my eyes, instantly confused. The white light was gone, so was the hallway. Instead I was standing in the middle of a quaint, homey little office. Cream colored walls went well with the worn-in mint carpet, and small photos of various children lined the walls.

"Really must have done a number on you," the voice, a girl, said again. "Most people start demanding where they are by this point."

Following the sound of her voice, my eyes guided me to the long desk at the end of the small room. Like everything else, it was worn in, small scratches and random flecks of paint staining the cherry wood. Behind it was a re-stitched leather chair, a petite older woman smiling pleasantly as she sat in it.

My eyes nearly bugged out of my head.

"Just what the hell is going on?" I managed at last, ungluing my tongue from the roof of my mouth. Taking a quick look around I added, "And where's Ari?"

The older woman gave a dainty little shrug, still smiling. At first glance, she seemed harmless enough; her clothes were circa 1920's, soft peach and carnation pink weaved together to make her dress and matching hat.

"Don't know who you mean, dear," she said airily. In her hands rested a tea cup and saucer, steam steadily rising from the decorated porcelain. She made a gesture to the chairs in front of the desk. "Please, have a seat."

I stared down to the three chairs lined in front of the desk, each one vastly different; the furthest to the left a plain folding chair, the middle a rich and plush red leather recliner, and the furthest to the right a white sofa embroidered with light gold stitching.

Arms crossed over my chest, I started to shake my head. "I prefer to stand, thanks."

"We cannot start until you pick one, Essallie." She took a small sip of her tea. "Please, take your seat."

I let out a heavy sigh and quickly sat on the folding chair, watching the clock tick the seconds away on the wall above the desk.

Another minute passed before the old woman spoke again. "Are you sure that's your seat?"

"Well it certainly didn't have my name on it, but I can fix that if you give me a Sharpie."

"What I mean to say," the woman said carefully, her voice freakishly even-toned. "Are you comfortable in that seat?"

I narrowed my eyes, ignoring all urges to fidget in my seat. "Yes, I'm fine."

"You're lying," she said in a sing-song voice.

"Dammit woman, who the hell are you and what the hell do you want?" I shot up from my chair, fists clenched at my sides, my knuckles covered in fire. "I just went through my own personal hell and back, lost the person who came with me, and now I'm supposed to just shrug it all off to sit down and chat with you over a cup of tea? Who do you think you are?"

Her expression never wavered, the calm composure keeping steady through every cuss word I could fling at her. She spoke when it looked like I had nothing more to spout at her.

"I've offended you, I see." The corners of her thin mouth pulled downward. "My apologies, Essallie. I can see I'm still reveling in the fun of having done this to Ari not too long ago." Setting her tea on the desk, she shakily rose from her seat in a polite gesture before motioning for me to sit again. "Please, pick a seat that you think suits you best, then we can begin and I can explain everything to you."

I watched her through narrowed eyes, thinking. What if this was just another ploy to get me to play her mind games?

Keeping the fire burning on my hands, I made my intentions clear. "Here's how we'll do this. I'll sit, you'll tell me your name, we'll do whatever it is your inner Wicked Witch wants to do, then I'll leave."

She nodded, sitting back into the worn leather with a grateful sigh. I moved across the room and sat on the white sofa, uncaring if I added any potential dirt or blood or sweat to the clean cushions.

Tea cup back in her hand, she hummed a little tune before a quick sip of the liquid. Delicate porcelain hiding her lips, she spoke in a sweet-yet-soft tone.

"My name is Louise." Her honey colored eyes held the distance of an old soul, matching the deep creases in her face and soft but frazzled mound of curls mounted on the top of her head. "I have been the *Arcanum* since the first Nephilim was born."

"Arca-what?"

"It stands for secret, dear." She held her hand into the air, a spoonful of sugar materializing in her palm. It went into her tea, stirring itself. "You'll find most things connecting to Nephilim have Latin-worded roots. However, that is not why you are here. You are here for the list."

I nodded, inwardly grateful she had cut a good chunk of chatter out to get right to the point. "Ari brought me here, said that the list would confirm if the person I suspect to have been my Watcher was true."

Louise nodded, rings of her curls rustling on her head. "He didn't lie, the list will tell you exactly who was or is your Watcher." Tea cup on the desk again, she opened a drawer and pulled out a large, white leather bound book. It pages were a deep cream, aged from thousands of years of repeated usage.

Flipping the book open, she cradled it within her lap, leaving me only to see the top gold trim of the book. Ironically, the same gold trim that matched the sofa. So that was why she wanted to know my choice; she had to have been testing me, but how I had no idea.

"Hrmm, well, that's curious." Louise glanced up at me over the book, a smile sneaking on her lips. "I'm surprised you're here to know about your Watcher. There is so much more we could have discussed if we had more time..."

I ignored her tease, leaning on the edge of the cushions with trepidation. "Do you have the name?"

Golden honey eyes met mine. "Leo Skripper."

It all rushed up to meet me; the first time Leo and I had met, the bonfire, our day in Charon, the night of his death. Like someone spreading a deck of cards before me, I witnessed each moment with him in glimpses just as they vanished under one another. His fluttering eyelids was the last memory to stack on the deck.

I took a deep breath, my chest heavy. Inside I had known all along that he was the one, and Kayden's words had only solidified that thought in my brain. Now I had proof, real and tangible proof that my clock was running out, and soon I would go up in a display of flames brighter than the sun. It may have only meant I had a time limit on my time with

Jayson, but knowing that made everything okay. I would make the best of what I had, and maybe even give Kayden his twisted wish of killing me himself.

"So that's it," I finally said, a sad smile on my lips. I made sure to tuck away all thoughts of Jayson aside, just for the moment. They would be revisited in private, when I knew the sound of my sobs wouldn't be heard by anyone but myself. "I am to die."

The sorrow on her face said more than enough. "Yes, my angel. You will burn before you can gain the key to your kingdom. Was there anything else you wanted to know?"

Images of wings, arched high and wide over a sun-blushed horizon, came to mind. "My father," I said quietly. "Will I see him before..?"

"That I do not know," she replied, worry and sadness filling every crease on her face. "No one has seen Michael in almost twenty years." Off her chair once more, she slowly walked around the desk to stand before me, reaching out to place a hand on my knee. "Do not be afraid of death, Essallie. It will pass before you know."

I offered her an absentminded nod, thinking of Ari's earlier words. Even most terminal cancer patients had a chance of survival, a sliver of hope. My only hope had been like a final straw, now dissolved and scattered to the wind.

Taking her hand off my knee, I stood and gave a polite half-bow. "Thank you, Louise, for the information. I'd like to leave now, if you don't mind."

The smile I first saw had returned to her face, all traces of sadness gone. "Of course, dear. The door's right behind you. You'll find Ari waiting for you just outside."

I turned around, sure enough, to find the golden door restored to its original glory waiting behind me. Part of me prayed I'd never have to set foot in this place again, not even if baited with the opportunity to see my father. Hand on the red knob, I started to twist it when one last question bubbled up onto my tongue.

"Louise? Why did I have to go through all the spooky junk to get to you?"

From behind, I heard her chuckle. "You never had to do anything, Essallie. The halls only project what the mind perceives, and your mind imagined a battle. You wanted to prove you were worth it, not just to Ari and I, but to yourself. The question you need to answer is, did you succeed?"

I opened the door, and blinding white light encompassed me again.

The floor vanished from under my feet. My body fell, hurling down an endless tunnel of black that reminded me oddly of the rabbit hole in Alice in Wonderland. I couldn't breathe, my chest tight and knotted, until with a crash I landed flat on my back, any spare oxygen squeezed from my lungs.

I could see the room spinning, voices of every volume ringing in my ears. My insides felt as if they had been reduced to the consistency of some kind of pulverized pulp.

Sitting up, I looked around to see I was back in the first room once more, the desk and small man exactly where I had seen them last. Moving to lay back down, I spotted a body next me just as the room stopped spinning about.

Ari was lying on his back beside me, hands cradled behind his head, eyes staring listlessly at the ceiling. His teal eyes seemed to glow in the dim lighting of the room, like a curious cat lurking in the shadows of an abandoned home. Something in his stare tugged at my heart, watching his eyes continue to stare into the abyss above as if he was searching for a memory long lost to the black.

"Ari?" I gently asked, leaning towards him until our arms touched. "Have you been here this whole time?"

His face scrunched into concentration, and for a moment I was sure I had disturbed him from some kind of trance. But then he rolled over onto one arm to face me, and I felt my chest tighten. At a glance his eyes were powerful enough, but the full force of his smoldering hued stare left me with the same feeling I had when we first met. Words like *naked, undressed,* and *exposed* came to mind.

Heartbreakingly beautiful to begin with, he only shined more with a crooked smile gracing his lips. "Probably should have known we both couldn't go at the same time. Sorry I couldn't be there," he murmured softly. Fingers reached up to touch one of the emerald earrings I still had on. "Did she...?"

Even with his ethereal looks, the easy tone of his voice and words couldn't save me from the gravity of his question. Like weight pulling me to the depths of the Atlantic, he brought my mind back to the reality of things. I had just been officially handed my personal death sentence. I had felt it in my gut for weeks now, but this was actual proof spoken directly to me.

"She did," I started to get on my feet, wincing. So much for thinking I wouldn't have leftover pain from the fall.

"And she said what?" Ari got to his feet before I could, and helped me up. I couldn't believe it; he looked completely unscathed, free from any injuries. Heat rolled off his skin in waves. Up this close and under the barely useful lights I could make out more than before. Tangled and curled strands of his platinum hair spread askew from his face, sticky strands clinging to his sweat-dampened skin. Perfect planes and angles of his face stood out, his skin radiating as if he were filled with a personal sun within.

I warred against myself to reach out and touch him, fear that making any sudden movement would ruin the moment and send my ethereal saint away.

I froze. Ethereal saint? Warring to touch a person? I

balked at my own state of mind; what was I, a boy-crazed twelve-year-old waging battle with hormones? I liked Ari, that much was obvious, but I certainly didn't need him. My life would continue without him should something happen. I was a half-angel with the clock ticking against me- there was no time to be thinking of budding emotions over another half-angel.

"I was right." The words sounded like a dull echo as they left my lips. "Leo had been mine. I will die."

For a minute, Ari said nothing. In answer, he reached out silently, wrapping his arms around me in a soothing embrace. The effect was like stepping into a tropical paradise untouched by man, left alone and beautiful in its wild state.

"We should go," I finally said, stepping away from him. Two small spots on his shirt were damp- tears I hadn't even been aware of collecting in the sides of my eyes. Nervous laughter painfully mixed with my words. "I'll need to be returning to Maine."

He seemed to regard me for a long moment, waiting to see if I'd crack under the weight of my world and initiate hysterics. I was stronger than that.

"It can be arranged," he said quietly, the zeal in his eyes dimming to burnt out coals. "I can get you to a safe portal home so you can be with your family." Reaching out for my shoulder, he stopped and thought better not to, instead gesturing to the door leading outside. "Come on, it's probably getting close to sunset."

Ari hadn't been far off; the door open, I could make out the faint glimmers of stars decorating the color-blended sky, navy blue crushing over oranges and yellows still fighting to linger on the horizon line. Even a city girl like me had to stop and stare. A delicious, chilled breeze swept at the skirts of my dress, far better than the heat we had originally walked through to get here.

"Coming?" Ari called over to me, impatience playing in his tone. "I highly doubt you want to spend any unnecessary time here."

I removed the emerald earrings and placed them in a small pocket fashioned on the seam of the dress. "Hold your horses, I'm on my way." Two handfuls of the skirts and a small jog was all it took to catch up to his slow and exaggerated stride.

"Technically I'm holding your horses, Miss I Can't Wait To Get Home and Explode Into Flames," he teased rudely, the grin on his face the only balancing factor to his words. "I really do wish you'd stay, Essallie. You never know, we could find a cure for you before it's too late."

"Are you afraid of death, Ari?" I asked with a growing suspicion.

He looked shocked, nearly colliding into a set of barrels outside one of the street shops. "What? I, no, heavens no. Why would you think that?"

It was as if someone had ignited a darkened part of my brain to life. At first, Ari's words over trying to save me from my assumptions had seemed noble, very angel-like. Still, there was a layer of wonder that left me curious if his aversion of death had something more to do with a particular black memory in his life.

"Nothing," I said hurriedly, but not before making a mental note to revisit the thought at a later time. "Just some mindful musings."

We kept going forward, reaching to the end of the main street. The packs and thick pools of people that had been there earlier were gone, no doubt home with family or friends to settle in for the night. I started to feel the familiar ache of missing my brother, couldn't help but wonder how he was. Was Abigail staying at home with him, protecting him just in case? Or did Kayden have anything to do with helping him?

Regardless of earlier conflicts with both, I couldn't see Kayden doing anything to help out my family, not when he was seeking my death for his freedom.

"Hey Ari," I started to say, about to ask him if he knew any neat ways to possibly set a demon on fire for all of eternity, when a loud scream cut off all other sound.

EIGHT
PRAY FOR THE WEAK

I spun around, bewildered. What little people that were left on the strip were scattering, running in every which way they could. Behind them, darkness surged in billowing black smoke, the silhouette of a Vens coming forth. This one was male, unlike the first one I had dealt with, dressed in the same all-black get up.

Ari took one look at the Vens before rounding on me, eyes nearly popping from their sockets with a jolt. "You weren't lying when you told Serena you were attacked?"

"What do I look like, the little girl crying wolf? And what the heck is with all this Men In Black crap?" I swore, grabbing even larger handfuls of the dress and running. Ari grabbed my wrist and pulled me along faster, turning us onto one of the streets off the main and rushing forward. "We need to get to a portal-"

A sharp silver dagger sailed past me, but not before it sliced into my arm. Pain rippled through my arm, and I screamed in the same moment my shoe caught something in the ground, ripping me from Ari's grasp and flattening me to the pavement.

Hands were on me in an instant, grabbing at my throat and digging fingers into the soft skin. I gasped and kicked about, connecting with someone's shin hard enough to drop me with force back to the floor.

I rolled over to my back, coming face to face with the Vens out for my blood. He gave me a petrifying smile before striking me with some kind of metal, and I blacked out.

Inside my mind, everything was underwater. A voice, urgent and afraid, continued to call out to me from above the surface, but I felt comfortable under the waves.

"It's nice in here, isn't it?" A voice, oddly familiar, said to my side. In the shifting colors of the water, I made out a face with long, sleek blonde hair and bottomless brown eyes stare back at me. She looked like a porcelain doll, perfectly made up from the even tone of her skin to her plump red lips.

I had to laugh; of course the face was familiar, it was me a year before Chase came along and ruined everything. My mind was playing games with a shrink version of me.

"Have you ever been out there?" I asked my carbon copy, pointing toward the surface. "It's violent as hell. I'm pretty tired of having to run for my life because my parents created a little bundle of unloved abomination."

"You don't have to go back, you know," the long haired me replied, shrugging her dainty shoulders with grace even underwater. "No one is forcing you to leave."

"But if I stay here," I trailed, frowning. "I'd never see anyone again. Jayson, Ari, Kayden, Abigail, Serena. They all mean something to me."

"Then go," she urged, but the smile on her face wasn't happy. She looked almost disappointed I chose to leave. "I'm sure we'll see each other another time, soon enough."

"Essallie!"

My eyes fluttered open, and I heaved a sigh of relief. Pain throbbed at the top of my skull, and something wet was running down the side of my cheek. I hadn't been moved from the pavement, which meant I had to have been out for five minutes at the most.

I struggled up and looked over to the sidewalk, where Ari and the Vens were at it. Ari's upper chest and shoulders had been covered by the white fire like the breastplate of a suit of armor, his arms encased in the flames as well. He and the Vens moved around in short, jittery moves, circling each other like men in a fighting ring.

Ari made the first move, lancing a spear of the flames at the Vens. He dissipated into black smoke, swirling behind Ari and reforming in time to make a critical blow.

Without thinking I raised my hand, an arc of the wild blue fire soaring through the sky and searing the Vens' arm. He screamed in agony before bursting into smoke once more, blue smoke trailing with his dematerialized shape. I took the opportunity to roll up onto my feet and over to Ari's side, hands pressed outward and ignited for the fight.

"Enjoying your final days before you burn, Nephilim?" The smoke laughed cruelly, small tendrils steadily forming limbs. "I knew it would only be a matter of time before you returned to this place."

"If you have a point to make, then *make it*," Ari hissed, flames rising off him in waves. His hair began to defy gravity, hovering off his face mystically. "Otherwise, it's time to barbecue you and move on."

The Vens burst into smoke, spreading out through and around us. Coils of it laced around my neck and forced up my nose, choking me worse than when he had grabbed me. I fell lightheaded, stumbling away from Ari and falling painfully onto my knees and palms. The Vens materialized instantly, one hand still smoke, the other grabbing my shoulder and roughly pulling me back to my feet.

"She comes with me, but don't worry, Nephillim, you'll join her soon enough," the Vens shook my shoulder. "Wave bye-bye, pretty girl."

Fire sparked off my back like quills exploding from a porcupine, shooting straight at the Vens. Once more he screamed and pulled away from me, only this time he couldn't vanish into smoke to save himself. The volatile blue fire wrapped around him like a boa constrictor, tightening and burning deeper into his skin. Ari ran forward, arms still covered in his white flames, and grasped the Vens around both shoulders.

"Who sent you?" Ari demanded, repeating the question when the Vens only answered in a soul-shaking scream. "Who sent you to kill Essallie?"

The Vens jerked his head, whipping it back and forth in a violent display. "Not kill, only capture. The Queen can't use dead blood, not for what she needs."

Queen? I felt the color drain from my face as I listened, Ari continuing to press him for more information. Flashbacks of the sunny afternoon in Belfast surfaced through my thoughts. He had to be lying, he couldn't be telling the truth. Perhaps there was another Queen who wanted my blood, but it couldn't be the one who had warned me of the dangers herself, could it?

"What does she want with me?" I fearfully asked, feeling my hands start to shake. "Why does she need my blood?"

"I'm not told these things," the Vens spat malevolently, still managing to sneer between his facial contortions of pain. "All I know is one thing; I was instructed to bring you back, alive and intact. If I don't someone else will. Either way, *Queen Lucretia will have you, Nephilim.*"

He gave one last shriek of unbridled pain before the fire fully consumed him. Flesh melted away in chunks, dropping to the ground before melting into puddles of putty, then to ash to carry with the wind. When it was finished, all Ari held in his hands were a set of black bones.

I stared at the pile of dark bones in his arms, numb. I wanted it all to be a lie; for someone to say that the Queen didn't hire him, that it was a case of mistaken identity, anything to make it better. I couldn't get over the fact that the same woman who tipped me off of Kayden's plans could be the one to set a price upon my head, payment for my blood. What could she possibly gain from having my blood? As far as I knew, Nephilim gifts weren't transferred from person to person through blood like a vampire bite would work, and my blood wasn't some curious color like green or purple to warrant wanting to bottle and display it for some bizarre and personal collection. So what could the reason be?

Ari came over to me, his arms still cradling the pile of black bones. He visibly winced seeing me closer. I had a good guess as to why; blood covered part of my face, dirt staining both the dress Serena had lent me and any visible skin, and I was pretty sure patches of purple bruises covered parts of my skin too.

"I'm pretty sure you're going to need stitches for that," he said with a sigh, motioning to the outskirts of Charon. "Come on, who knows how many more of them may be looking for you? We need to find shelter."

I had already started walking down the street, eyes scanning the houses on either side for any shady onlookers. The warmth of my fire was swirling inside my stomach, the sensation like I had placed hot rocks in a circle around my belly button on my abdomen. But nothing could offset the pain of my head, the ache in my bones. Bone-weary didn't even start to touch how I felt.

"We could go to Serena," I suggested, glancing quickly over my shoulder to see if he was keeping up with me.

He appeared lost in thought, holding one of the longer bones in his hand like a knife. Where his fingers touched the bones began to turn green like moss, spreading and growing until it covered the it whole. A gasp caught in my throat as I watched budding flowers spring out from the mossy substance.

"Hopping habaneros, what the heck did you just do?" I was caught between amazement and delightful shock.

Ari's eyes looked up to meet mine, all amazement vanishing from my face. He looked haunted, the normal wistful and bright glimmer in his eyes lost to a vacant and hollow stare. It had been as if someone sucked the life right from his own bones and left him to wander alone.

I turned around and came over to him, worried. One touch of his skin had told me he'd gone cold, like an iceberg floating among the Atlantic. "Ari, what's wrong?"

"If I told you," he started to say, then cut himself off with a shake of the head. Strands of hair covered part of his stare as he searched my face carefully. "You should go, Essallie. Find a portal and go home."

I frowned, clearly not on the same level of thought he was. "I'm sorry, I don't think I understand."

"What don't you understand?" He scowled, brushing past my shoulder and continuing down the road in a rigid stance. "You've made your place in this world clear. You have no intent to fight, no intent to do anything but waste away in a mortal world with a half-sibling you know nothing about, now go."

I caught up to him easily, grabbing an upper arm and spinning him around. "Hey, you don't get to talk to me like that. You have no idea what I've gone through to get here-"

"Like hell I don't, Essallie," Ari nearly shouted, the hollow in his stare replaced with a bright and hostile look. "It's always about you and your brother and how your clock is running out. Have you ever thought for one single moment of all the lives placed in danger just to help you succeed?"

"You leave my brother and my personal problems out of this!"

"How about I start when you stop using it like a crutch?" He demanded spitefully, throwing the black bones and green one covered in flowers. "What, do you think I don't know your pain? That I haven't experienced family loss, or friend betrayals, or outcast sensations, too? When are you going to learn this isn't just about you? We're chess pieces in a much bigger plan here, and you're the prized Queen of the opposite color." He pointed a wild and shaking finger toward the main street, chest heaving up and down in sharp breaths. "Lucretia is going to keep attacking you, she wants something from you. No amount of you saying you're just 'waiting to die and spending time with my brother' is going to stop them."

"It's a mistake!" I half-screamed, but I couldn't cut the doubt out from my words. "That Vens was only saying what it could before death, you don't know if he was lied to or-"

"Or what?" Ari challenged with a snap. He dug into a pocket and pulled out a scrap of black fabric, the same the Vens had been wearing. This piece had a patch on it, a thickly embroidered red heart with spikes emanating from the outer design, purple filled in the center. He threw it at my feet bitterly. "So sure he was lying now?"

I picked up the patch, turning it over in my hands. My voice was quiet. "Who's is this?"

"Who else, but Queen Lucretia."

A wave of lightheadedness passed over me, my throat drier than a desert as the sharp realization of things started to set in. Ari was right; no one was going to simply leave me be because my clock was running out faster than others. Going home in the middle of this unfinished would be putting everyone I knew in danger.

I wasn't sure how much more of this truth unveiling I could handle before I passed out. A shaky, ragged breath rattled my chest. "I'm sorry."

Arms wrapped around me, holding me close. "It's going to be okay." His body stiffened, muscles tensing in his arms like tightly bound wire. "We need to leave here, it's been too long. Come on." He let me go, taking me by the wrist and pulling me along the street.

"Wait, where are we going?" The heart shaped pendant around my neck started to glow.

"Just think of it as a safe house," he said in a hushed tone, taking us further out than I had ever been in Charon. The buildings had started to turn to darker and deeper shades of grey. For the first time I saw abandoned and damages homes, garbage scattered among the unkempt lawns. Thorny vines, black and deep red, twisted over any unused fixture.

I nearly tripped on the hem of Serena's dress, and cursed her out. Next time I'd make sure if she gave me clothes to only accept pants and shirts.

"It's right here," he said after what felt like an hour of navigating under the darkened sky. Now it was a striking dark navy blue, stars sprinkling the sky to provide a meager source of light. Against the night, I could barely make out the house, but the silhouette stood loud and clear, and left me breathless by the display.

NINE

ANGELS AND DEMONS

"And here I thought the biggest house I'd ever seen was in Maine," I observed in awe at the giant home looming above us.

Ari hadn't been leading us to a safe house, he had been leading us to a freaking *super-huge mansion*. From what I could make under the dark, the building had to at least be five stories tall, stretching on both sides like an oversized rectangle. Small windows held candles inside them, casting an eerie glow within each room.

"It puts Ursula's place to shame, at least for this lifetime," came an all-too familiar voice from the open doorway. I didn't need any magical glasses or super sleuth to tell me who it was.

Kayden was leaning against the frame of the door, his facial expression decidedly amused. Since the last time I'd seen him he looked well; the tan color of his skin had returned, his eyes bright and dancing with the need to be mischievous.

I started to run to him, then stopped. There wasn't a

chance that I was ready to forgive him for his actions, not yet. Keeping my composure in check, I made sure to walk with intentional grace and steadiness.

"Going out on a limb here and saying this isn't your place?" I asked Kayden, giving him a minimal acknowledgement. He deserved that much, I guess.

He gave a low chuckle and shook his head. "Not a chance. Lilix called me as soon as she spotted you. She had a feeling you'd come here sooner or later."

I took the four steps leading to the door carefully, but made sure to stop in the doorway and get a closer look at Kayden. He was wearing the same thing I would always picture him in; a black ribbed turtleneck, tan pants, and a pair of black Italian leather shoes. On anyone else it would be decidedly snobbish, but for him it worked.

"Good to know you haven't changed one bit from your lazy ways," I remarked coolly, sniffing with feigned distaste. "At least Ari here gave a genuine damn if I lived or died."

Ari had been right behind me, giving Kayden the same suspicious regard. In the end he said nothing, giving a curt nod before stepping inside. I followed after him, leaving Kayden to trail behind both of us.

Following Ari, we walked down a series of hallways, all with similar decor on the walls. Any door that was open had a completely different mix of things within it; some had weapons both crude and current; some had drawing rooms, old as colonial times in America; some had bedrooms, mixed furniture making it appear caught between two worlds at the same time.

Ari ended up turning into a large drawing room, the furniture reminiscent of Victorian times. A fire had already been started in the grate. Taking one of the seats closer to the fire, he seemed to sigh with relief as he sunk into the cushions.

I collapsed with a thump into one of the chairs across from Ari. Pain pulsed as I moved about against the chair, my back still sore from the beating I had taken today. I didn't even dare ask about my head, figuring that as long as I wasn't passing out there wasn't a problem.

"Where's Lilix?" I looked around, seeing nothing but books and random brass objects displayed on various tiny tables throughout the room. "Is this all real Victorian era furniture?"

"Of course it is," Kayden answered with a laugh, mocking me with a roll of his eyes. "Hasn't your little angel buddy told you how old Lilix is?"

I gave a small shrug of the shoulders and met Ari with a sideways glance. "No, he didn't."

Kayden stood in front of the fire, blocking it from my end of the grate. He waved a dismissive hand. "We can save that for another time, then. I'm just surprised she remembered the first time we met in Greece. Togas baby, gotta love 'em."

My hand twitched compulsively, the pressure of fire budding in my fingertips. I reigned it in, for now. "So why, in the name of anything sacred, are you here?"

He jerked a thumb over his shoulder to Ari, a dull expression on his face. "Rumor has it this twit can't save you from a Vens." He leaned in closer, narrowing his gaze questioningly. "Believe me now about the Queen and her psycho antics?"

"If you're here to gloat, I'm leaving," I snapped, getting up from the chair. Everything around me turned blurry and tilted sideways before I collapsed back into the chair.

Ari moved to get up, but Kayden stopped him. He came closer to me, centimeters left between us. I felt my chest tighten and stopped breathing.

His fingers hovered dangerously close to my skin. "Essie, pull in your fire for a minute. Your head looks like hell."

"Gee," I rolled my eyes. "Flattery will get you everywhere."

"Don't roll your eyes at me. Haven't you read that darker shades book? You'd never roll your eyes again after that."

I made a mental note to figure out what the hell Kayden was blathering about. "Okay, fine. Ari," I leaned over slightly to the side, just to see his teal eyes. "Burn him if he tries anything."

I took a deep breath, feeling the fire flex inside my veins. Pictures of waterfalls, cooled incense sticks, and ice bergs all played in my mind, forcing the fire deeper and deeper into my chest until it was only tightly wound around my heart. I gave a nod to Kayden but warned him, "Go slow."

Very gently, he brushed at the wound on my head. Pain instantly flared down my neck as he did it, and I lost control on the tense coil of power wound in my heart. Fire erupted on Kayden's fingers, singeing him and racing up his arm with speed. With a swear he dissipated into thin black smoke, swirled around and reformed in front of me.

"You might want to get something on that before it festers," he pursed his lips and ran a hand through his black hair. "I'm sure your little golden boy can manage that much."

"Do you mind?" Ari finally jumped in, hands on his knees curled to fists. "You don't hear me mouthing off about you and your demonic spawning."

"Oooh, he's a keeper," Kayden stage-whispered back to me, winking for extra effect. "Really knows how to defend a lady."

"How about both of you are being freaking ridiculous?" I spat, using the back of the chair for support as I stood. "Neither one of you can behave like grown men, can you? I'll talk to both of you in the morning, and you'll both be civil, or I'll char you both to ash."

Against his better judgment, Ari snickered and opened his

mouth to speak. "Technically speaking-"

I raised my eyebrows, one fist curled in display. He decided it wouldn't be worth it to make his point, after all.

I nodded, turning sharp on my heels and making for the door. "Right, goodnight to both of you. I'm going to find the nearest bed, pass out in it, and tomorrow morning we can take care of the loose ends."

Kayden materialized in front of the door before I could reach it, hands up automatically in a display of harmlessness. "Lilix wanted you to use her room while you stay here. Second floor, left hall, two doors on the right."

"I'll have to thank her when she shows up," I said, breezing past him through the door and straight down the hall. After today, a bed sounded like the best thing next to getting a hold of the Queen with my bare hands.

Lilix Morgan was gorgeous, even before her death. Now, three hundred years later, that still hadn't changed. I watched her in the mirror as she slowly wrapped a strand of cultured pearls around my bare neck. She was dressed like a woman from the 19th century, right down to the shoes. Her corseted dress was of a deep, rich crimson, accented with gold and black. Small, off-white laced gloves covered her hands, little ribbons tied at the edges in bows. Her soft, platinum blonde hair had been spun in soft curls, piled high on her head. Even now she reminded me of a queen, or a duchess, ready to make her appearance to her people.

Only she wasn't the one going to meet people, not this time. No, she had said it was my turn to make an appearance. I was brought here for an important reason, a duty to fulfill. It was my time to join a family, to become betrothed. That should have bothered me more than anything, to be tied down forever, but it didn't. In fact, nothing bothered me, not even the fact that I was wearing a white corseted dress with golden accents from the 1800's.

Lilix tied the back of my necklace, looking up in the mirror to meet my eyes. I only had a couple of minutes left now. The bare, whitewashed walls of the dressing room suddenly became small, confined.

"You look beautiful," Lilix whispered, placing her hands on my shoulders. I had to admit, she was right. Only an artist could have taken my pallor complexion and turned it into something as beautiful as it was now.

"Thanks. You look gorgeous, too."

She scoffed, rolling her eyes like she always did. "Please. Even in my previous life I didn't look as pretty as you do right now."

We stared at each other through the mirror, neither of us speaking. I vaguely wondered if my eyes were going to sparkle as much as hers did when this was all over.

Lilix sighed, walking to my side so she could look me directly in the face. "You have to go now."

"I know."

"You'll be fine. He's a good man, Essallie. He'll take care of you."

I wasn't afraid of not being taken care of, that I could manage perfectly well on my own. No, I was more afraid of what would happen once I looked in his eyes, once he spoke my name. I could never go back after that. Not unless I wanted to die. "I know," I repeated, sounding like a broken record.

Lilix nodded, like a person sealing the deal with someone else. I rose from my chair, grabbing fistfuls of my skirts so I could walk my way out. I managed to get to the door before I heard her running to me.

"Wait," she called, and I spun around with a little too much enthusiasm. Something reminded me he was waiting outside, waiting for me to show. Maybe if I stayed in here long enough he'd leave, defeated. Slim chance.

"You forgot this," she held out the small bouquet of white and red roses to me, seventeen roses in total. Taking both of my hands,

my skirts dropped as she wrapped my freezing fingers around the bouquet. "There. Now you're ready." She smiled, only this time it looked painful.

I couldn't speak anymore, so I nodded, turning and opening the door.

All around me, the atmosphere changed. Fire laced up the walls as thick black smoke clogged my lungs. Air rushed into the room, fueling the fire as it pushed out the small quarters into the main hall. Somewhere behind me I could hear the sound of voices, screaming in agony as I'd never heard before. My name was called, pleading, but I knew to go back meant turning my back on everything when I was so close to the truth. I fell to the floor and crawled to escape the fire, my vision going hazy from the smoke. I covered my mouth and screamed a name, flinging a hand out into the darkened miasma surrounding me.

My eyes snapped open, a hand reaching for my throat. Short, painful gasps of air pressed through my lungs, as if I'd been running in the scalding, southern summer heat with no reprieve. The sheets clung to my damp and sticky skin, a thin sheen of sweat covering every inch of me. Now would have been a good time to have a window to crack open in my room.

Oh, you know, except I couldn't because some psycho monarchy inbred of a woman decided she wanted to have me and my blood for some reason. Hence the lack of windows in my room. Because you never know when someone is going to try breaking in and running off with me tossed over their shoulder a-la old fashioned humor movie. I sniffed and made a face.

Slowly I sat up, using one arm for support against the mattress. I was too tired to get up and face the two boys just yet, but the idea of going back to sleep and possibly back into that weird dream seemed far worse. For a split second, I half expected to fall back into the dream, or worse, wake up to flames all around. I thought back, trying to recall the startling noises and scents, but only came back with the images of blazing fire and putrid smells of burning wood. The images were vivid, tangible to the point of reaching out and touching them. I distinctly remembered a part that involved a white room, but what exactly was said in said room slipped from my mind, like sand through my fingers.

Stupid dreams and their stupid premonitions. These days my dreams were always caught halfway between pure premonition based warning and nightmares bordering on driving me mad. Neither one left me feeling like a bag of joy in the morning.

Groaning, I rolled out of bed. I had a date with some stitches, a demon, and another Nephilim. And to think, two years ago the worst thought on my mind had been if I'd get a new car come graduation or not.

I took a quick look around, getting a good look at Lilix's room for the first time since Ari and I had arrived at the mansion. Her room had to be at least as big as a suite in a hotel. The walls had been trimmed in a rich blue and painted white, the same royal blue color used for the plush carpet lining the floors. Two doors, a bathroom and full walk-in closet, showed a matching taste for the carefully decorated tastes of Ari's demon friend.

Taking one look at the blue dress from Serena, I took it off, glad to have the blood and dirt stained piece of cloth off. It only took me a few minutes riffling through Lilix's clothes to find a comfortable pair of jeans, dark blue blouse, and socks to wander. I'd worry about the shoes later.

Out in the hallway, the smell of something sweet and delicious caught me. Judging by how strong, it was just around the corner, so I followed after it. Sure enough, down the end of the hall was an open kitchen and dining room combo, a marble-topped island in-between both for smaller parties.

Ari was standing in front of the stove, flipping pancakes without a spatula. He took one step back, held the pan out, and gave a quick flick of the wrist to send the flapjack sailing into the air before landing smack back in the middle of the pan. For the first time since I'd met him, he looked truly relaxed, the expression on his face genuinely happy as he moved around and cooked. I was almost sad to interrupt, but my stomach couldn't handle waiting much longer.

"Any eggs?" I called out to him, still having not moved from the end of the room.

He looked up, any trace of the happiness I first saw vanished. Now he was guarded, drawing into himself and shutting the door.

"Don't really care for eggs," he said with a shrug. He pointed to a set of plates already set with three pancakes on each at the marble island. "But I made you some pancakes if you're up for it."

"Thought you'd never ask," I replied quickly, crossing the room in two strides and taking a seat. I didn't even care to cut the pancakes; instead I drizzled on some syrup, jabbed it with a fork and piled a whole one into my mouth to chew.

Ari watched me with a cross of awkward and surprise written on his face. He started to shake his head, muttering something under his breath while fighting not to laugh. "Do you want eggs?"

Swallowing a chunk of pancake I asked, "Do I eat that much like a wild monster?"

"You have no idea, Essallie," he bit his lower lip, still trying not to laugh. "Have you never been fed your whole life?"

"My hips bones are cunning little liars."

Ari cracked, a chuckle escaping from his lips. Before any

more could get by, he turned around and opened the fridge, pulling out a carton of eggs. "Scrambled or sunny-side up?"

"Wait, I want to make them," I said, hopping down from my chair and rounding the counter. Ari had started to move towards me, handing out the carton, when we bumped together, the carton dropping onto the floor between our feet.

"Oh, shi-" I looked up at Ari, afraid. "I'm so sorry, I didn't mean to-"

But Ari wasn't mad, not in the slightest. His teal eyes looked up at me under thick and dark lashes, no trace of anger in them. A crooked smile dashed his lips, his chest still shaking from the bottled laughter.

"Relax Essie, it's fine. There's another carton in the fridge," he said, only it sounded more like a gentle whisper to me. It suddenly dawned on me that we were close, close enough that I could make out the details of his face perfectly. I stared at the sharp line of his jaw, the perfect curve of his throat, his soft and lightly colored lips. Part of me wondered what it would be like to nestle in the crook of his neck, or kiss those lips.

"I... I think I should get a mop," I fumbled out, my eyes darting between watching his bright teal gaze or the grin hitching on his lips.

He tilted his head to the side, and for a moment my breath caught in my throat. "You sure?"

Somewhere between the ogling of his lips and eyes, I shook my head. Ari leaned forward, lips dangerously close to mine-

"Those pancakes have salmon in them?"

I froze, eyes wide. From the corner of my frozen stare I could see Kayden, dressed in funeral style black, sauntering into the room like a king to his throne. He squandered my seat from earlier, digging into my plate without a single question.

Ari pulled away first, mumbling something under his breath about cleaning up the mess on the floor. He averted my eyes as he scooped the carton and moved to dump it into the trash.

I turned my gaze to Kayden, furious. Who knew just how long he had been standing there, waiting for the right moment to drop in and mess with me, like always? I had a right mind to deck him in the face and let him see how to felt to have on the other end of a sucker punch.

Kayden swallowed a chunk of pancake and syrup, grimacing and nearly gagging. "Mortal food, how positively revolting. No matter how many times I try and eat it, it always tastes like dirt."

"I bet you know exactly how that tastes," I snapped. "Since your behavior has you on the end of someone's boot more often than not." What a shame I didn't own a pair of boots. I wondered if Lilix had a spare pair in her room...

He rolled his eyes, sighing with boredom. "Must you be so hostile in the morning, Essallie? I haven't done even done anything yet today."

"Other than hijack my breakfast."

His eyes looked down in horror to the plate in front of him. "No wonder it tastes like death- your germs are all over it."

I started around the counter, fire sparking over my knuckles. Ari's hand snaked out of nowhere and grabbed my wrist, shaking his head while holding me back.

His gave flickered from mine to the demon. "Why is he here again, exactly?"

My shoulders slumped. "It's a long story."

"Well, whatever it is, it can wait." Ari said, stunning me. He wasn't exactly Kayden's number one fan; the idea of even tolerating him seemed completely beyond his charming persona. "We have bigger things to think about. Like why the

Queen wants Essallie."

I gave Kayden a sharp shove with my elbow, knocking him off my chair and setting him on fire in the same breath. A small smile curved my lips as I watched him explode into smoke and recover, cursing in a language I didn't know.

"Like I know," Kayden shrugged, his tone surprisingly nonchalant. "It's not like all us demons share a same brain. She's not even a full demon, anyway."

I snapped my fingers, a light bulb going off in my head. "What if it has to do with the fact that she isn't a full demon?" When neither one of them caught on, waved my arms. "You know, she's part demon, part Nephilim, like Serena said. She carries our blood."

"Then why not him?" Kayden nodded towards Ari. "He's Nephilim, just like you. Same blood."

I shook my head, the smile spreading on my face. "He's not. We come from different angels." I reached into my blouse and pulled out the small, wire-wrapped glass heart around my neck. "Supposedly my father was Michael. This was his gift left to me. The emerald earrings were also from him, but given to another Nephilim he had created."

Ari took this in bits, eyes darkening with thought. The second he said it, his suggestion rang true. "Maybe it has nothing to do with Essallie, and everything to do with her father."

"A legacy of vengeance, and on kids no less? Maybe you are a little dark, after all," Kayden said, giving Ari a wink. He walked around me, careful not to come in contact, and made for the fridge. His rummaging inside dearly drowned out his words. "So she's a pawn in the chess board, and us boys are like her bishop and knight or some crap like that." Head out of the fridge, he held his prize up into the air; a fish, most likely freshly killed. "And now she's being made to wade into the battlefield without flanks."

I turned away from the smell, nearly gagging. "If that's the case," I continued, nose pinched and face pointed down at the ground. "Then she isn't going to stop. We have to get to her first."

Kayden smacked the fish onto the island countertop. He dug his knife-like nails into the skin, peeling it off with ease as he drew back. "Easier said than done, Essie dear. The Queen's doesn't do as much as she used to. More often than not she's in the center of her castle, ticking off the hours by eating mortals for satisfaction."

I saw Ari shudder. "What ever happened to good old parties?"

Kayden glowered at him. "I'm sure this is going to be hard for you to grasp, given you're what, nineteen at the most? But parties in Charon aren't exactly as much of a hot commodity as they used to be. When you attend the same string of parties hosted by the same people for the last 300 years, the words 'drab' and 'suicidal' start to mix in sentences."

"Even the better ones?"

"Better ones are repeated, of course, but eventually those get boring too. Think about it. Imagine if it was your birthday every day all year long. I bet you'd want to inject rat poison in your cake just to avoid another one." Kayden ripped a strip of pink meat off, examined it briefly, then tossed the uncooked chunk onto his plate. "Could you imagine seeing the same people attend those parties- or worse, seeing a former lover everywhere you went for the last 300 years? Now that's sting worthy."

I removed myself from the island countertop, lingering in the far end of the kitchen where the hallway and entrance frame met. Thankfully, the smell wasn't as bad with the distance between us.

"I don't know," I pondered aloud, throwing Kayden a

narrowing stare. "I'd imagine it would be the opposite. At some point, a connection was shared, and when they die, so does a part of you. If it were me, I'd want to keep them close for as long as time permits."

Ari and Kayden exchanged glances, eyebrows raising all around. "How typical of a woman," Kayden said, knocking the breath from my lungs. "To cling to anything even if it only offered a drop of pleasure among a full glass of pain. If I didn't know how simple-minded you are, I'd say you were one hell of a plotter and revenge-planning wench."

My eyes flashed, and fire burst from my hands and arms, growing with rage. I could barely talk from how pissed I was. "I'm typical? Funny coming from a demon who sees it okay to manipulate a girl to save his own hide." I turned my gaze to Ari, livid. "Discuss with him whatever you want, I'm done talking to the child of the group."

I stalked out of the room and down the hall, fuming. Who was he to think it's okay to call me out and consider himself a saint? For a centuries and beyond aged creature, he had one hell of a funny way to play selective memory bits to his advantage.

Of course, I assumed he wanted nothing to do with the memory of our kiss, and it didn't take a genius to figure out why. Nothing was in it for him. My only playing card was the beating heart in my chest, and that had a limited time left. Sooner or later my guard would no doubt drop, and he'd slice me in half easier than he cut his fish.

Footsteps sounded behind me, but I had no desire to look back. If it was Kayden, I would light up faster than a Roman candle and take the whole hallway with me. If it was Ari, I'd probably find Kayden and still do the same thing.

My fingers jabbed at the elevator buttons when Ari's hand caught me by the wrist. "Ignore him, Essallie. He's just some flimsy air-headed demon."

"Don't talk to me," I hissed, yanking my hand free. I started down the opposite hallway, deciding on a random door to open and get away from him. "I don't want to talk to you, or that *demon* or anyone. Back off."

Ari ignored my protests, following close enough that I could feel the heat of his skin. When I reached out for a door handle, he caught me and spun me around quicker than I could resist. "You can't go wandering these halls alone. There's more behind some of these doors than you'll be able to handle."

"Let me go!" I struggled in his grasp, kicking aimlessly at his legs.

"I'm serious, Essallie!" The tone of his voice caught my attention, and when I looked up at his eyes I found them hard as steel, colder than ice. "Some things in this place aren't meant to be seen."

"Speaking from experience?" I countered, sneering childishly. "What, am I going to find dead bodies stored away for a rainy day?"

Ari didn't answer me.

I ignored the way my skin went cold, goosebumps rising high off my arms. I had seen enough dead bodies to last me a lifetime; I didn't want to go stumbling upon more. "Look," I said with a quivering tone. "All I know is you had damn well better take me to a room where I can set something on fire. Otherwise I'm going back and kicking that smirking smart-aleck so hard in the face he'll be tasting ass for months."

He stared at me for a moment, eyes searching my face, but for what I didn't know. "I think," he started to say. "I know exactly where we can go."

Taking me by the hand, he led me back to the elevator in the center of both halls. We used it to go down several floors, but when the doors opened it looked identical to the hallways we had just left, save for the small painting on the opposite wall depicting a dungeon entrance.

Ari continued to guide me down a small stretch of hallway, coming to a stop at a door just like all the others in the hall. A creepy feeling of dread rolled through me, and I had half the nerve to ask Ari if Lilix got her decorating ideas from The Shining.

Opening the door, he ushered me inside, coming in behind me and shutting the door before I had a chance to look around. No lights were on in the room, catapulting us into an abyss-like black and I got the eerie sensation that most of the room was empty, spacious.

I could feel Ari's breath hot on my neck, warm hands touch the sides of my arms. "Go ahead," he breathed softly. "Let the flames begin."

I didn't need to be told twice. Fire lit over my hands, exploding to life with ease. The glow from the flames casted jagged shaped shadows along the walls and brought the front of the room to light. As soon as I saw the small pillar shapes, I grinned.

Releasing the tension in my shoulders, I breathed out a sigh of relief and moved my hands forward, fire shooting off and lighting the wicks. In less than a minute every candle displayed on a counter top, shelf, false chandelier, and notches on the wall was lit, rich candlelight casting the room in a sultry, soft glow.

The fire died from my hands as I watched, amazed. The whole room was nothing but candles in patterns and rows, forming a display unlike anything I had ever seen.

"Ari, this is beautiful," I whispered, transfixed on the wavering glow and flickering shadows. I turned my head up to meet his gaze. "How, where did you find this?"

His fingers ran down the sides of my arms, clasping my hands in his. He brought me further into the room with him, centering us around the swirl of dancing flames.

"When I first met Lilix, I was going through a painful moment. She brought me to this room and told me to light every candle by hand until I wasn't mad anymore."

"Did it work?"

"Not really," he shrugged and laughed. "I ended up doing it five times over before I finally calmed down and admired the way the room looked fully lit."

I stood there in front of him, very aware of how he continued to watch me closely. His eyes stood out sharp amidst the dim light, two little sparks of life among a swaying wave of flame.

"Hey Ari? About this morning," I managed to get out before he leaned in closer to me with half-lidded eyes. I stepped back with a jolt, knocking one of the candles to the floor, hot wax spilling all around the floor cresting my heels. I lost my balance and arched back, falling right onto a whole table covered in candles.

In one steady move he closed the gap between us and caught me, arms wrapped around my waist, safe and secure.

He hovered so close, to the point nothing could come between us. Suddenly everything came into perception; the weight of his body pressed against mine, the way my hands twisted like vines around his neck, refusing to let him go. His eyes had darkened to a smoldering turquoise. I could feel his rough hands moving gently over the small of my back, cradling me. It felt like every part of me belonged there, steady in his embrace.

"I can't..." Against every screaming cell in my body, I pulled out of his arms. Instantly I felt cold, empty, and I wanted nothing more than to run straight back for his warmth.

He looked confused, but didn't question my choice. "Okay." Taking my hand, he gently ran a thumb over in small, soothing circles. "So, who hurt you?"

Laughter twisting between nervous and afraid, escaped my lips. "What makes you think someone hurt me?"

"You're going to laugh." His head turned downward to stare at our joined hands.

"That corny, huh?" I tried to keep the conversation light, but his hesitance only made the twisting in my gut more intense. "Spill it cowboy."

Slowly, he turned back up to look at me, his scattered blonde hair like a framing halo. His eyes were piercing, brutally truthful. "One look in your eyes and I just know." The faintest of blushes bloomed on his cheeks. "Someone dragged you through the mud."

I felt my breath catch in my throat. Where the room had been warm before, now it was as chilled as a frozen tundra. I hadn't planned on peeling back the layers of my damaged past. I wasn't ready to be this exposed, this raw and vulnerable.

Swallowing, I found my voice. "Not mud so much as blood and personal gain."

Something in his eyes wavered, and for a second I saw it. He knew exactly who I meant when the words 'blood' and 'personal gain' left my lips. "Well, don't worry," Ari said, tipping a finger under my chin and bringing my gaze to his. "You don't have to do anything you don't want to. But, I do hope you get past it one day. It would be a shame to see such a beautiful woman go to waste."

I kissed him; a quick peck on the cheek was the most I could control myself over. "Once again my past surfaces to light." I shook my head, frowning. "Why don't I ever learn anything about you?"

"Because my past is... nothing worth talking about," Ari struggled to say, his skin paling slightly. He straightened us both before pulling back, making for the door.

I did like he had done to me; grabbing one of his wrists, I

turned him around, shaking my head. "Oh no, it doesn't work like that. You said you want me to stop using my past like a crutch. That means we have to talk about other things, and it makes sense to talk about you. I know almost nothing about you, but I'm supposed to trust you. It doesn't work like that."

He chewed on his lower lip, and I could see the war in his eyes. If he said no, he would be backtracking and giving me room to continue my moping existence; if he said yes, he'd have no choice but to tell me a bit about himself.

Good won over evil. Ari scowled and crossed his arms over his chest, bitterness written in every inch of his stance. "What do you want to know?"

"Anything really," I confessed, hoping it didn't sound as desperate and vague as it did in my head. "Where you're from, family or friends, where your Watcher is. You're like a mystery to me, Ari."

Tension kept his shoulders tight, but his expression flickered with an ounce of sadness as he spoke. "I came from the South, a little spot in Nebraska. Mom died early from a massive car crash."

"And your Dad?"

"A Vens killed him." A haunted look hollowed out his eyes.

"I'm sorry." My hand rested on his own, cold to his hot. "Any siblings?"

He shook his head. "No. Only child from the start, only child to the end. As for friends, I really only had one. Her name was Bethie, short for Bethanie. She was a real angel, not because of magic in her veins, but the compassion in her heart. She told me a little quote I'll never forget."

"What was it?"

"We always reach for the light for clarity, but it's the dark moments that shape us and give us vision. It's the dark moments that makes us into who we are."

I stood there in the silence, staring at our joined hands. His words sounded so clear, like I was finally pushing past the surface of the water and gasping in air. But the shattered look in his eyes told me there was something deeper to his words. I wondered if this was Ari's first love, or a crush he carried a torch for.

"Ari," I said, a horrible thought coming to mind. "Was Bethanie your Watcher?"

His head shook again. "I can't, Essallie..."

"Yes, you can," I pressed, gripping his hand tighter. "Tell me about your Watcher."

The effect had been like telling Ari to jump off a bridge with no rope. His shattered gaze crumbled, revealing a broken and exposed soul.

"Yes, Bethanie was my Watcher. She's been dead for four months now."

TEN

SLAUGHTERHOUSE

When I got back to my room, it had already begun to rain. The bright, sunny morning sky had been replaced with a grey, wretched overcast as thunder rumbled in the distance. I flopped onto the unmade bed, wondering about everything.

So we had a vague, and still unproven, theory for why the Queen was out for my blood. It certainly didn't make me feel any better, especially since now there wasn't a chance for doubt. Until this all resolved, I couldn't go home to the one person I wanted to see. And because of this problem, I was stuck with two boys, one who twisted my heart into something dark and one who thought it fair to make me fall for him.

I wanted them both to go away; I didn't need either of them. Kayden was just a pain, constantly reminding me of how I fell to a petty game. Ari was pulling more rabbits of his mysterious wizard hat than I could keep count of, between his dead Watcher or crush or whatever and family and weird grass-growing ability. Both were two very difficult pills to swallow at the same time.

I grabbed a nearby pillow and shoved it into my face, groaning. It shouldn't be this hard to fix a problem! Why couldn't I just find out the next time the Queen would be out at an event or mostly alone, drop in and kick her ass, and move on in life?

Excitement caught me so fast that I rolled off the bed and smacked onto the floor. "Bingo!" I shouted, and took off from my room to go down the hall.

As soon as I rounded the corner of my door, I nearly ran head-first into Kayden. He jumped back in shock, but not before his hands flung out between us and brushing over my skin. Like a match striking to light, fire crackled between us in a dazzle of warning blue sparks.

"Essallie," he breathed, his dark eyes brimming with excitement. His chest rose and fell rapidly, and I realized he had been running down the hall when I crossed into his path. "I was just coming to get you."

I could feel myself instantly splitting into two, like always when I became involved with him. Half of me wanted to shun him for the jerk he was, cold shoulder him harder than dry ice. The second half preferred the idea of daydreaming a second kiss with him.

I mentally shook the second half of me out of the picture. This wasn't the time to swoon or sway or whatever lovesick idiots did. Not that I was one of those. Narrowing my eyes with discontent, I did my best to appear disdainful of him. "I'm extending you an olive branch when I say I suggest there's an apology involved in this conversation?"

"For what?" He cocked an eyebrow, the action instantly bringing the heat in my veins to a growing boil. "For saying what was on my mind?"

"For calling me a calculating bitch, for starters." I kept my gaze icy. "We can settle you manipulating me later with some flowers or melting your face or something."

He kept his face expressionless as possible, but I could spot the carefully masked twitches of his face fighting to grin or laugh. "Oh, Essallie, when are you ever going to learn?" His head shook, black hair swaying with motion. "It's sink or swim in this world. Even your closest friend will have an ulterior motive somewhere in their back pocket. If you're looking for begging or some sniveling act of pleading for forgiveness, you've got the wrong guy."

"I see," I turned to head back to my room, refusing to meet his eyes even from the sideway glance. "Then I guess this is it."

"This is what?" His words were hard.

I didn't respond, praying the element of surprise would play in my favor. In one move I had uncrossed my arms, fire blazing over them, and grabbed Kayden by the neck. With a sharp thud his body stood pinned between me and the wall, spirals of blue flame rolling over his skin like a fast-spinning web.

"I'd choose your words carefully," I warned him, locking eyes with him. "You'll find I'm incredibly forgiving when the right words are strung together in a sentence."

"Really? This again?" He snickered shortly before grimacing in pain. Horns started to peak through his forehead, his true form appearing under the stress of the flames. "You tried killing me before, remember? You don't have the heart for it."

Adrenaline twisted inside my body, my heart taking off with fervor. It was like someone had doused my flames with gasoline; blue and black fire began to run off my hands and over Kayden, burning him with a sickening smell.

His eyes briefly widened, the first flicker of fear. "Essie-"

"Make it count, Kayden." It was all I could say, my brain seeming to have disconnected from the rest of me. An odd haze clouded my vision like a thick film, and for a second I felt nothing but a hazy weightlessness in limbo. One heartbeat later, it all came back into perfect clarity.

Kayden still had his eyes on me, the fear still present. Something else was there, too, but what exactly it was I couldn't place. His back arched as he let out a gasp of pain, the fire spreading further and digging deeper into him.

"I know how we can get to the Queen," he spat out with a gasp.

I felt my eyes widen, the shock disabling the overruling power of my flames. Acting on impulse, Kayden exploded into fine black smoke, snaking into my room and away from my fiery grasp.

I stalked in after him, his body filling back to normal near the vanity at the other end of the room. Pink and raised scars covered his body, yet already they started to fade. But I could barely get past the fact that he had said exactly what I had been thinking just as I went to leave my room. Hesitation laced my words as I spoke. "What do you mean you know how to get to the Queen?"

"Exactly what I said, silly girl." His eyes sparked back to life the second he spoke, a mischievous and wickedly dark glint in those swirling orbs. In his hands was a paper I hadn't seen at first. "I found an in to Lucretia. There is a socialite ball in a week, one she is required to attend."

"You're full of bull," I cracked back at him, the fire still running over my hands and arms, brushing over my chest and neck like a self-knitting turtleneck. "You're only doing this to get at me. Congratulations, you've pissed me off. Now *leave*."

"Not until you listen," he declared, his voice dark and rumbling. "I came here to help, and dammit that's what I'm going to do."

"I'll believe it when I see it-"

"After this morning's discussion," he continued over my mutterings, eyes thin as slits. "I thought about things, specifically how to get to the source of the problem. It hit me like the Great Wall falling on me-"

"Oh, how one can wish *that* was real-"

"Lucretia attends one key party, every year. And I bet you'll know why the second I show you this." Kayden was over at my side in a flash, spreading the paper out so I could see. It looked like a poster I had seen before, one that reminded me eerily of myself...

I snapped my head up to meet Kayden's gaze. "The play?" I couldn't believe it. The one time I stumble into Charon and embarrass myself beyond normal standards and here it's the tie to a party to get to the Queen. I was starting to smell one too many coincidences keeping the air clean.

"The very same. Come on," he reached for my hand, freezing centimeters from my skin. Fire crackled between us, daring the contact. He pulled his hand away and made for the door, catching my eyes over his shoulder. "I've already told Ari to meet us in the drawing room again to discuss a plan."

"Hold on," I beat him to the door, putting myself between him and the exit. With one good shove, the door snapped shut. "We're not finished yet." It was now or never, I told myself. If I didn't stand my ground, Kayden would continue to play tennis with my heart. Too much felt up in the air, floating at a dangerously high level, ready to collapse and crush me at any given moment. "Why are you really here?"

His expression shifted, irritation blending into his facial features. Somehow, he looked even more gloriously handsome while bitter and snippy. "Did you not hear me? I came here to help."

"No, I heard you. But I don't believe you." My voice was high and sickly sweet, like poisoned honey. "The last time we saw each other, you told me to my face that you knowingly manipulated me."

"I know what I said," he interjected. "I'm here to remedy that."

"Now you show up offering to be just as helpful as you were before your underhanded actions caught up with you." I pressed past his words, staring straight through him as if he had never materialized. "How can I trust you?"

"Essallie, please." His pained expression shocked me, catching me completely off guard. The strain in his voice was thick, his lips quivering as he struggled to grasp for words. "I need to explain."

I took a step back from his twitching hands, taking note of how tense he had twisted himself in a matter of seconds. "Explain what?"

He swallowed, closing his eyes as he took a sharp inhale of breath. "There are three things I have ever known in all of my existence. One, always have the upper hand. Two, never turn your back on an enemy." His lips pressed shut, thin and hard.

The pause prompted me. "And the third?"

Kayden's shoulders didn't move, leaving me to wonder if he was still breathing. His eyes opened and instantly locked on mine, a look so smoldering I found my heart quieting in my chest.

"Three, never let your emotions control you."

He closed the gap between us instantly, hands cradling my face as his lips met mine. Fire bloomed over my skin and onto his, enveloping us in the blue blaze in seconds, yet he continued to kiss me with hungry lips. His teeth nibbled at my lower lip before his lips traced over my jaw in a frenzy, then down my neck and collarbone.

My mind stalled, heart exploding in my chest. I barely had enough control to put my hands on his chest and shove him back as far as I could, trying to save him from the flames that began to burn deep into his skin. "Kayden, *no*."

The second he stepped back, his body burst into smoke. It

hung lazily in the air, swirling around in a half-hearted tornado before his form began to take shape. As he filled in I noticed his skin had turned lighter and paler, pink scars littering his body once more. His eyes held the perfect mix of hauntingly sad and conflicted, a combination that made me want to reach out and kiss him again.

My breath came in short, choppy gasps. I could hardly force the anger into my words. "Are you insane? What the hell has come over you?"

"I don't know, Essallie," he confessed pitifully. "All I know is I've wanted to do that since the night in your bedroom when I saw your breaking in half. I wanted to fix you."

"Stop," I hissed, shaking from head to toe. Every inch of me screamed to run back into him. "I don't need you, or Ari, or any man to be whole and alive. Just because I'm the only girl around doesn't mean I have to be kissed and fawned over!"

His eyes betrayed every inch of the pain in his heart. I could see the armor he had so precariously built up cracking under my words, crumbling into dust.

"Essallie..."

"No," I turned around and fumbled for the door, yanking it open. I couldn't look over my shoulder, not with him standing there watching me, wondering if I'd cave and let my own armor crumble and fade. "Stop trying to think you can fix me. I'm not broken."

I stalked to the drawing room without him, making sure my eyes stayed strictly forward. I could feel the crumble starting in my chest, an aching feeling rippling from within.

It wasn't fair; Kayden had done exactly what I wanted, opened his blackened soul to me and let me in, and I had to be the right one and push him away. He was a demon, a lying and manipulative bastard who sought out only things that brought him gain. How could loving me, or whatever it is his emotions were telling him, play in his favor now? It felt too easy, like he was giving me exactly what I wanted. I would be cautious until I figured out his motive.

As soon as I stepped into the drawing room, my eyes spotted Ari. He seemed to have been waiting for a while, arms crossed over his chest and one foot tapping impatiently. He had traded in his earlier clothes for an all-black get up; black pants, black t-shirt, and a black track jacket with two yellow stripes running across the left side of his chest.

"Have you seen Kayden? He told me to meet him in here as soon as he got you," Ari placed his hands behind his head, stretching. Through the mid-afternoon high sun lighting the room, I could see a thin layer of sweat over his skin.

I made sure to keep my eyes off of his, unsure if I would give away what had transpired in my room with Kayden if I looked Ari in the face. Ungluing my tongue from the roof of my mouth, I searched for an excuse buried in my brain. "I, I think he-"

"-is right here," Kayden's voice finished, and I looked up to the door. Sure enough there he was, the wounded expression I had seen on him last traded in for a cold, indifferent gaze. He barely offered me so much as a nod as he strode past me, coming to a stand between Ari and I.

"I was just sharing with Essallie in the hall that we have a way to the Queen," he said smoothly, not a single hitch in his voice. Ari regarded him coolly, nodding while he continued to stretch his back and arms. "Our earlier mention of parties reminded me of one event she never misses; a party for the new play of the moment."

"That Nephilim and demon play?" Ari asked, and I wondered if he had seen the posters too. "Ironic, given her blood status. How do we get to her? I imagine she'll be crawling with her personal guard and Vens alike."

"Easy," Kayden gave a cold, humorless smile. "We drop into the castle, get into her quarters, and wait for her to return after the party. The event is held on one end of the castle, and her quarters are on the opposite end. We'll have little trouble mingling in with the rest of the crowd there."

"Correction; you'll have no trouble, but I can't imagine the only two Nephilim in existence flying under the radar," I added.

Kayden didn't look at me. "You have your trinkets to blend in, that will cut you out of the vision of most. It's the guards and higher Vens that we'll have to dodge."

"And how do you propose that?"

"A blanket of haze, a-la vile and vicious demon," Kayden said with a bitter zest, dramatically bowing for extra effect.

I wasn't convinced. "So, you want to hover over me like a cloud of smoke? How the hell is that going to help?"

"Honestly, Essallie, have you no faith in me?" He rolled his eyes.

My teeth started to grind. "Actually, no, I don't." My gaze turned to Ari, eyes narrowed. "You're okay with this? No complaints about throwing me in the lion's den? Pretty sure going to the home of the big bad villain is the number one thing they say *not* to do in the books."

"If you're against it, fine," Kayden replied sarcastically. He now stood over near the windows, one hand lightly pressed against the pane of glass. "You said you didn't want to be treated like you're the squishy, unknowing human in some girly vampire novel. Here's your chance, so let's chop up this pretty lamb and serve it raw."

I looked from Ari's wary expression to Kayden's turned back. If there had ever been a moment I wanted to punch both of them, now would be the time. Thunder struck in my chest as the hairs along my back stood straight, my skin prickling with precognition.

"You want a death wish, you got it. I have no problem taking as many down with me as I can."

Kayden looked at me from over his shoulder, confusion buried between his eyes. He turned around fully, a dark laugh escaping his lips. "No one's saying you'll die."

"No one says I'll live, either," I pointed out with a wry smile.

Kayden's mood turned black. "We're confronting her, not slaughtering her in a pool of blood."

"Says you, the manipulating demon," I continued to battle with him. The room turned hot and stifling, and the fireplace jumped to life with a gust of ash and flame. "But you forget, I have a score to settle. If that means making a mess of some body parts, I won't mind."

The rest of the week rocked in limbo, like a person floating among a raft in the Bermuda Triangle. Kayden, Ari, and I all somehow managed to completely avoid another, catching only glimpses of one or the other passing through rooms.

It had been the first time in days that I'd had a moment to myself, one that didn't involve passing out or crying from heartache. Lilix's mansion was large enough to hold over a thousand people at any given time, yet I felt enclosed and cramped. No amount of lavish decor or carefully spaced rooms could keep the feeling at bay. It was almost as if I constantly felt like a pair of eyes rested on me, watching my every move while taking subtle notes.

As the days went by, I found myself exploring rooms within the mansion. Part of me had hoped opening random doors would bring Ari out from the shadows, bringing him to talk to me, even if only to say I wasn't allowed to explore. Instead, all I found was a crushing silence greeting me with every open door. The contents of most were barren; left over furniture draped in white sheets, broken violins and cellos, empty notebooks and abandoned half paintings. One thing did catch my eye though- a broken, aged wooden desk, the kind you'd find in an abandoned schoolhouse. I wasn't exactly sure what Ari had been trying to warn me about, except maybe that Lilix was just a messy housekeeper.

After I grew bored of exploring useless rooms, I started investigating the grounds around her mansion. No one had exactly told me how much land Lilix owned, just that most of the land in sight was hers. Turned out her property line extended as far as the eye could see, claiming rolling hills and a small river just a mile from the mansion.

I decided to take a sketchbook and head out to the river, soak up a little sun while finding a place to ground my head and heart. Making sure to sit a little ways off the bank, I found a cozy spot among some grass and flowers and took a seat.

The sight was beautiful; flowers identical to the ones in the floral shop Serena and I had been in were in full bloom. Mixing hues of tangerine and smoky violet brought to life the patch of grass along the river. While the sun, sitting high and bright, would have normally scorched me, a gentle breeze made the outdoors inviting and pleasant.

I flipped open my sketchbook and began to draw, starting with small, smooth lines across the page. Instantly I began to feel calm and relaxed, stress melting off my shoulders and leaving me with a weightless sensation. No pressure, no call to action, just a beautiful setting with open room.

As I continued to draw, I felt my mind slipping into a familiar limbo. Images, both good and bad, phased in and out of my head as segmented sentences paired with each photo. I thought of Ari, and how mixed up I felt with him and his awkward actions, yet couldn't deny the magnetic pull I felt for him. He clicked with me perfectly, understood exactly the kind of misery I did, two birds of a feather.

Then there was Kayden. A brooding, mysterious, borderline psychotic bastard who thought it was okay to play with my emotions. One minute he was colder than the Arctic, the next he would be reaching for me, an aching look in his eyes begging for me to step into his arms.

Both of them were ridiculous, that much was for sure. I didn't see the need to get wrapped up in another person when I could barely manage myself and my own pile of problems. Having someone else in my life, no matter how perfect or imperfect they were, wouldn't solve my own issues. It wouldn't save me from dying.

I pulled myself out of my head with a rough shake, a huge sigh escaping my lips. My eyes stared down at the sketchbook in my lap, another photo of an eye staring back at me. I must have drawn it in the midst of my half-hearted musings over the two boys.

Voices sounded off in the distance, whoops and yells and laughter filling the serene setting with noise. I stared off toward the house, spotting two familiar faces dressed in all black racing through the field, tackling each other on and off. My stomach immediately clenched, the thought of a Vens coming to mind. I dropped my sketchbook with a thud and rose to my feet, calling out fire to my hands and arms.

The figures came with alarming speed. One lanced into the air, sharper than a diamond-tipped arrow, heading straight for me. The other ran in a hazy blur, shifting from left to right in less than a blink of an eye.

"Lilix, don't land on her!" Ari's voice came from the running blur. My mind froze; Ari?

The second I put two and two together, he came into clarity. Ari was running, sprinting faster than anything I had ever seen. His short, platinum blonde hair laid flat against his head as he ran, allowing his startling blue eyes full exposure. His run reminded me of a cheetah dashing across the hot plains, locking on its prey with the intent to catch it at all costs.

Lilix on the other hand was graceful, a swan among buffalo. From her springing leap into the air, to the arching of her body, to her cleanly tucked landing, she was never without poise. Her hair had been pulled back into a loose ponytail, stray pieces pressed to her skin as she worked against the breeze. Her eyes were equally captivating like Ari's, only in a different way, for I knew these were from witchcraft, not a genetic gift.

They both landed in front of me, inches apart from another, laughing from the exhilaration of the sprint. Lilix placed a hand on Ari's shoulder and smiled warmly, pearly whites taking place on yet another piece of her that was perfect. A bubble of annoyance built in my chest, the beginning of something rude forming on my tongue.

Lilix beat me to speak. "Enjoying the fresh air?"

My rude retort slithered back into my throat as I fought not to laugh. Lilix may have looked gorgeous and had a perfect setting in her home, but it seemed she forgot to cast a spell on saving herself from speaking like a ditz.

I forced a smile onto my tightly stretched lips. "Oh, yeah, loving it. Nothing like a little pollen inhalation to brighten the day!"

Ari stifled back a laugh, his face twitching with exertion.

Lilix grinned, fighting to giggle herself. "Ari and I were just about to start some battle practices. You know, fighting techniques and that kind of thing. Care to join us?"

"Uhhh, sure?" I shrugged my shoulders, figuring there wouldn't be much harm in playing a little sparing with the two of them.

"It would be useful," Ari said, his eyes sparkling from the

sunlight. "In case the Queen tries to pull a fast move, or if someone makes a move on you at the party. Though you already seem to have a good dose of defense down from what I saw against that Vens."

Ari was right; I wasn't exactly clumsy when it came to fighting. I had the proof in the two Vens I had managed to kill with little help. Although most of the time when push came to shove, my body did more than I realized, like some instinct buried within the memories of my skin and bones. Still, it wouldn't hurt to know what to do when my instincts didn't kick in.

Lilix took me by the hand, pulling me away from the river's edge and further into the field of flowers. She left me in a patch of blue tulips, putting ample distance between us as she stepped further in-field.

Finally, she was satisfied. Her voice carried on the wind as she called out. "Call out your fire."

I did as she told. Pressure built in my chest and flowed through my veins, spreading through my arms and building into the tips of my fingers. With only a spark for warning, blue fire blossomed over my fingers and hands, rushing to engulf my shoulders and chest until it licked my upper half like a mid-cropped turtleneck.

"Good," I heard her appraise me. "Now attack me."

I faltered instantly. I didn't like the idea of attacking someone without provocation. "Lilix, I-"

"Too late," her voice echoed like a whisper of a ghost. I blinked, and she was gone. A faint whistle sound touched my ears just before she collided on top of me.

We collided in a heap, Lilix instantly pinning me to the ground. Fire lashed at the flowers and grass, incinerating it with puffs of black and white smoke. I gasped, struggling to free myself from her iron-clad hold with kicks and thrashes of my arms. Nothing worked.

Something snapped in the back of my mind, and instinct took hold of me with force. Like storm waves crashing onto a beach, I blazed fire off my chest in a gust of heat, throwing Lilix back high into the air.

She spun in mid-air, catching herself and landing perfectly on her feet, just like a cat. I could spot several small cuts and burns from my fire, part of her long bangs burned to a black crisp.

I shot out my hand, a burning strip of fire flinging like a whip. It lassoed around one of Lilix's wrists, spiraling up her arm and shocking her with waves of pulsating fire. Three pulses into it, she dropped onto her knees, eyes rolled heavenward, and collapsed.

Watching her pass out instantly snapped me from my instinctual rage. I extinguished my fire with a single pause, running over to her small, crunched in frame.

"Lilix? Holy crap, Lilix can you hear me?" I repeated frantically, turning her over onto her back.

Her eyes fluttered open, a taunting smile playing on her lips. "Nicely done, but you forgot one thing."

I blinked, confused, until a pair of warm hands wrapped around my neck without warning.

Ari's voice whispered in my ear, teasing me the same way Lilix had just done. "You turned your back on the enemy."

"Dammit, you two are no fun," I scowled, turning around with a fist full of flames to smack Ari in the face with. He let me go and leapt back, laughing as he dodged me a couple of times. My heart felt light and free, like a bird released from its cage. I had forgotten what it felt like to truly smile and live in the moment.

Tackling Ari onto the ground, Lilix cheered me on. I had brought my hand inches from Ari's face when he called everything to a grinding halt.

"Essallie, what is that?"

My eyes traveled from his face, worry etched deep in his eyes, to my hand. At first I didn't see it, but then I stared closer. My fire, blue and beautiful, was now turning black at the tips.

Pushing off Ari, I got up to my feet, using my free hand for support. All the while, I couldn't take my eyes off the shift in color of the fire, it's change distracting.

"Huh," I said to no one in particular. I twisted my hand from one side to the other, marveled by the stained flames. "And here I thought I was beyond surprises."

"What kind of surprise?" Kayden's voice came from the side. I turned to see him standing alongside Ari, having materialized from smoke.

Holding out my hand, I gestured to the black fire with shrug of the shoulders. "It's kind of cool, actually. Though I was expecting white after seeing Ari's fire." Fire snaked up my arm like a protective barrier from the world. "When did your fire start to do this, Ari?"

Ari stared at me, frozen in shock. With difficulty, he turned to meet Kayden's equally dismayed stare. They both turned back to me, staring for what felt like an eternity with the same soul-crushing, sorrowful stare. Both of their eyes gave me the impression that they were burying an emotion deep, down under the surface. My skin began to prickle, a cold ache settling in my bones that had nothing to do with the large cloud passing over the sun. And that's when it hit me.

They didn't have to say anything, because Ari's fire never turned black.

Ari had never been dying.

I was.

ELEVEN
DEFYING GRAVITY

"You need to eat something, Essallie."

"I'm not hungry."

"You have to eat before the party. Last thing we need is you playing the Fainting Damsel in the Queen's quarters."

The day had finally come, a week having passed in a whirlwind of death markers and uncomfortable bits of silence. In a matter of hours, I would be playing myself into the Queen's castle. The thought alone brought a whole new wave of nausea to it.

The last two days of the week had been hellish, and that was putting it lightly. After the display of my impending death in the grassy fields, I'd locked myself in Lilix's room without contact from everyone. At first I thought I'd only need a minute to put a brave face back on. The two days of sleeplessness and uncontrollable shaking soon proved otherwise. I had known I was dying for weeks now, but never actually saw proof of it happening before me. Seeing the black fire had been like waking up in hell itself, surrounded by searing lava and creatures of death, unable to free myself for all of eternity.

It had taken Kayden and Ari both to coax me out of the bedroom for the party crashing scheme. Now, sitting at the island countertop in the kitchen, I was wishing I hadn't.

"I always had a nagging suspicion you were a closet anorexic," Kayden said, trying his hand at livening the mood. "You not eating that sandwich is only solidifying my thoughts that you're going to need a cheeseburger and ice cream binge night soon."

Glaring silently at Kayden, I kept my mouth shut, looking back to the plate in front of me and grimacing. He had done his best to make a sandwich fit for human consumption; ham, tomato, spinach and mustard on two slices of white toast. On a normal day, I would have happily swallowed it whole. Today, not so much.

"I can't eat this," I said with a sigh. "I just don't have the stomach for it."

He leaned in across the countertop, serious. "Think of that sandwich like the Queen. Defeating that sandwich will only make it tastier."

My lip twitched. "That made no sense."

"But it did get you to grin."

"Don't know what you're talking about."

"I bet a joke on bakeries and muffins will fix that."

A half-choked laugh caught in my throat. I grabbed the sandwich off the plate and shoved a bite in my mouth, savoring the first bit of food in days. "I'm so nervous about tonight."

Kayden met my eyes for a moment across the counter, his hands digging into another freshly sliced fish. "Panties in a bunch over the Queen boiling for your blood? Don't be."

"Why not?" I asked.

"She won't do anything," he snickered, shaking his head. "She's the type who likes to play up on the drama. Draw it out, you know, like all vengeful high school-brained girls do."

This time, I let out the laugh that had built in my chest. Ari came into the room just as I finished my fit of laughter, his face carefully neutral as he swept his gaze from over the two of us.

He took the seat two over from me, pulling at the collar of his white button-up. He had already gotten dressed for the party, a full tuxedo that made him twice as handsome and dashing.

Taking a fork, he stabbed at a piece of salmon in the frying pan and pulled it out to eat. Kayden shot him a mixed glare of anger and surprise. "Let's run over this one last time."

I ran down everything I knew. "All three of us are heading to the Queen's castle, you and I, and Kayden separately. We're going to try and keep our noses clear, then wait for a moment to dodge out to her private end of the castle and wait for her. I confront, figure out why she's out for me..."

"And then you kill her," Kayden said simply.

Ari and I both stared at him. I envisioned fighting her and her shadows, their icy touch sucking the life of my fire right out from me. "Just one, teeny tiny, small problem; even if I could get close enough to her, I can't kill her."

"Why not?"

"Her shadows," I replied in a low, nervous tone. "They can strip me of my fire at her command. If we go in there, and she wants to fight or hold me, I won't make it out."

Ari looked livid, eyes burning with a bold and emblazoned fire. He sat straighter in his chair as he spoke, "You will make it back here, I promise you. We will come out together. As for the blending in part, we know the earrings and necklace won't shield you from her, so Lilix gave me something for you last night." He procured a small, thin green vial from thin air, reaching out to give it to me.

I took the vial gingerly, an uneasy feeling rolling in my

stomach. "What is it?"

"A camouflage potion, so to speak. Lilix graciously donated some of her hair at the chance for you to play her."

I shook my head and shoved the vial back at him, adamant. "No, nuh-uh, not happening. I am not getting involved with all these magic potions and junk."

"Look, do you want to get in there and know why she's after you or not?"

"Well, yeah-"

"Then go get dressed in one of the gowns in her room, and meet us in the drawing room."

I stomped off to my room in a huff, muttering something about knocking both of their skulls into their heads if they ever tried anything like this again.

Inside my room, I went through Lilix's closet, not for the first time since I'd gotten here. The girl had everything from mortal high-end labels like Louis Vuitton and Chanel, to other brands in various languages I didn't even try to pretend and comprehend. Each cabinet and separate closet had a unique set of colored bags sheathed over the clothes stored inside, and I ended up going through four closets of red, yellow, purple, and green sheathed clothes before finally finding all the gowns in a closet with blue colored bags.

Each dress was an elegant masterpiece, decorated with the true craft of a professional, one-of-a-kind designer. The more bags I unzipped, the greater the detail on the dress; elegant, hand-stitched swirls embedded with real gems, trains of taffeta and satin cut expertly to frame a unique figure. All of this, for Lilix. The younger, former fashionista within me squealed in delight, knowing all too well that if you owned a dress specifically made for you, you had all you needed in life. Or so I had originally thought.

On the fifth dress unveiling, I heard a polite knock on door leading into the room. I let out an infuriated, irritated sigh.

"Ari, Kayden, if either one of you comes in here I swear, I'll remove your organs and make pretzels out of them."

"And if I'm neither of the offenders at hand?" A soft, higher voice came from the bedroom.

I craned my neck out of the blue-bagged closet, spotting a blonde ponytail, followed by an even more familiar pair of glowing blue eyes. Lilix had been hovering in the doorway, dressed in a buttery sundress, blue flowers patterned on the fabric. For a brief moment she reminded me of a southern blonde of a famous vampire TV show, if only her skin had been tanned and a gap between her two front teeth.

Lilix smiled, showing off her perfectly aligned and evened pearly whites. She joined me in the vast and roomy space of her personal closet, eyes settling on the cabinet of blue slipped bags. "I heard you were hunting for an outfit for tonight?"

"Something like that." Gesturing to her vast collection I was in the process of destroying, I continued. "I've found everything but the brown potato sack in here."

She rolled her eyes, the corners of her mouth twitching to fight back a smile. I automatically thought of Kayden and his brooding, rapidly altering moods. "I see you've been hanging around Kayden a lot, silly half-blood. Essie, right? That's what he calls you."

"Essallie, he calls me Essie for short."

She gave a small, thoughtful nod. "Your mother didn't happen to be high when she gave birth to you, did she?"

My face flushed. "No? Why?"

"Creative names like that typically warrant use of things like LSD. Not that your mother used anything of the sort," she hurriedly added at the sight of my face and clenched fists on the bed. If I didn't think she could fix a broken nose with a spell, I would have punched her. She sighed. "I keep going off topic. I came over to help you get ready, and here I am insulting you. I'm sorry."

I shrugged; I didn't really care about the rude remark. It was the fact that hearing about my Mom could still bring out something in me that hurt. The fact that my birth was one giant intentional breeding fest on my father's part. But some things just weren't meant to be shared, especially with the relatively unknown.

"Actually, I think I could use the help. Any idea what would blend in well with tonight's party?"

Walking over to the cabinet, she seemed to think about it, running her fingers over each bag and letting them rest for a moment before moving along. Then she grabbed one of the bags in the back, pulling it completely free from the closet and zipping it out from the bag.

It was gorgeous; a white corset detailed with golden thread, gold lacing in the back, the cut perfect for a woman's frame. It looked like a cross between a princess gown and delicate wedding dress, yet held something dark and forbidding. I envisioned myself wearing the dress, pairing it with a white, jeweled mask made for an evening of old socialite gossip and secret kisses on the wrist.

Judging by Lilix's smile, she must have approved of my gaping shock. Unlacing the back half of it with one hand, she beckoned me closer. "Come here, let's get you in this."

It took a little wiggling, but I managed to slide into the dress without a bodice and minimum gut-sucking. On my regular frame, the dress sat awkwardly, too loose in the chest and hips. Apparently, I was no Marilyn Monroe with a figure eight to boast about.

Lilix took to lacing up the back of the dress, tying to pre-fit it where it would sit perfectly after my change. She had me sit in front of a mirror, grabbing a spare vanity chair from her bedroom. A chilling, nagging sensation itched at my neck, hairs standing up on their ends. I felt like I had done this before, the ghost of the memory creeping over me.

"Ah, there it is," I heard from the other room. Lilix walked back in, holding a strand of pearls in her hands. She wrapped the strand gently around my neck and fastened it together, looking at me through the mirror with satisfaction. "Perfect. You look heavenly."

I watched her through the mirror, a hand reaching up to touch the pearls around my neck. "This is all so beautiful. Thank you."

She laughed. "Don't thank me, thank whoever I had commission this two hundred years ago." A dreamy look melted into her eyes, memories playing like a sweet lullaby in her head. "I'm pretty sure it was for a ball of some sort. No doubt I was chasing after a prince in some vain attempt to feel normal with the royals of England."

I was astonished, eyebrows raising high on my forehead. "How old are you, Lilix?"

Her eyebrows rose high on her head. "My, don't you know to never ask a lady her true age?" She placed a hand on her cheek, staring thoughtfully up at the ceiling. "Honestly, I've lost track. It's been some time since anyone's actually asked me how long I've been around."

"But you were here long before you met Kayden?"

"Oh yes, without a doubt," she nodded in affirmation. "I can remember up to the 1300's with perfectly clarity. Anything past that is a little hazy."

Unbelievable. I was standing in front of someone with over 700 years under their belt, and still she looked like she could have passed for my younger sister. "I thought witches were just humans practicing the craft."

That got her to laugh loud, her hands hugging her body as she let it out. Her head shook. "No, but that's what movies and books lead you to believe. There are actual witches, ones with the bloodline built deep within them, and there are mortal who play with silly little spells and incantations you can find on the internet. A real witch never ages, never dies, and carries the mark of her kind. But I'm not a witch." She pointed to her glowing eyes, showing the cats eye shape of her pupil. "See these? They are the mark of my people, a race far different from anything Earth has to offer. Though I have been accused of being a witch many times. Apparently if you're good with potions and have a gift for surviving the impossible, you're a witch. Who knew?"

I stared at her, bewildered. "Then, if you're not a witch, what are you?"

She seemed to pause for a moment, eyes drifting with the look of lost time. When she stared back at me, the weight of thousands of years pressed against my subconscious. "The human language doesn't have a word for our kind, but the closest is guardian."

"You said Earth as if," I hesitated, tethered to the last bit of my thought. Lilix's gaze had swallowed me whole, sucking me into a soul-searching gaze. "As if you're not from here."

"You're right, I'm not." She said without shaking her head. "Our kind came here long before mortals were putting blood on stone, back when the mystics of this world were the majority. Few living today know we exist. We are a dying race, not by choice, but by destiny. It is a true, tragic fate."

I felt ashamed, my cheeks burning with indignation. The first few times I had met Lilix, I could have sworn she was completely dumb, giving blondes everywhere a bad reputation. The more she spoke, the worse I felt on my horrid assumption. She had been prime witness to empires rising and falling, kings and queens making all the wrong choices, and in the end she would die, just like me. Yet there could be no comparison. Standing next to Lilix, I suddenly looked like a whiny child, a far cry from the teenager shelved with a great opportunity to take out a violent evil.

"I'm sorry," I whispered eventually, feeling the all-too familiar ache settle in my chest. "I can only imagine all the things you've had to see. The pain you've had to endure."

"Not all of it was bad, you know." Her eyes began to lighten, releasing me from her soulful stare. The smile to me through the mirror showed she meant it. "I've met several Nephilim in their time, and tons of demons like Kayden. I've fallen in love, had friendships stronger than diamonds, seen things that the world will never bear witness to ever again. I refuse to regret a single moment of my life."

The moment she said Kayden, my heart gave a weak beat against my skin. Hesitantly, playing with part of my skirt, I asked. "Kayden, has he always been like he is now?"

"Like what?" Her eyes went cloudy with confusion, her fingers running through the end of ponytail out of habit. "You mean snarky and moody?"

I nodded.

"Not always. He used to be much, much worse," her tone lowered, and I strained to hear it. "You never would have wanted to be around him after he lost his love to the Queen."

My eyes widened, a cold running over my body that had nothing to do with bare arms and exposed shoulders. "He loved the Queen?"

"No. The Queen killed his love." Lilix looked uncomfortable talking about it, shifting her weight from one foot to the other. "She had been a mortal, and the Queen had just taken the throne. She explicitly forbade all relationships with mortals, unless it was out of need, like a vampire for blood. Kayden ignored her, and the Queen found out."

"What happened?"

"The Queen had a vampire turn her, and she ran into the sunlight, set herself on fire, and died."

I stopped breathing.

"Kayden loathed the Queen, wanted her dead. But with

Lucretia being part demon, part Nephilim, he was useless against her. That's when he went underground, and found me."

The ache in my chest spread, and I took a small, shuddering breath to ease the pain. It had only been a couple of weeks since my grandparents were murdered by one of the Queen's personal Vens, and I could hardly stand it. To exist for centuries, carrying that kind of burden, had to be maddening. "How could he live like that, knowing the person who killed his only love got away with it every day?"

"I'm not sure, honestly." She let out a sad sigh, meeting my eyes in the mirror. Something in them was haunting and hollow, and I wondered if Kayden was the only one who had felt the power of the Queen's wrath. "Death would probably feel better than whatever he feels thinking about her."

I opened my mouth to speak when she placed both hands on my shoulders, shaking her head. "We could go on about this all night, but you have to go."

We started to walk out the room together, when she stopped in her tracks. "Hold on." Making a quick turn back into the room, I waited for her in the hall as she emerged with a familiar, small purple vial.

"I've seen that before," I said. "At the apothecary."

Lilix gave the bottle a slight twist with her fingers, grinning. "One of my personal best." Placing it into a spare hidden pocket within the folds of the dress, she nodded with satisfaction. "There, now you're all set."

"What is it?"

"Insurance." She winked. "You'll know when to use it. Now let's go! Any longer in there and they'll start thinking we're making lesbian moves on each other, or whatever it is boys dream of in their spare time."

Somehow, I had a feeling she wasn't far off.

We walked out of her room together, making for the

drawing room where Ari and Kayden were waiting. As soon as I stepped into the room, I watched both of them stare at me in wild fascination. I did my best not to roll my eyes; boys and their slack-jawed idiocy.

Ari and Kayden had both traded in their typical mash-up of black t-shirts and pants for full tuxedos, bow ties and all. Ari had a small white rose bud pinned to his jacket; Kayden sported a red rose with black tipped petals.

"We wondered if you got lost in that closet," Kayden snickered, a corner of his lips twitching in delight. "I was just about to batten down the hatches and go in after you. But only once Ari secured a video camera."

Lilix and I looked at each other. Yep. Spot on.

"Nice to see you too," I replied humorlessly, face neutral.

Ari held out the tiny, green vial to me once more. "Ready for this?"

"As ready as I'll ever be," I muttered, uncorking the small glass tube in my hands. With one gulp, I downed its contents, the liquid thick and slimy.

I handed the vial back to Ari, and held my breath. My stomach let out a low, nauseating rumble, shaking my entire body. I could feel myself altering, my bones reshaping under the effects of the potion. Holding out my hands in front of my face, they began to shrink, turning small and soft with faint white scars etched in the palms. As the shaking stopped, I turned to look at Lilix. She smiled wickedly, picking up a round mirror from the mantle and holding it up for me to see. Sure enough, an exact carbon copy of Lilix stared back at me; gone were the under-eye circles, dark brown eyes, and short blonde hair. Now my hair was long, soft and beautiful, my eyes a glowing blue, and not a trace of tiredness touched my face.

All three of them were grinning at me. Even I couldn't help the grin spreading on my lips. "This is pretty awesome.

And hey, the dress sure fits better. I actually have boobs now!"

Kayden was the first to laugh, startling all of us. "So much for not being vain. Come on, let's go. I'm sure the carriages are waiting outside."

I nodded, taking the mirror from Lilix and placing it back on the mantle. Without warning, everything around me turned blurry and tilted sideways. I latched onto the edge of the mantle and stared straight ahead, concentrating on the in and out rhythm of my chest as I struggled to breathe.

Ari's voice sounded in my ear instantly. "You okay?"

For a second I thought I wouldn't be able to answer. Then the room suddenly snapped back into sharp clarity, all traces off dizziness vanished. I felt oddly light, like I was floating.

"Yeah, I feel fine."

And my eyes rolled into the back of my head and I blacked out.

TWELVE
SMOKE AND MIRRORS

Sound was the first thing that came back. It came to me in waves, slowly growing from a faint whisper to a full breath.

Ari spoke first, panic clear as wedding bells. "How long has she been out?"

"Five minutes." Kayden seemed far less worried.

"We can't do this, look at her! She can't handle it."

"Not exactly sure what I'm supposed to be looking for, seeing as she looks like Lilix right now. Unless you mean under her skirt?"

Lilix growled. "Kayden, keep your perverted hands off of her before I relocate you to the bottom of the Atlantic."

Ari's voice continued to strain with worry. "Lilix, don't you have something to... you know..."

"Stave off death? There is no such thing, dear. Death is inevitable. Death waits for no one."

Through the thickness of the dark, I forced my lips to move. "I can hear you."

There was a small stretch of silence before both voices clamored in my ears.

"Essallie, this is too much-"

"We need to call this off-"

"*No,*" I said as firmly as I could, forcing my eyes open against the weight of the dark. I was on the floor, Kayden and Ari on either side of me on their knees, hovering freakishly close over my face.

"What do you mean no?" Ari was the first to ask.

Pushing up onto my elbows, I bit back a gasp of pain. I must have fallen backwards when I passed out. "Help me the hell up, we're going to be late," I hissed, eyeballing both of them. Turning to Lilix, I gave her a plead. "Can you have the carriage brought to the front? It'll be easier to get in that way."

She gave me a sharp and steady nod before leaving. "You can do this. Don't listen to these two worry warts."

"Didn't plan on it."

Kayden helped me up without complaint, his face kept decidedly neutral. Ari continued to be stringent, watching me with disbelief.

"Essallie, just look at you! You can barely stand. Who the hell knows what'll happen when we get there," he protested angrily, putting his arm out to block my passage out of the room.

"Ari, it was one tiny little blackout. Big deal. I haven't slept in nearly two days, that's probably what's wrong," I said, ignoring the shaking, unsettling rattling in my bones. Quitting now would be a mistake, one I wasn't about to make. This wasn't just about me and what I wanted now. This was about Kayden, Ari, Lilix, and Serena. This was about everyone the Queen had held onto and squeezed until nothing was left to draw from. Plus, I was itching for a little bloodshed.

Doing his best without taking me up into his arms, Kayden helped me to the carriage waiting outside for us. His face told me he didn't care that he burned as he helped, just that I stayed conscious and alive. Ari, on the other hand, was furious, following behind us with every intent of sounding like the muttering, whining, pain in the neck he was becoming.

As soon as I was in the carriage, I let my body collapse in a heap of fabric and flesh, deflating like a hot air balloon. Kayden hung on the edge of the door, waiting until Ari was in before he spoke. "Ari will stay by your side the entire time. Remember, you're Lilix tonight, not Essallie."

I sat up a little straighter, pressing my back into the chilled, deep green fabric lining the private and intimate compartment. "Where will you be?"

"Around," he said simply, winking for added effect. "Try not to miss me too much."

"I wouldn't dream of it." Rolling my eyes, I reached over and pulled the door shut, and with a jolt, the carriage took off.

Ari and I rode in silence, the only sound between us breathing. He refused to meet my eyes, staring straight ahead with a cold, hardened silence reminding me of the angel statues in the cemeteries.

I was the first to break the silence. "Ari..."

"Don't," he cut me off, a hand raised in silence. "Please, don't."

"What is your problem?"

"My problem? You're pushing yourself to death, Essallie. Don't you see how fast you're moving the clock, winding it to your undoing?"

"Excuse me, but you're the one who told me not to stop," I said with a snap, anger building to a blush in my cheeks. "You're the one who told me a cancer patient doesn't quit. I may not have tumors, but the end result is still death, and I'm still not quitting."

"I didn't ask you to engage in a violent, burning death

wish."

"What I am doing is not a fiery death wish, it's a bloodbath."

"Your attitude is terrible."

"Oh? Pardon me, I thought I was all sparkles and sprinkles."

"Dammit, Essallie," Ari looked pained, his fingers pressing into the side of his temple. "Death or not, didn't you ever think some of us aren't ready to watch you die?"

My confidence faltered. "What- what do you mean?"

"I'm saying you're going about this the wrong way." His words hung in the air like a haze of smoke around a volcano. "I'm saying... two Nephilim are better than one."

"Ari, I'm going to die." I reached over, placing a comforting hand over his. "We're all going to die. Maybe not today, maybe not tomorrow, but eventually we all will pass."

"And you're... you're okay with that?"

I gave him a small, gentle nod of the head. "I think part of the reason I was so twisted after Leo's death was because I couldn't accept someone not being there ever again. Maybe part of it had to do with me being scared of my *own* death." A nervous bubble of laugh escaped my lips, yet somehow it felt comforting. "But I've accepted it now. If I'm meant to die to save even just one person, then so be it."

Ari opened his mouth to speak, but couldn't think of a word to say. With resignation he closed his mouth, reducing himself to biting his lower lip. Dark swirls of pain, fear, and something else stirred in his eyes, and in that moment I knew exactly what he was trying to say without actually saying it.

He didn't want me to die, because he had fallen in love with me.

Realization sank into my chest like a knife, knocking the breath clear from my lungs. Something colder than ice froze my veins, and I dared to sneak a glance at Ari.

His eyes were focused on the outside, one hand parting the curtain keeping out the glowing lights from streetlamps lining the way. Even though he appeared calm, waves of something stronger rolled off of him, leaving a bitter, upsetting taste to linger in the air.

I looked back down to my hands on my lap, bewildered. How could I have missed it? One minute, Ari was someone virtually unknown to me, someone with a drive and goal I could barely understand except that he needed to be with me, the only other Nephilim on the planet. Now it felt deeper, like he ached to be near me emotionally, an attachment formed. I had to clear the air, had to tell Ari that now just wasn't the time to be thinking of where my heart could lie.

The carriage came to a sudden, jolting halt, rattling both of us from our seats. Ari gave me one quick, small glance, a smile on his lips that didn't touch his eyes. "We're here. Remember, you're under disguise. We're here as a pair of great, close friends."

As he said the last part, I couldn't help but feel another stab of pain as I watched the sadness soak into his stare. Close or not, friends was the last thing he wanted to be.

The carriage door opened with a strong swing, a gloved hand held out for me to take. I took it and stepped out, taking a moment to revel in the beauty of the fortress I had just stepped into.

A castle crafted entirely out of pure, unblemished white marble spread out before me. The east half of the castle shined with a bright light inside, small windows opened to let air ventilate the stifling party rooms. Turrets twisted high and intimidating, their tops covered in tan shingles, reminding me of upside down ice cream cones. But that was the only sweet thing about this place.

I quickly took notice that the party was taking part on not just one, but two floors. The first level was all indoors, thin veiled curtains billowing out toward the night, sounds of excitement in the form of laughter and cheering brewing inside. The second level was outside in the form of a large, fully exposed balcony, soft sounds of a string orchestra playing for the couples dancing along the stretch.

Ari came around the carriage, extending his arm with a stage smile in place. "Shall we, Lilix?"

I gave him a faint, innocent nod, linking arms with his. "Let's make the most of this beautiful night."

His eyes flashed, the corners of his mouth playing with a teasing smile. "To make the most of it, we'd have to go somewhere private."

My jaw locked, and I bit back the urge to say something nasty. Although, I did make a mental note to repay him for his remark later with a good kick to the shin.

Ari led us inside, taking the lead, as I had no idea where the heck to go. From the large marbled steps leading into the grand foyer, a long plush and rich red carpet lined the way. Three chandeliers larger than school buses hung above, crystals dripping in decoration while thick tapers created a romantic illumination. All around me, men and women walked around with a sense of stuck up aristocracy, men sporting cigars and brandy in tiny glasses while women dressed in every jewel they owned. I couldn't help but feel we had stepped backwards in time, where old style riches in flashy displays like parties and personally handcrafted drapes were all the rage. That, and that I was underdressed.

"All of this," I spoke in a low tone to Ari, keeping my eyes on surveying the room for any familiar faces. "For a play?"

"Of course." Ari replied simply, as if it was a common thing to throw multi-million dollar parties for plays. "You don't understand, this is the Queen's favorite play."

"Why?"

"Because no one wins in the end."

We moved through the crowds, passing every creature you could imagine; vampires, dressed to the nines in gold and black, fangs carefully exposed; faeries, bright bulbs of blues and pinks reminding me of jellyfish in open ocean waters; werewolves, all carefully avoiding the silver cutlery and serving plates; and demons, each dressed with a different hint of their most favored time in history.

Time passed, varying degrees of jubilant and dulcet music playing from all angles. Ari steered me to several people, whispering quickly who they were and a general synopsis about them so I had something to grasp onto for conversation. For the most part, I held my tongue, letting Lilix's pretty face do most of the talking.

"We must be going now," Ari said suddenly, knocking me from my stare at the man's three-wide purple chin in front of me. "I promised Lilix we'd take a small spin around the balcony before leaving for the night."

The man, a warlock of some kind I was told, gave a small bow. "I'm sure we'll talk soon about the mechanics of proper potion ingredient arraignment. You always do find yourself in the apothecary."

"Indeed she does," chimed in another voice behind me. Ari's shoulders visibly stiffened as I looked over my shoulder to see who it was that spoke.

It was Bernard, the owner of the apothecary, his wife Lorena in tow. Both were as overdressed as the rest of those present, Lorena in a low cut, navy blue velvet gown that flared out past the hips, large diamonds hanging from her neck. Bernard, like all the other men inside the first floor of the party, held a cigar in one hand and glass of alcohol in another, his grey tuxedo fitted and sharp.

"Ah, Lilix, I thought you weren't the type to dally in these sorts of social events?" Bernard took a drag of his cigar, blowing smoke straight at my face.

I did my best not to cough, but couldn't stop my eyes from watering at the musty cloud. "Not typically, no. Ari convinced me it would be best to get some air for the day."

Bernard's face darkened, eyes refusing to look at Ari. "Mixing bad blood among the crowd, I see."

"You know I have no problem with them, Bernard." A familiar pit of fire sired in my gut. While I would have been okay insulting the oaf and jabbing him in the eyeballs, I knew Lilix took the high road. "It's best we agree to disagree on this one."

"Yes, well, I guess we will continue to reach an impasse on this discussion." He took a sip of his drink, followed by another puff of his cigar. Almost instantly his mood lightened. "I do apologize you didn't get to see Jessica tonight. I know you both had been working hard at finding something to cure her... aliment."

Jessica? My blood went cold. Could he had meant Jessica, the girl who had a seizure before vanishing from Belfast the night Kayden arrived? I mentally shook off the idea, inwardly laughing at myself. There were tons of girls named Jessica in the world. Chances of this Jessica being of one and the same were slim to none.

I played along with the conversation. "Yes, it is sad. How is she doing?"

"Well, given the circumstances. We plan to bring her home as soon as the female Nephilim is caught by the Queen."

If I had been cold before, it was nothing compared to how I felt now. A family, torn apart because of my existence? What did this Jessica have to do with me? "Why not bring her home now?"

"You know why." Irritability etched into his face.

"Surely there must be another way," I tried, frowning.

Lorena cut in, her mood having darkened worse than her

husband's over our conversation. "You know there is not. As long as Essallie lives, Jessica will continue to have prophesies of the Queen's fall by her hand. Until Essallie is in the Queen's grasp, Jessica's life in danger."

A snippet of memory called in my mind. Abigail hadn't denied Jessica was a part of the tangled web surrounding me, but she hadn't said just what role she played. Was this it? A prophet, marking me as the Queen's slayer? I had more questions than answers, and they were all the same piece of the puzzle, unwilling to fit with each other.

"Yes, well, as I had said to the gentleman beforehand, I promised Lilix a spin on the balcony. Excuse us, please," Ari took me by the arm, pulling me away faster than I could say goodbye. Within a minute he had us on the balcony, breezing past people in a blur of dresses and lights spread across the expanse.

A soft, gentle song began, and Ari began to move us to the soothing sounds of violins playing in harmony.

"Ah, wait a second," he stopped us, pulling out a dead flower from his pocket. Within seconds, the bud bloomed back into full, vibrant life, pink petals richer than any I had ever seen in the wild. Tucking it into my hair just over my ear, he gave me a soft, crooked smile. "Much better."

"Will I ever be able to do that?" I asked curiously as we danced, my skirt swaying with the movement. "You know, bring things to life."

"You could," Ari gave a light, fluid movement of his shoulders. "I don't know exactly what you're capable of. History tells us that all Nephilim have a different gift. Some can create life, like me, and others can do things like manipulate elements, or procure the truth without violence. Things like that."

"Do you think I'll find my gift before I die?"

His footing slowed, jostling me into him. He quickly

resumed pace. "I'm sure you will."

"Let's try a new topic, like how exactly you're attached to that demon, Kayden."

Now it was my turn to slip on the footing. I accidentally stepped on Ari's foot. "Sorry- what about Kayden?"

"How are you connected to him?"

"It's a long story."

"I've got time."

"It's not something I really like to talk about, okay?" I snapped, instantly regretting it. My head shook and I sighed. "He was summoned to kill me by my ex-boyfriend."

Ari paused, watching me intently as the seconds ticked by. "Summoned to kill? As in-"

"As in I was the intended sacrifice." Saying it out loud made it feel like I was reliving it for a second time, watching the blue fire dance off my skin for the first time. "When I didn't die, Kayden's charge wasn't fulfilled. The end result, he's still here."

"Waiting for you to die."

No sound came out, but my lips still formed the word. "Yes."

"And he hasn't tried killing you yet?" Ari asked, spinning us for a moment before carefully dipping me low. With a quick, smooth move he pulled me up and against his chest. When I refused to meet his eyes, he pressed further with the questions. "Or he has, and you're still keeping him close for some stupid reason."

My heart leapt into my throat, pounding faster than if I had been sprinting from an enemy. I thought of Kayden's lips, warm and inviting, the heat he created in my body that had nothing to do with the fire in my veins. "It's complicated."

"The hell it is, Essallie. You have a demon following you who can turn on you at any moment."

"And he hasn't," I lied. I wasn't going to offer the

191

complication with Leo to the argument. "He told me from the start that the Queen was no good, and I chose her words over his. For what? For two dead relatives, two attempts on my life by her personal Vens, and needless strife."

"I don't trust him," Ari's tone was sharper than a new blade, eyes bordering on black. "And neither should you."

My voice became cold, icy. "Then why did you let him join us in this?"

His contempt turned to hurt in a heartbeat, the sting of his sadness worse than his anger. "Because of the look in your eyes."

My body went rigid, the breath gone from my lungs. I didn't dare answer the statement, not if I wanted to break Ari's heart. Or my own.

Pulling free from his arms, I moved to the edge of the balcony, pressing my hands onto the cool metal fencing lining the end. Below, a drop of at least twenty feet rested, small shapes of bushes and bunches of flowers standing out amongst the dark.

Ari's words burned at my insides, making my squirm where I stood. Had he seen the look I gave Kayden when I wanted nothing more but to lay in his arms and let the world melt away? Had he read my mind and knew how I wanted Kayden to come to bed with me, rather than sleep alone?

I knew better than to say my inner thoughts out loud. The last time I had acted on my feelings, Kayden had used me like a cheap parlor trick, pushing some kind of persuasion on me to forget about the bond forming between Leo and I. A bond that, with a little more time, would have saved me and my life. But I couldn't deny that his kiss had brought out something within me I hadn't felt before, something raw and untamed, something that made me want to love him more than stay in love with my own misery.

"Pretty sure I'm supposed to be the only one who can

make you look that torn in two."

I didn't have to look back; there was only one person in the world whose voice could bring me to tears and a fist fight in the same breath. "Not sure if I'd be proud of such a notion, Kayden."

He came closer, standing beside me, careful not to touch me. Sneaking a small glance, I saw he was still perfectly dressed, playing his part well.

"I saw you left your shining angel over there," he said, giving a small nod of the head to where I had abandoned Ari. A quick look over my shoulder told me he was gone, probably hovering nearby and giving me space. "Take it he didn't like that you don't kiss and tell on the first date."

"Kayden, please," I begged, closing my eyes to fight back tears. "Not tonight."

"Maybe you should tell him you don't want to get into anything with an expiration date posted on your soul." His thoughtful muse was lost on me, but he continued to smile sarcastically. "Everyone knows pity is given to the dying chick."

Something in me snapped. I turned to face him, fire blazing in my eyes. "When do we see the Queen?"

"I can take you now, the guards are all here. Why?"

"Because I've decided enough is enough," I said, hands clenched in tight fists at my sides. "I'm ready to kill her or by damn I will die trying."

THIRTEEN
IN THE END

Kayden look startled by my sudden demanding revelation. His black eyes lightened to a molten hazel, flecks of green standing out among the dark.

"Not that I'm not for suicide or anything," he said, still blinking in shock. "But why the big need to kill her? I thought you said you couldn't."

I walked past him, keeping to the edge of the balcony as not to bump into couples dancing past us. Sweet, cheery music continued to play, a far cry from the way I felt inside.

I was tired of being labeled; first it was the freak, then the nosy Nephilim, now the dying girl. If I wasn't being ridiculed by my dance with the devil, Kayden, I was gossiped about by the likes of Bernard and his wife. I had a feeling they weren't the only people whispering things behind my back, spreading lies and rumors about me.

Killing the Queen would put an end to all of this, for she was the source. It was her who sunk her claws into the people I was surrounded by, her who moved them all like puppets to the tune of her play.

Too bad she didn't factor me standing up. Too bad she

didn't factor me not going down without one hell of a fight. I wouldn't let her steal my life, what little of it I had left to claim. I wasn't going to stand there helplessly and let her kill me.

I had made it inside the castle, sparing no time to admire the old decor and pleasantries the Queen wanted to familiarize herself with. I wanted to feel her cold, dead fingers try and fight back as I squeeze the life from her until nothing remained.

Kayden appeared instantly beside me, keeping pace against my shuffle of skirts with ease. "Why can't you be in a hurry like this when anything else goes on?"

"Take me to a half off everything sale at Abercrombie and you'll see me speed like I was on drugs."

"I know a good dealer in Charon, but I can't promise you'll still have hair."

We approached the end of hallway leading to the grand foyer, where just beyond the landing connecting to the steps lay the Queen's quarters, empty and dark. Two Vens, dressed in typical all black, stood guard at the grand French doors leading to the dark half of the castle.

Kayden was the first to react. "Essallie, they will take one look at you and see right through the potion."

Fire blossomed over my knuckles, blooming into my palms with a raging fury. "Fine. Let them."

I started forward, pre-planning to take out the one on the left of the doors, when something in the corner of my eyes caught my attention. Fair, platinum blonde hair and the sound of a soft, lilting voice. I stopped charging forward and looked down the stairs, breath catching in my throat.

Ursula looked regal, dressed in a tightly wound gown of all black. The top half was patterned lace, barely covering her pale skin underneath, the bottom half flaring out in a fishtail shape. A tiny gold locket rested against her chest, while two small gold teardrops hung from each ear. Her hair had been piled high above her head in gentle curls, revealing her beautifully shaped face that needed no makeup to appear flawless.

She chatted animatedly with a gentleman at the entrance doors, a hand placed on his upper arm in a gesture of affection. Then, with a small nod, she didn't make her way up the stairs like everyone else, but to a small door on the west end of the wing, to the dark half of the castle.

My fire extinguished in a gust, and I looked at Kayden with a growing, dark glee. "We don't have to fight. I just saw another way in."

"So did I," he said, and I knew he meant that he too, had seen Ursula. "Quick- follow the one with too many chemicals in her hair."

I ignored his jab and ran down the stairs, holding my skirt up to avoid a full on face-plant. No one stopped Kayden or I as I opened the small, grey door to the other end of the castle, and followed inside.

The door shut behind us with a quick click and snap, leaving both of us shrouded in darkness. Only the sound of my breathing filled the silence pressing between us.

"Did you bring a candle?" I asked in a hushed tone to Kayden.

"Do I look like a pack mule to you?"

"I'm sure you can mutate into one if it tickled your fancy."

"Let me just pull one right out of my-"

"Oh for crying out loud." I held out one of my hands and watched the fire spark to life from my skin, swimming over my fingers and palm. Light from the blue flames created an eerie, aqua shade to everything, giving just enough light to illuminate the way.

I pushed past Kayden in a hurry, darting down the wide

hallway without a care. My heart hammered in my chest, pounding with enough force to burst from my rib cage. Behind me, I could hear Kayden's soft footsteps keeping up, the only noise to show he retained a solid form.

Turning to another hallway, I stopped short, Kayden bumping into me, cursing as fire crackled over his outfit.

"Essallie, we're never going to get anywhere with every little bump setting me on fire," he muttered angrily in a low tone, but I shushed him.

I could barely speak the words. "Kayden, we have company."

"What?" He peered over my shoulder, one of his arms reforming from black smoke. The hallway looked much like the last one we'd run down, only this one had six figures unfamiliar to the last hallway.

Vens, part of the Queen's personal arsenal, stood shoulder-to-shoulder, a horrifying never-ending sheet of black.

I barely had time to process what was happening before everyone leapt into action. Kayden grabbed one of my arms, flinging me behind him and onto the ground as he screamed something. Three Vens instantly descended upon him, and I watched Kayden vanish under a tangle of limbs.

Scrambling up to my feet, one of the remaining three Vens made a grab for me. Fire ignited with fury on both my hands. With a single swing, I clocked one of them, fire burning at the skin with a sickening smell.

Smoke curled around me, forming into a solid shape. Hands wrapped around my upper arms, a voice whispering in my ear, and I screamed. As if it reacted to my fear, blue fire laced up my arms, ensnaring the Vens that had locked onto me, boiling his hands. He released me, dropping to the ground in a flurry of screams and shouts. He swung at me, connecting a burning fist to my temple and throwing me to the floor.

For a moment, everything swirled in a daze. All six Vens were ganging on Kayden, dancing around him in a tight circle. Kayden's lips moved, eyes shining a sparkling obsidian as horns began to grow from his forehead, his true form coming forth. No one paid attention to me.

Something hard pressed at the inside of my left thigh. I fumbled through the fabric, finding a hidden pocket I hadn't known. A small, purple bottle had been stowed away inside the dress, identical to the one I had seen in the apothecary.

An idea seized my mind, one wild enough that it would end all of this, once and for all. Standing, I uncorked the purple bottle and held it out in front of me, eyes narrowed on the tip. Fire curled over my fingertips, the purple bottle growing hot in my hand.

Kayden snapped his eyes up at me from over his shoulder, shock quickly turning to wild horror. As if on cue, all six Vens turned around to watch me too. Fire bloomed on my hands, the twisting blue and black working in slow motion as it swirled over each finger before reaching the bottle. It raced up the sides, diving into the liquid as a new, hotter fire began to spiral skyward out of the bottle.

"Essallie, no!" Kayden turned to rush for me. But it was too late.

With a final breath in my lungs, I felt my wings explode from my back. The bottle shattered at my feet, setting everything ablaze.

I accepted this; death would be a welcoming gift to end this maddening war. I would stop the world from burning out by setting it on fire.

Only a second went by before the explosion rocked the hallway, sending everyone flying in different directions. But I didn't care. I only knew one thing.

We would all die.

FOURTEEN
MONSTER

Bodies were everywhere.

The hallway looked like a building after a raging, uncontrollable inferno. Destruction littered everywhere; broken and burning pieces of timber lay splintered, chunks of marble scattered on the floor, the smell of ash and burned flesh heavy in the air. Blood splattered every surface. Smoke clouded like a thick, unyielding haze.

I tried to take breath, but found only ash coating my throat. I coughed, trying to clear the burning taste from my mouth. Something was pressing on my chest, making breathing impossible.

"Essallie..."

Two eyes, swirling with a molten amber and raven black, met mine.

"*Kayden,*" I forced out, pushing him off of me. He landed beside me with a groan. Already I was getting to my feet, amazed at how little had hit me from the blow. "What happened?"

He said nothing, rolling onto his side, and I instantly understood why. His back had been shredded in the blow, the glass and marble acting like a monster, eating at him alive. He had protected me from the blow, throwing himself on me in the last moment of the explosion. Crouching down against the broken glass and blood, I tried to ease him into a sitting position.

"Why didn't you let me die?" I asked out of my bewilderment, my voice hoarse. He could have easily let me fall prey to the Queen without a blemish on his non-existent soul. "You could have finally been free."

His voice was dry, but the words he spoke sang with an unparalleled truth. "I gave up trying to imagine a world without you."

I watched the expression in his eyes turn soft, dim glimmers of something kind shining inside them. He reached out to stroke my cheek, his thumb igniting sparks from my skin, like flicking a lighter on. "You remind me of someone." He paused. "For a second I thought...maybe part of them was reincarnated into you."

I studied him carefully, running my eyes over the cuts and burns that littered his body. He looked like a giant mess of ripped tissue paper. I wondered if the blow left him delusional. "Who do I remind you of?"

He shook his head, the broken look on his face nearly crippling me. Rising to his feet, he stumbled and gently swore. "Doesn't matter who. What matters is that where this person went, it isn't possible to come back."

"Don't stand up," I started to say. I'd barely made it to my feet when he spilled forward, collapsing into my arms. Adjusting my stance to save us from a spill into broken glass and blood, I muttered under my breath. "You have got to be the heaviest thing made of smoke. Ever."

Leaning off of me, Kayden grinned like a jackal, blood smeared across the bridge of his nose and cheek like blush. If we weren't in the middle of a pile of dead bodies, I might have smiled too. "Admit it," he said. "You like this. You wouldn't know what to do without me."

I ignored his words and the hammering in my chest, doing my best to keep him from dragging us to the ground. Alarm bells rang in my head, reminding me that Ari was still missing from the party. "How exactly do you get better? Because there's no way I can carry you like this forever."

For a second his gaze returned to the serious Kayden I was accustomed to. "Do you really want the answer to that?"

I locked eyes, prepared to dish the first retort on my tongue, and stopped. Even with his brooding stare my heart felt like it could explode at any moment. I didn't want to look away from him, because what if that last time I saw him was his last? If he died right now, how far did I really think I could get before I'd break down and sob? I realized that while I told Ari my scars were his to guard, Kayden had the same right, maybe even more. I couldn't see the final picture without him, couldn't stand the thought of letting him go. And yet, if I didn't...

"Essallie?" Kayden tilted his head to the side.

Something screamed inside of me to respond. Something, anything. Anything that didn't involve flinging myself into him and kissing him like I'd never see him again. I had to hate him, hate him to the very core so Ari wouldn't kill him. So my heart would survive the break. Demons and angels didn't mix, they couldn't. No amount of love could fix something like that.

"What a pity to interrupt something so *lovely*."

I looked up in shock, staring through the heavy smoke blanketing most of the destruction. Two figures, outlined in black, came into view. Fire instantly blazed my knuckles, Kayden wrapping his arms around my shoulders as I let him free from my grasp.

Ursula stood alongside the Queen, both wearing elegant

black gowns and hair styled to sit in twisted spirals above their heads. But where Ursula looked soft and beautiful, the Queen looked composed and assured, smiling knowingly to me.

"My, what a mess you've made of this place. Still, how nice it is to see you again, Essallie," the Queen purred, half-lidded eyes regarding me curiously. Gesturing to the blown open door on her right, she turned to walk inside. "Come, I'm sure we have much to discuss."

The pounding in my heart froze, replaced by a slithering sickness swirling in my gut. One look at Kayden told me we had no choice- to run would mean death for both of us, and while I had no qualms about using myself like a human bomb against the Queen, I wasn't about to put Kayden and Ursula in the middle of it.

Following the Queen inside, I waited until the door clicked soundly shut before I breathed. We were standing in a room almost as large as the balcony, its walls and floors the same shimmering black from the bookkeeper's. Five small pedestals, all evenly spread out, stood in the center of the room, a floating blue orb dimly glowing just above.

The Queen gave a dismissive gesture to Ursula. "Take Kayden and leave. I'd like to speak to the Nephilim-"

"*Essallie*," I corrected with a snap.

She paused, only the faintest of twitches betraying her calm demeanor. "-Essallie, in private."

Beside me, Kayden gave a the Queen a smile. His stance was strained as he visibly tried not to attack the woman dressed so elegantly before us. "Now isn't the best time. We're both injured, thanks to your idiot squad. You'll do better by letting us go."

"And ruin all my fun? You have no say, Kayden darling," the Queen replied sweetly, smiling. With a flick of her hand, Kayden exploded into smoke, hurtling out the door with Ursula sauntering in tow.

The door sealed behind me, I found myself alone with the Queen. A woman who wanted me dead, for reasons unknown. Fire lit on both of my hands, the burning in my stomach spreading to every end of my body. If she wanted to start anything, I would be ready to take her down in a fight of flames.

Walking with unparalleled grace, the Queen moved carefully through the room, putting the floating orbs between us. Her gown was much like Ursula's; a tightly fitted bodice, wrapped in swaths of black shining fabric cut in a daring low neckline, the bottom flared out with layers for extra flow. Around her neck rested a small, red pendant heart nearly identical to my white one.

When she spoke, her voice was boring, like a drone reciting an age-old quote. "I see you found your way back to Charon."

"Hope you didn't waste too many brain cells on that one."

"And still just as snarky as the day we met." Her tongue clicked in disappointment. "Tell me, is that Kayden's influence working on you, or all your own?"

I stiffened, the fire on my hands burning brighter. "If you wanted to keep me on your good side, you should have made mention that it wasn't the world who was out to get me, but yourself. You play a good game, Lucretia."

She stopped moving deeper into the room, her bare shoulders rising in a display of controlled anger. They dropped as she turned, any signs of her rage masked. She reached out to touch one of the orbs, fingers running down the side and back up.

"No one has spoken my name to me in such a manner in over three hundred years." Her words seemed to betray her bitterness, but her tone of casualty off-set the mood. "It's almost refreshing to hear someone rebel against me for a change. Of course, that still doesn't change the outcome of our conversation."

"Which is what?"

Her eyes met mine, a frightening smile revealing sharp teeth. "I always get my prize, Essallie."

"Yeah, well not this time." I felt my bones begin to rattle and shake, the potion's effects wearing off. Like a snake shedding its skin, Lilix's appearance washed off of me, leaving my true self unveiled to the Queen.

The Queen appeared unfazed by my declaration of resistance. If anything, she smiled a little wider, relishing the idea of a battle to obtain whatever it was she so desperately wanted from me. "I take it my two favorite Vens won't be returning for future assignments?"

"Don't know, want to ask them yourself?" I stepped further into the room, the glow of one orb cast on my face. The reflecting shine of a gold plaque, posted on the black pedestal, caught my eye. A name I didn't recognize, Rinae, had been etched in dark red. "Why are you sending people to capture me, Lucretia?"

"My desire was only to bring you to me, never to hurt you," she said gently, moving closer to me. Her fingers lingered over another orb, whispers growing in my ears each time she touched one. "My intentions are more noble than you think."

"I'm sure they are," I spat, putting as much sarcasm into my voice as I could. "Except the evidence between the Vens attacks sort of put a hole in your promise of peace."

"You wouldn't understand." Her tone turned sharp and dark. "You've never come so close to having everything you've ever wanted, yet still be so far."

"What the hell are you talking about?"

With a flick of her wrist, two black bands snaked out of the dark, binding my wrists, immobilizing me. I struggled against the bands, the black burning into my skin as my fire did little to slice through them.

"You are a miracle, Essallie. A miracle I have been dreaming of for over three hundred years. Your very existence is proof that I have not waited in vain on the word of a madwoman, but a true prophet who told me that one day I could have a child again."

"Wait a minute, you said you lost a daughter. But you can't have children," I stared, shock spreading on my face as the pieces of the puzzle began to fall into place. "Unless she wasn't yours to begin with."

"She was not mine, but a gift given to me nonetheless." Fists formed at her sides. "When she perished, I lost everything. All that remains of her now is a memory, a tiny spark in my dark heart. I was destroyed, knowing my line would die with me, a disgrace to my family.

"A woman approached me one night, wild with the fever of a premonition. She spoke of a Nephilim who would be able to give me the thing I searched most for, all I would need is her blood and mine to mix."

I jerked against the bands, twisting my hands and wrists in futile attempts. "News flash. Even if I could give you wanted, my clock is running out. I'll die before you can do anything with me."

"That's where you're wrong, Essallie." She nearly darted across the room to put her hands on my face, nails digging into my cheeks. "It's already beginning. How else do you think you've lasted this long? On *faith?*" She let out a dark, harsh laugh. "You're smarter than that, think Essallie."

"I don't know-"

She pushed my face away in disgust, stalking off across the room. Shark-tooth shaped burgundy scales grew from her unblemished, pale arms, creating the illusion of sleeves. "Funny, how blood ties into everything in our lives. It defines

OBUMBRATE

relations, connections, unspoken words performing the impossible. Everything always boils down to blood." She paused, reigning in the rising wild sound of her voice. "What a shame, Chase couldn't leave you be that night at the circus."

"Chase was a madman who only thought of himself," I hissed, the thought of him alone bringing my fire to a brighter blaze. It wrapped up my arms protectively. "He has nothing to do with this, he's dead."

The Queen didn't move, the scales on her body inching up and around her shoulders and neck. "Curious, that he knew exactly where and when to find you. Especially when you made the decision to attend the event at the last moment."

"He was hunting me!" I shouted, writhing. "Sooner or later he'd of found me."

"And yet he chose that moment, that part in time, to seek you out and attack you in a full house." She paused. "Shocking how no one leapt to your defense but your little crew."

I began to argue with her, the words sinking in. She was implying something very heavy, a damning thought that Chase's attempt to kill me was set up from the start. I licked my dry lips. "I bet there's only a few in all of Charon who could stun a whole room, and even fewer who could find piece of my past and use them to have me killed."

"Alas," she clasped her hands together, elation spreading on her face. "She's finally putting it together."

My skin began to turn cold, ice water running in my veins. The fire on my arms and hands dulled, pulling into the skin until only sparks remained. "It was you. You orchestrated the whole thing that night. Because of you, Leo is dead!"

"And what a pity that is, truly." For a moment, she looked remorseful, but it quickly vanished under her mood-altering mask.

"You're just as bad as Kayden." I shook my head, refusing to let tears pool in my eyes. I would not give her the benefit to see me cry. "Why are you bringing this up? Why now?"

"I'm curious as to how you survived." Her voice had gone soft, probing. Tilting to her head to one side, she came to stand in front of me, leaving only inches between us. "Everyone knows demon poison to Nephilim is a sure death sentence. What makes you so special that you lived?"

I thought back to that day, ghosts of the screams ringing in my ears, faded images of blood and fire clouding my eyes. "I... I don't remember. Kayden said Ursula gave him something-"

I froze, all air leaving my lungs. One brief, tucked away memory surfaced, like a hidden body rising to the top of a lake. A tiny vial, as small as my pinky finger, filled with a thick, dark red liquid. The vial opened, held over my screaming mouth, and the pain washing away.

"*That was your blood*." The words crashed over me instantly. I could barely speak the words as they left my lips. "Your blood and mine, mixed."

The Queen's exalted look brought air back to my lungs, blotches of rage coloring my cheeks. The moment I said it out loud, she gave me a full, frighteningly beautiful smile. "Little unknown secret of a demon-Nephilim hybrid; our blood works as an anti-venom against both Nephilim fire and demon poison."

In that tiny, blink of a moment, everything changed. I was no longer in control of my life. Someone had already moved me across the board, placed me in the direct line of fire, and had left me to fend for myself. Any strength I had left vanished. If it hadn't been for the bands holding my wrists, I would have collapsed onto my knees.

"Don't look so stunned, Essallie. It'll all be over before you know it," the Queen soothed, reaching out to touch my face again. This time it was gentle, caressing my cheek as if I was her favorite new pet. "In a matter of days, your soul will split, and I will finally have my wish. A daughter I can call my own."

"I won't let you," I started to scream, pushing away her hand with a swift shake. "I won't let you use me like this."

"Darling," her voice carried through like a mist, clouding my mind as darkness swelled overhead. "You don't have a choice."

READ ON FOR A PREVIEW OF

RIVEN

| THE ILLUMINE SERIES, BOOK THREE |

PROLOGUE
HIDING

Thunder sounded off in the distance, a faint reminder of old tales on how each time lightning struck, it was an angry and wrathful god seeking redemption or vengeance. Lorena privately shared a dark laugh; the only vengeful god she had ever met had been a woman who dealt with dark magic beyond her control. A woman who only sought to corrupt and swallow every person within her grasp.

A flash of light briefly illuminated the small hospital room, Jessica's pale face glowing amongst the dark. At first glance, she appeared peaceful, like a coma patient submerged in the confines of a peaceful dream. Upon closer inspection, the set of her muscles showed she was not lost under the ocean of her mind, but was fighting to stay underwater. Fingers twitched as they wrapped further into the white sheets, knuckles nearly blending with the over-bleached fabric. Eyelids fluttered as small, panting gasps sounded through barely parted and cracked lips.

Lorena reached forward, her hands only inches above that of her daughter's. Yet, she couldn't press further. To touch her unprotected could bring a wave of sharp hallucinations-premonitions of anything from death to life, love to loss. Even the smallest gesture of comfort without a barrier of gloves or clothes could render her only daughter frozen with the knowledge of her Mother's death.

"Mother?"

Lorena startled in her seat, hands flung backward in a show of palms. She hadn't heard Jessica move, hadn't noticed the slow movement of her head as she turned to face her Mother fully before asking the question with her rough, shaking voice. Her fingers continued to linger, thin pianist hands extended towards the place her mother's hands had previously rested.

"Jessie darling," Lorena's breath came in a startled gasp, clearly caught off guard. "Is everything okay?"

Her daughter reached out further, delicate fingers hovering inches before her mother's eyes. She made a sweeping motion with her fingers, mimicking the crescent shaped bags under her mother's startled, yet shatteringly beautiful blue stare. "You haven't been sleeping." She phrased it almost like a question, voice light and eerily detached from this world. "What's troubling you?"

Lorena hesitated, lower lip pulled into her mouth as her teeth nibbled on the already-raw flesh. In her mind she had been playing over the options on what she would say in this moment, how it would turn her already unstable world even more shaken, until like wet sand drying out, it fell out between her heartbroken grasp.

"She's gone, Jessie. Essallie is gone."

She was unable to meet her daughter's gaze when she heard the sound of a small, yet undeniably sharp gasp of breath in the room. Lorena could feel the pressure on her tested body as she sat there, as if the weight of Charon had been deposited on her in one fell swoop. But it vanished just as fast as it arrived, the same time her daughter's unmistakable laughter broke the tenuous silence that had wedged between them.

Looking up, Lorena stared in shock, eyebrows lost high in her frazzled hair. "You're laughing?"

Jessica nodded, the laughter leaving her gasping for air. Of course, she had known for the last two weeks that the half-angel had been captured, along with her demon lover-pet thing, and had been stowed in the high tower quarters while her body betrayed itself as the Queen's blood did unspeakable things to her. She knew, because she had been the one who told the Queen it would happen, just as it had all been planned since Essallie's birth. But Essallie going free had not been part of her vision, nor the Queen's, and she now understood why her mother was so nervous; the Queen's failed plans meant she would be returning to Jessica, and punishment would surely follow. Between shallow inhales, she managed to ask. "How... did she get... free?"

"It doesn't matter how she got free," Lorena snapped, her voice rising and falling like the Berlin Wall. "What matters now is how soon we leave."

"What happened to *lying low and staying quiet?*" Jessica bitterly asked, mimicking her mother's low tones with mock. "Wouldn't moving your precious daughter ruin that?"

Lorena bristled. "You don't know what you're talking about, child. This is a change of plans, nothing more."

"Oh shut up," Jessica spat, all traces of humor vanished. Under the mask of illness and exhaustion, a burning fire of rage and anger flared. "When are you going to admit it? That this, all of this hiding and stalling was for nothing?" She waved a pale hand around the room with a jerk. "It's time you face facts, and let me go. I need to find Essallie, *we* need to find Essallie-"

"*No!*" Lorena screamed, then quickly clamped a hand tightly over her mouth. When she lowered it, her voice had returned to the silence, shaking noise it was before. "I will not allow you to put yourself in the Queen's hands like that. What's done is done."

A growing irritation colored Jessica's sigh. "We can't keep doing this, Mama."

Lorena forced her gaze down to the edge of the bed, staring at the off-white sheets with increasing interest. "I'm not quite sure what you mean, dear."

"Liar," her daughter retorted, breathing labored. Pinches of pink colored her cheeks. "You think she doesn't already know where we are? As if she isn't keeping tabs on us. The Queen will find us eventually. Perhaps not today or tomorrow, but she will come."

"She will not!" Fear brought a high-pitched quiver to Lorena's voice.

"She will!" Jessica shouted back with fever. "Unless you choose to forget the day she branded me." When Lorena didn't answer, Jessica yanked the thin sheets back, exposing her pencil thin legs. Black shadows ensnared them, caressing the skin as gently as a twisted vice could. With each tremble of Jessica's skin, the shadows moved, re-grouping over her feet and lower legs exactly as they had been on the Queen's. "Do you remember now?"

For a split second, Lorena could feel it all slipping away, her life and world no longer in her hands. Unsteady eyes found her daughter's, and she stared bleakly at the child she had brought into this world with the hopes of seeing her thrive, not struggle like she had. And now it was too late for them, too late to find the sun within the shadows, to savor the breaths of life they had left. "I will not her have you, used like some toy in her pretty treasure chest. I refuse to let her use you until-"

"Until what, Mama?" Jessica's voice remained low, an eerie tone of calm making her words carry more weight than her mother's screams. "Until I give her exactly what she wants? Until I tell her where her incubator half-angel has ran off to, where the last piece of her puzzle rests?"

"She will not have those things." Lorena hissed in fear, eyes wide and brimming with tears. "We'll keep moving you, stay low as long as we need-"

"When are you going to learn?" Jessica said with growing exasperation, hands relaxed and no longer white knuckled. Her eyes had opened, two beautiful orbs of color brimming with the vitality one as young as her should have had everywhere. But her eyes were the only source of her youth, the rest of her body having fallen prey to the crippling effect of her growing supernatural power. "All of this is going to happen, no matter what you do or say. The prophet warned me, warned *you,* that keeping us from Essallie would only bring about the end to us all. Now look where we are, exactly as she predicted. I am servitude to the Queen, our last hope is running in the unknown, unaware of what will befall her, and yet you continue to believe in the madness that if you hide me from it all, that it will vanish." Her words turned sharp as ice, bitterly cold with truth. "Is that what you desire?"

Jessica's words acted like a loaded gun placed over her mother's heart, safety off and all. Lorena turned her watery gaze to the glass behind her, staring unseeing at the brewing storm, its violent mauve and oil black clouds a classic painting of warning to an oncoming disaster.

Minutes ticked into the silence, Lorena's eyes still watching the twisted braids of clouds and shuddering trees outside. "She will use you until you break," her voice sounded faint. "Use you and throw you away like she has everyone else. You mean *nothing* to her."

"I mean more to her than I do to you."

Lorena whirled back to face her daughter, and in one swift move, struck her daughter across the face.

The effect was instantaneous.

Jessica's eyes flew open wider than possible, irises melting to a clouded white. Her hands slammed against her mother's chest, fingers digging into the slippery silk of her clothes in a grasp of violent desperation. A wild, uncontrollable scream tore from her throat as the flashes of red, white, and black burning into her mind, forcing her to watch the newest way her mother was set up to die.

"Jessica!" Lorena shrieked, clamping onto her daughter with fear. Arms wrapped about Jessica's writhing frame. "Oh god, Jessica stop, please stop!"

"Let me go!" She cried out between screams, the images coming faster as her mother continued to hold onto her. Flashes of Lorena holding a knife, pressing the sharp blade against the soft flesh of her wrist. Lorena standing outside the Queen's castle, chanting in defiance of her while a guard takes aim with a bullet of black fire from a castle window. Claws, crossbows, swords, poison, fire, glass, water; they all blended into one, crowding Jessica's mind as she screamed in unrelenting agony, the visions beginning to split her levels of consciousness into different realities.

Jessica jerked back in a jolt of pain, Lorena's hands flying off her as she rocked back into her chair with a sharp thud. She watched, knowing in horror that she had broken the very rules she had set in place to protect the fragile relationship she had with Jessica. For a moment, the frail girl sat upright and frozen, screams pouring from her throat. It was all Lorena could do but hug her daughter and cause more pain.

Minutes pass as the frozen, soul screaming madness continues. Then, just as suddenly as it had started, Jessica collapsed back onto the bed, whiter than the sheets surrounding her, barely breathing.

Her mother barely spoke. "Jess-"

"Don't," her daughter cut her off, exhaustion running

deep in her veins. She no longer sounded like the bright, jittery teenager having awoken from a nap, but of a woman fractured by the stretch of time. "Please, don't."

Lorena ignored her, pressing on. "Don't you see? She has done this to you, done this to us. Jessica, my baby, my only daughter, you're mean everything in this world to me. Please, don't let her take you away."

"You mean like how Rinae is all Essallie has? All she will ever have in the end?" Jessica lamented with sorrow, the weight of her knowledge insurmountable. "But she'll never know just how important Rinae will be to her, not with you continuing this useless play against fate and destiny."

A voice drawled softly. "Now, I wouldn't say that."

Something colder than ice froze in Lorena's veins, the breath extinguished from her lungs. Her eyes swiveled around the room, landing on the darkest corner that seemed to rebuff any light. She knew the voice from anywhere, and knew that it would only be a matter of time before the owner of the voice would try and come for her daughter.

Shapes formed from the dark, stretching out in a flowing river on the ground before rising to the ceiling to take shape. A body, with lean shoulders and a sleek black dress, formed from the darkness. Waves of midnight black hair framed a petite, sweetheart shaped face, two eyes black as coal standing alien against pale skin.

Blinking her dark almond eyes, the Queen gave a rich, malicious smile of sharp teeth. "Lorena, what a lovely surprise. Counseling your child to do right to save her skin?"

Lorena froze, all sense of what to do vanished. Before she could think, she reached for her daughter with a cry, hands flinging out at the cotton sheets with a fevered desperation.

With a flick of the Queen's hand, Lorena stopped, shuddering in mid-grasp. Lucretia let her dangle for a moment before tossing her against the wall, listening to her body collide against the plaster with a sickening smack before dropping to the ground, unconscious.

Jessica raised a hand. "Mom!"

A stilled silence settled upon the room, only broken by that of Jessica's continuing gasp for breath. The Queen turned to face the frail child lying in bed, a mask of expressionless quiet perfectly in place. Slowly she came closer, closing the gap between them until the shadows swirling in her skirts licked the edge of the bed frame.

"I had planned to make this trip short," she said with a sneer. "But complications have risen in my faults. No matter." The Queen extended her arm, black satin covering her bone-thin fingers and hand, stretching all the way up to her elbows. "Tell me where she is."

This was it, Jessica knew; the moment of her personal fork in the road. To give the Queen what she wanted would bring her life to an end with a sharp suddenness, and yet if she didn't give it she would be equally damned to an early death. Options tumbled in her mind, like a deer standing in the middle of a dark road on a foggy night, and she knew she had to make the choice to jump into the woods and save her skin, or admire the glow of oncoming headlights and meet a brilliant demise.

Jessica shook her head. "I refuse." Defiance gave her a delicious glow, lighting her eyes brighter than she had in weeks. "We finally stand a chance to be free. Three hundred years of your scorn has been more than enough. The time has come to watch you fall and lose your crown."

The Queen's knowing smirk twitched, a crack showing in her perfect facade. Just as quickly as it was seen, her face smoothed out, an expressionless vacancy in her eyes standing out against her forming mask of demonic blood. "Is that so?" They narrowed to slits, her lips pursed as she weighed her next words. "Perhaps you have forgotten your place, Seer."

Jessica had not forgotten. "I would rather die," she whispered with a giddy malevolence. "Than give you anything."

Lucretia pulled her hand back, fingers curling to form a fist. For a second she stood there, glowering in the scorn from a frail half-human. Her words stirred the potions of vengeance deep within Lucretia's heart, echoing with sharp precision in her ears. The girl really thought it would be so easy to defy the Queen of their world.

When her mouth opened to speak, no trace of discontent was to be found. "I had hoped," she began in a lilting tone. "That it would not come to this." Reaching into one of her sleeves, she drew a long, auburn needle the length of her forearm. The needle glowed, swirls of blood red and burnt orange warring within it. "But you leave me no choice." She drew the needle back, as if in slow motion, and plunged it into one of Jessica's legs.

The frail girl cried out, screaming louder than ever before. Lorena, listening to her daughter's unbridled cries of pain rattling the room, stirred on the floor, raising her head. Pain lanced above her left eye as something sticky and wet clung to her skin and hair. Reaching a hand into her hair, she pulled back fingers stained with blood, just as the glass panes behind her spiderwebbed into fragments before exploding. A rush of the violent storm rain and wind poured into the room, drenching the monitors and equipment until the burst in puffs of choking smoke and wild sparks of electricity.

Between the frightful screams of her daughter, malevolent grinning of the Queen, and the collapsing scene around her, something snapped in Lorena's mind. Her fingers fumbled for the small, silver dagger tucked under her shirt at her waist, unsheathing the blade and gripping it tightly in her quivering hand. With a wild scream she lunged forward, thrusting the blade deep into the back of the Queen's shoulder.

For a moment, time seemed to pause, silence echoing in Lorena's ears. All eyes in the room transfixed on the hilt of the blade. Lorena's gaze flickered up to the Queen's, bottomless black eyes meeting her fearful gaze with a twisted delight. The Queen reached up, wrapping her fingers around Lorena's hand as it still held the blade. She gave it a twist, continuing to smile as the blade dug deeper into her flesh, then pulled it free. Dark blood, black as ink and thick as tar, bubbled from the small yet deep wound. She rolled her shoulder with barely a wince, the wound vanishing to a thin white scar before blending seamlessly into her skin, as if she had never beeb stabbed at all.

Holding the dagger in her outstretched hand, she examined it with mild interest, tilting the blade back and forth as she ignored the screams from the bed behind her. "Curious, what did you plan to do once I had died? Take the throne for yourself? Or perhaps you thought that by killing me, maybe somehow your daughter would be spared an early grave?"

Lorena barely had opened her mouth to speak when the Queen fastened her hands onto Lorena's face, the dagger clattering to the ground. Her palms pressed against Lorena's face, nails scratching the skin of her temples with each increase of pressure. With a jerk of her hands, she made sure the mother's eyes met hers before she spoke.

"Shame, you will never know such pity from me."

The Queen's nail grew, tips sharpening to jagged edges and cutting deeper into the skin. Needle-thin, startling white teeth filled her mouth as she gave a sickening smile that stretched from ear to ear. The unmistakable crunch of bone echoed within the room as the Queen flicked her wrists, breaking the protective mother's neck in one fell swoop.

Jessica screamed even louder, wailing in agony as her mother's corpse collapsed to the ground with finality. Bitten-down fingernails clawed at the needle steeped deep into her leg, frantic to pull it free. Lucretia came closer, storm winds whipping her hair in snake-like streaks across the room. With a single move she secured both of Jessica's hands, pressing them firmly against her wounded leg, driving the needle home.

"Do you know what this is, Jessie dear?" Lucretia asked with wicked glee. "It's a spike from a demon tail, filled to the brim with poison. A little insurance, if you will." She ran a gloved hand over the needle carefully, the swirls of red and orange within it turning to a wilted purple. "I've stuck it in the prime artery within your leg; if you pull it free without my magic, the poison will stop your heart in less than minutes. Do you understand?"

"Monster!" Jessica screamed, writhing within her confinement. "Kill me now, I'll tell you nothing, nothing, you murdering creature!"

The Queen came closer, hand hovering against one of Jessica's cheeks. Heat built between them, an unbound friction reminding Jessica of the first time she clashed with her Mother over her cursed existence. Every touch was a double-edged sword; sweet comfort of knowing she was human, cursed bitterly to see their future with every brush of flesh.

"Tell me where she is," Lucretia said in a tense, low tone. Her voice quivered with every syllable. "Tell me where I can find the girl."

Jessica closed her eyes, shaking to the point of rattling teeth. Taking a deep breath, her words came out slow. "Burn in hell."

Lucretia snapped; she let out a wild scream, and plunged the needle deeper into Jessica's leg. As the girl cried out, Lucretia smashed a hand over her mouth, silencing her with the thin satin separating them from a rush of visions. Jessica lay there, stunned in fear. Her mother had once spoken cryptically of the Queen's power, citing how the cities surrounding Charon had been reduced to rubble and ash because her true daughter had been killed over three hundred years ago. Never in her mind did she think she would bare witness to her raw abilities.

The longer she watched, the more Jessica began to notice just how far from human the woman before her truly was. Bloody fingernails tore from the flimsy fabric covering the Queen's arms, ripping in rippling waves until it all peeled back from the skin. Stained crimson scales covered her arms where pale flesh had once been, while rivers of green and black twisted like vines pulsating with dark life as they wrapped about her fingers.

"One last chance, halfling," Lucretia called to Jessica, hovering her lips inches above the girl's ear. "Tell me where she is." Jessica shook her head, biting her lower lip hard enough to draw blood. Roaring in fury, the Queen shed the last of her protective gloves, and with a single move slammed her hand onto the Seer's chest.

Jessica screamed as loud as her vocal chords would allow, her body bucking on the bed. Outside, the winds picked up with ferocious intensity, rain heaving into the room in swells of bruising waves. Lightning lit up the sky, arcing in a display of dazzling forked wings. If Jessica ever needed a sign she was doing the right thing, that was it.

The visions began to pour into her mind, her eyes pooling to white. She continued to scream, flailing against the Queen's iron-tight grasp as she too screamed, repeating the same question with a growing, ravenous panic.

"Tell me, Jessica! Tell me where the girl is!"

Pushing against the waves of images, Jessica fought back the screams long enough to give one solid retort, the last she'd ever give. "Give Essallie my best," she hissed, daring to kiss the Queen's cheek in a snark of defiance. Sweat and rain drenched her, and despite the hollow bruises under her eyes and sallow look of her skin, she never felt so alive. Her hands tightened around the needle. "When she lights you on fire."

And she pulled the needle free.

Hell is cold.

For the longest time, I thought I understood what they meant by those words and just how real it was. A barren wasteland, lost of anything living and good. Scrapped raw by something dark and foreign, an unholy ground for the devil to ponder and grow. A chilling hell that sits deep in your soul, festering like an untreated wound unable to be cured.

There's just one problem. I think they got it wrong.

They don't know about tasting divinity, only to lose it in battle. To breathe with unbridled clarity, unaware of the smog creeping in the shadows. To feel passion running over your skin like a desired fever, yet be unable to act on those feelings.

Whoever said that hell was cold was wrong, oh so wrong. They don't know what the real hell is like, and how scorching hot it grows. How badly it burns.

Death is cold, not hell.

Hell is here, inside of me, cooking me alive.

And there's nothing I can do to stop it.

ONE

ANGELS

I opened my mouth to scream, water filling my lungs. It burned, racing down my throat as my body thrashed, starving for oxygen.

I hate water.

Okay, maybe I should re-phrase that; I hate bodies of water. Lakes, ponds, seas, rivers, they're all the same to me. A mess of gravity and pressure, a mysterious expanse of hidden secrets, beckoning you to test your fate each time you dip into its space. It's a cruel, unkind place that takes its victims without care, and spares those it feels deserve a second chance to fight. No rhythm or rhyme, just chance.

Hands pulled my head out from the small, rusted metal basin with a sharp jerk, nails scratching at my already tender scalp. The second I broke the surface, the pain in my chest intensified, each heave for air worse than the last. And to think, this had only been going on for the last ten minutes.

"I'll ask you again, Essallie," Ursula whispered in my ear with her sickly sweet tone, reminding me of honey drizzling over a box of rat poison. "Which will it be, the wrist or the ankle?"

I gave her a moment of mock pause. "Depends. Do I get screwed like all your other significant others afterwards?"

She shoved my head back into the basin, letting me linger until my chest felt like it could spontaneously combust. Black spots blotched my sight when she yanked me back up for air, her breath hot on my face.

"Care to repeat that?"

I shook my head against the pressure building in my temples, nausea rolling my stomach flat. "Of course not, Little Miss Loose Legs. I must aim to please you, just like all the other disposable men and women have through time."

Ursula swore in a language I didn't know before tossing me to the floor, laughing as I collapsed in a limp heap. Rolling onto my side, I heaved instinctively, my teeth rattling as my body shook in convulsions. I wanted to hit her, scratch the malevolent grin off her face and toss her immortal corpse to a pack of starving lions. A mixture of sweat and water clung to my skin in a sickly sheen film, the only barrier between me and my enemy.

The sound of her stilettos clinking on the cobblestone floor grew closer, the air shifting as she bent down to my level. "You talk big for a prisoner, Essie. But without your little demon lover and lost puppy Nephilim counterpart, you're weak."

Anger blazed in my chest. I rolled over to face her, tossing both hands in the air. Blue fire flared from my fingertips, suctioning to her face faster than she could react. She fell backwards to the floor, screaming as I burned her face for the second time since we met.

I scrambled to my feet and stumbled for the door, throwing it open in a single swing. All I had to do was make it to the end of the building. Racing down the hallway, I recited the plan in my head. *Three hallways, two left turns, kill anyone in the way.*

The first left turn held three Vens, each armed with thick, black swords twisting with violet smoke. Ashpods, I already knew, extremely poisonous and paralyzing to whoever is cut by one. Exactly my weapon of choice.

One of the Vens screamed, pointing a finger at me in astonishment. Flicking my hand, I continued to charge towards them, fire cresting off my hand to form a half-shield, my other hands brandishing a sword crafted of flame. Slamming back into the wall to avoid the first Vens, I sliced at his extended fingers, watching his hand drop to the ground before fizzling to black bones.

The other two leapt into action, ashpods drawn. I ducked between the two, tossing my shield above my head to avoid both blows. Blue fire and purple smoke mixed, creating a frenzied haze in the hall. I used it to my advantage, pulling back my blaze long enough to sneak behind one of the Vens and wrap my hands around his neck. Fire lit up my palms, my hands twisting with a rough jerk until the sound of his neck snapping in half rang true to my ears.

A bolt of black cut through the smoke. I held up the Vens' fresh corpse, watching the blade bury into his chest, black fire racing over his skin faster than a flick of light. My hands fumbled for the dead Vens' ashpod, grasping the handle just in time to swing upward at the first Vens. Under better situations, I probably would have made a jab at his new stump.

Ashpod blades bounced off another, purple smoke dashing the air like hazy radio waves. I took another stab at him, nicking a pinch of flesh on his arm. That was all it took; he seized almost instantly, turning rigid before collapsing to the ground in a shuddering heap. He would stay there until someone administered an antidote, granted only if he'd live long enough to receive it.

My sigh of relief was cut short as the cry of the last Vens came from my left. I turned in time to block his swinging blade, the force of his hit knocking me to the ground. A quick tumble backwards and I was back on the balls of my feet, determination burning in my fire. Tossing the ashpod to the side, I dropped my fire shield, locked both hands in, and launched a fireball the size of the whole hallway. He didn't even have time to scream.

I wasted no time for the fire to settle and clear the air; scooping up the black blade once more, I charged down the second hallway, scanning every inch of the way. At first, I thought it was luck no one heard the commotion of three guards and a prisoner fighting it out in the hall. My second left turn proved otherwise.

Standing at the end of the last hall, the only thing keeping me from my freedom, was an army of Vens deep enough to fill an auditorium. At the head of the pack, sporting pink skin flecked with ugly red burns, stood Ursula in all of her over-done couture glory.

"Really, Essallie? We're going to do this again?" She said with a roll of her eyes, boredom written all over her face. "When are you going to learn, there is no freedom for you?"

I gave her a quick look-over. "Probably when you realize that those hooker heels are so 1980." I added a wink for extra effect. "What's the matter succubus, face meet stove? Might want some ointment for that burn."

Rage boiled in her stare, a new shade of pink having nothing to do with her burns tinting her cheeks. "I cannot wait for the day the Queen finally takes care of you, you little half-breed scum. Shame you won't be around to see the world under her new rule."

I feigned dramatic shock. "Oh no! Me, dead? You promised me you'd keep my fortune cookie a secret."

One of her stilettos began to tap impatiently. She gave me

a twisted, malicious smile. "Give it up, drop the blade and I promise not to let the guards be too rough with you this time."

"As if," I laughed back. Taking stance, I beckoned them forward with a wag of a finger. "Come on, pretty girl. Give me something worthy of my time."

Ursula laughed, then moved faster than I had ever seen. Her hand whipped forward at me, slicing at my cheek. The familiar feel of warm, wet stickiness ran down my cheek and under my jaw. I didn't need to touch it to know it was blood, that Ursula had struck me quicker than I could even register the hit. Eyes on her, I watched her wiggle her fingers at me, taunting me with the stain of my own blood on her hands.

"Guess it wasn't the wrist or the ankle today, but the cheek. Shame," she faux-pouted. "I kind of liked your almost perfect face." Ursula turned to the nearest Vens and gave a curt nod, seemingly satisfied. Swiveling on her heels, she sauntered through the cluster of them, her platinum blonde head disappearing in the sea of black clothes. "Have fun!" Her voice trilled from the mass, wicked laughter filling the silence as the Vens began to shuffle forward, each armed with their own black blade of poison.

I had the distinct, familiar sinking feeling that this wasn't going to end well.

———

Hours later, they tossed me back into my cell with seemingly no effort. No sooner had the door shut was I back on my feet, hurtling fire balls at the steel door with a scream.

"Is that the best you've got?" I yelled, curling another ball of flame in the palm of my hand. It smashed into the door, fire licking the edges of the metal for a second before vanishing into a puff of smoke. "Tell that witch of a Queen to show her damn face!"

I waited for something, anything, but only the sound of silence greeted me with open arms. I slammed a fist into the wall, screaming as hot tears ran down my dirt-covered cheeks. Death would have been better than the cryptic, mind-numbing silence they continued to torture me with.

Back pressed against the heated door, I slid to the floor in a pile. Not for the first time I looked around my confined space, counting cracks in the slate grey rock walls and dingy, butterscotch cobblestone floor. The cluster of sheets and blankets in the corner was as close to a bed I had slept in for the last two weeks, and food was something of an entirely different matter. Well, at least they were generous enough to provide me with a bucket.

My eyes squeezed tight enough to see stars. One day of this had been horrible, one week had been torture-worthy, but two weeks left me feeling lost. I opened one eye, staring at the wall across from me, six small scratches marring the rock. Getting to my feet and crossing the room, I placed my index finger against the jagged rock, digging the nail against it until a seventh mark fell in line with the rest. Seven attempts to flee, seven attempts failed. I was beginning to see a trend.

Standing in the middle of my small confinement, I could feel the itch to pace beginning to raise my skin. Each day I spent in this place felt like a year, and I didn't know how much longer I could take. With the exception of Ursula's sporadic visits to force blood out of my veins for some sick gain, I was left alone. No guard would speak to me, no one would tell me a thing. For all I knew, Kayden and Ari were dead, captured in the mess of our break-in, and I didn't doubt she'd eventually hunt down Abigail and Jayson, maybe even my mother, and wipe us all out.

Shivers shook my shoulders, but it wasn't from the cold. Visions of my brother, bloodied and bruised on the floor, rose the familiar taste of bile to the back of my lips. I barely made it to the bucket in the corner in time before I heaved everything I had eaten for my last meal. My head hung along the side of the bowl, hands gripping the sides for some kind of stability as the all too-familiar empty sensation began to spread from my stomach to the rest of my body.

"Congratulations, you're officially starving yourself to death," I whispered to myself, pushing back from the bucket and onto the floor to lay eagle-spread.

A pitiful mock-sigh came from somewhere in the room. "Please, you call that food? Try something a little more tasteful, like bacon or brownies."

Crap.

The hallucinations were back.

Well, not exactly *hallucinations*, but one hallucination.

Sitting upright, I searched around the room until my eyes found her. She was sitting on the pile of blankets in the opposite corner, lips turned into a frown that didn't quite touch her eyes. Still as utterly ethereal as she was the first time I had imagined her, my carbon copy excelled in looking graceful. Her long blonde hair had been tamed to tight spiral curls resting on a backdrop of her v-neck, black velvet top and matching black pants. Unblemished, youthful pale skin reminded me of the perfect china doll, right down to her curious brown eyes.

Having spotted me sitting up, she gave me a playful smile. "On second thought, how about just brownies baked with bacon?"

"Go away, silly figment of my imagination," I sighed with exasperation, lying back on the floor. "And stop teasing me about bacon. It's just cruel."

"Not as cruel as you're being to me," she whined. Out of the corner of my eyes, I watched her get up from the pile of cloth and stand beside me. "I have something cool to show you."

I stared at her through half-lidded eyes. "My imagined version of my younger self has something to show me that I don't already know?" The sarcasm was barely held back in my tone. "Oh, this ought to be good."

Taking that as a yes, she weaved her fingers into her hair, pulling out a chunk of midnight black colored hair. Eyebrows wiggling, she did nothing to contain the mischievous sparkle dancing her her stare. "Check it out!"

I scooted to a sitting position on the floor, biting back a sigh. "I see we're experimenting with hair colors now."

"Nope," she beamed with pride. "Not hair colors, hair color, just one." Fingers stroked the long silky lock of hair. "I like it. It'll help tell us apart for the future, aside from having different names."

Her words sank into my mind as I gave her an absentminded nod. The first day of my captivity she had appeared to me, but after a while I grew tired of calling her my carbon copy. She insisted on being called Ebony, saying it would be exactly what her mother would have wanted. Too bad she didn't know her mother was a deranged basket case, locked in a quiet little white room where the biggest stressor would be what color paint she'd use for her next work of art.

Then again, since she was just a product of my growing insanity, maybe she did. After all, I was ultimately the one in control; my subconscious was probably having a ball coming up with a friend for me to talk to. Next it would let me believe I can talk to squirrels and mice, maybe even sew a nice dress for a ball where I could don a glass slipper and-

This time, I let the sigh deflate my chest. "Ebony," I started to say, when the sound of keys outside the door hit my ears. Instantly I stood up, fire erupting over tightly clenched fists.

Ursula quickly came into the room, shutting the door with the blink of an eye. Instead of her usual get-up of laced corsets and princess skirts, she was dressed in a maroon turtleneck and black jeans. Her hair had been pulled into a tight ponytail high on her head, heels replaced for combat boots.

"We don't have much time," she spoke in a rush, tossing a pile of clothes at me. It was the exact same outfit as hers, right down to the ribbed fabric in the turtleneck. "Get those on, but watch it. There's a vial somewhere in the pants."

I took a quick look around the room, no sign of my gorgeous hallucination. Setting the pile on the floor, I wasted no time stripping out of the dirty white gown I was still wearing from the night of my capture. "She bought it?"

"Yes, but I can't trust that she'll buy it for much longer." Ursula paced the room, fingers twitching with each passing moment. Hints of stress touched her face. "Your powers are growing, way too fast for it to be normal. We have to get you out of here. The Queen can only believe you'd be overtaken by Vens so many times before she starts to see how fast you're incinerating them. Who knows what else is stirring inside of you with her blood."

Head through the turtleneck, I fumbled for the sleeves. "What do you mean?"

"I mean you need to get out of here and save us, all of us, before whatever her blood does to you finishes you off."

I paused, one leg in the pair of black skinny jeans. When I spoke, it was quiet and carefully controlled. "So you knew." When she didn't answer immediately, my blood began to boil. "You knew that vial wasn't from some medicine woman."

"No," she said sternly, finding my gaze. A mixture of shame and something I couldn't place had turned her face sad, withdrawn. "I didn't know. Some crazy green-looking hag on the street in Charon gave it to me, and told me I was to use it on the injured Nephilim. I thought it was a beggar, or someone who had one too many at the bar, how the heck was

I going to know it was for you? I must have carried that vial for the last sixteen, seventeen years. It wasn't... until later that I found out the hag was a consort of the Queen's."

"You didn't think to go to the Queen about it?"

"Of course I did," her tone grew short and bitter. "You want to know what she told me? *Do it, or what you love the most will die.* I laughed; the only thing I've ever loved the most was long dead. When I didn't take her bait, she waited. Waited until I met you to show me her little prize. That's when I knew I had to do it, no matter what I learned about you, about Kayden, anyone."

Boots on and laced, I stood up to stand directly in front of her. Up close, I started to see just how bad the tolls of things had taken to her. Ursula's pale skin looked wrinkled and aged, dark bruises cresting her eyes as if she'd never slept a day in her eternal life. No longer was she the pretty, perfect immortal, but a damaged and blackmailed pawn in the Queen's never-ending game of chess. But that didn't explain why she would be so torn over Leo's death. Wasn't he just another man in the breath of her life?

"Why?" I asked, almost as a challenge. "Why should I believe a word you've just told me? How do I know she isn't outside that door right now, waiting to point and laugh in my face at my gullibility?"

Her petite hands clenched to tight fists. "Because she has what I love the most."

"Leo is de-"

"Not Leo, you stupid girl," Ursula moaned. Fear flickered in her eyes, tears threatening to run down her face. "She has Euriel. My brother."

I stared at her in shock, disbelief riddling coloring my cheeks. Flashes of the day I stood in her house with Kayden by my side, pushed to the front of my mind. "... you told me your brother was dead. He was mortal."

When she opened her mouth, Ursula let out a harsh laugh of anger. "Funny, the longer I live, the more I see that nothing is as it seems." Her eyes were dark, images of pain and anguish weaved inside.

I reached out to comfort her, but thought better of it. "When did you find out?"

She hiccuped, tears rimming her eyes. "That night I ran into you. After the... after the bonfire incident with Kayden, she came to me. He's been in servitude to some vampire for the last couple hundred years on the Queen's debt." A rivulet of salty tear ran down her cheek. "She knows I can't do anything. If I approach him, they'll kill him, and he can't leave because he needs his master's blood to live."

Great. So there were vampires in this messed up world, too? What next, Sparkling werewolves? Unicorn-vampire hybrids? I didn't even try to pretend I understood vampire rules. "That's why you're helping me, isn't it? You want me to find him and somehow save him."

Ursula stepped closer, lingering far enough to leave a hint of space between our faces. Between the waves of anguish and sadness mirrored in her eyes, fire stirred a deep-seated flare of vengeance. I knew how that look felt; it was the same look I had worn the night I went for the Queen. She, too, had been through enough to harden her delicate skin to iron, stitched with staples to hide the invisible wounds she kept pressed against her heart. She had been stolen the one thing no one should ever have taken from them, family. The thought of someone taking Jayson from me, lying to me that he was dead for years, only to reveal he was hostage by the Queen's doing? I would have died trying to get him back. It wasn't that huge of a surprise that Ursula would do the same for her own.

"For years I have been told that you, a Nephilim, would destroy the beautiful balance Lucretia had given our land, that you were the enemy and she was our salvation. But all she has done is manipulate, slaughter, and incarcerate those who truly hold the key to saving us." She paused, taking a shallow breath that wheezed in her chest. "You have to find him, Essallie. Find Euriel, he can help you kill the Queen."

"He can't help me."

"If you find him, he can."

I dared ask. "How?"

"Remember how I said that library was his, the one we had together?" She waited for my nod. "Before we moved here, before I relocated to Maine, our last home had a library four times that size. He knew every book inside and out on those shelves-"

"This isn't the time for a monologue."

"There was a book," Ursula said with growing urgency, eyes burning bright as the memory blossomed in her mind. A fierce, triumphant smile brought her tired face to life. "On Nephilim in our original sacred library. It spoke of bondings, and Watchers; it was one of the original texts the True Queen owned, and when she passed we took it before her tainted daughter could burn it. I believe it holds the key to saving your life."

There was a pause, a moment that lingered between us as our eyes locked. If she was telling the truth, if I stood a chance of ever finding a way to save myself and everyone at once, this was it. As much as I loathed the idea of putting my faith into the hands of the woman who unwittingly put me here, I figured she had to believe in me if she was here, risking everything.

Giving her a single, short nod, I said the words. "Let's do this."

The fire in Ursula's eyes flared intensively, the smile on her lips spreading. Stepping back, she held out her hand. "Give me the vial."

I reached into my jeans pocket, pulling out a corked, thin

glass tube. Purple liquid sloshed within. Before I could ask what it was, Ursula had taken it, uncorked it, and swallowed the liquid in a single gulp.

She stumbled back with a gasp, colliding into the wall. I watched her body shake, skin stretching and bending to the sickening snap of re-forming bones just underneath her superficial layers. The straight, waist length platinum blonde hair she was known for turned short, falling off until a crop cut remained. Her body jutted like an improperly assembled jigsaw puzzle, stretching and shortening until the girl standing before me looked nothing like the immortal succubus I had come to know.

The girl before me was most definitely Ursula, only she looked like me.

"Judging by your slack-jaw stare, Lilix's potion worked again," she said, wincing. Her voice, normally soft like a sea breeze, was now strained and tense. Did I really sound like that? "Enough with the brain-dead behavior, we need to move."

I shook my head, still in disbelief. "You do realize, out of all the people I imagined you'd turn into, I would be the last. You know, being the *prisoner* and all."

She ignored me, turning to face the door as she pulled something out from under her shirt. It didn't take me long to see it resembled a grenade. Wires with different colored liquids wrapped around it, held together by what looked like a piece of clockwork. "That's the point, idiot," she hissed. She looked over her shoulder, meeting my shocked stare. "Get against that wall, take cover."

I backed into the wall, dropped to the floor and pressed my palms tight over my ears. Ursula twisted the the clockwork, counted to three and tossed the grenade through the small window on the door, running for me. She had just reached my feet when the explosion rocked the hall. Chunks of destroyed concrete and torn metal flung around the room, dust spiraling like a inside-born storm from the bowels of the Dust Bowl.

Ursula wasted no time, rising to her feet and making for the gap in the wall the explosion had created. "I'm sorry for what I did to-" She paused, turning back for a split second. In that last look, I read more in her stare than I ever had. It spoke of fear, the kind that submerged you under ice water and told you to breathe. The words that tumbled off her lips seemed choked as she grabbed at the fabric near the base of her throat. "Tell Ari we're even."

ALIVIA ANDERS is the author of the bestselling Illumine Series. Born and raised in PA, she fell headfirst into the world of writing at thirteen with the discovery of internet fan-fiction and RPG-forum boards. A lover of chinchillas, mexican food, and coffee, she spends most of her time drumming up new ideas to spin into tales to enchant readers everywhere.

www.ingramcontent.com/pod-product-compliance
Lightning Source LLC
Chambersburg PA
CBHW021231130626
46554CB00004B/1438